MOST DEADLY DESIRE

"You are still too much in awe of me, Tandra," Orram said. With a few quick motions he undressed and stood nude before her. "Satisfy yourself that I am alien."

Tandra studied his taut brown body, explored it with her hands and stepped back.

"Surely you are not done," he said. "I thought you were anxious to establish my alienness."

"There doesn't seem to be any alienness to establish."

Suddenly Orram grabbed her hands. "You refuse to see, Tandra! You must learn now! You must know without doubt that I am *not* human. I am alien to Earth! I am varok!"

"Yes . . . you are varok. You are also . . ." She stopped speaking, afraid of her thoughts, *you are also male.*

> But Orram had read her thoughts, understood their meaning—and knew that they spelled his doom. . . .

A PLACE
BEYOND MAN

CARY NEEPER

A DELL BOOK

Published by
DELL PUBLISHING CO., INC.
1 Dag Hammarskjold Plaza
New York, N.Y. 10017
Dell ® TM 681510, Dell Publishing Co., Inc.
ISBN: 0-440-16931-3
Reprinted by arrangement with Charles Scribner's Sons
Printed in the United States of America
First Dell printing—February 1977

For Don, who knew Conn first—
with thanks to those
who have contributed invaluable guidance:
Bonnie, Betsy, and George.

Contents

A Place Beyond Man

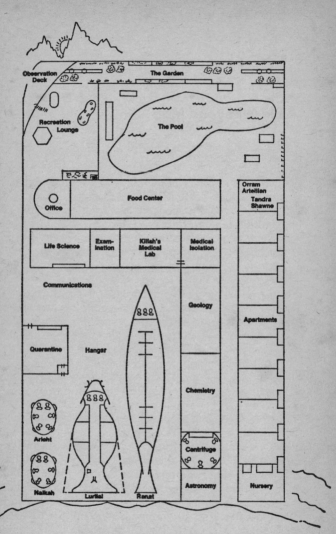

ELLL-VAROK OBSERVATION BASE

1
To Trust a Stranger

Beyond the moist, vibrant Earth and pocked Mars; past wild Jupiter and its living stepchild, Varok; and far from the cold regions of skirted Saturn and the track where lonely Pluto rides, there is a hollow black void that silently envelops nothing but minute particles and cosmic debris in an ethereal shroud so vast that it transforms the giant, explosive masses called suns into mere specks of light. Empty space occupies most of this enormous blackness; but buried in the midst of the gloom, lost in the statistical deviations of mathematicians, and hidden from the eyes of astronomers is a ball of condensed matter, a ball not so large when measured against Earth's sun or even Jupiter, but large enough to glow dimly in the deeps with its own internal warmth—and yet small enough so that powerful creatures could evolve out of its mild ooze to lounge and play in its heavy waters.

And lounge and play on their warm moist planet they did through the eons while nature toyed with them: reducing their form to reasonable dimensions, enlarging their wit to ridiculous extremes, and adding unnecessary but charming decorative touches until there emerged upon the face of that great ball—Ellason it was called eventually—handsome creatures known as ellls, creatures with an enormous capacity for joy. And occasionally a capacity for much more.

Occasionally an elll like Conn came along—one of the mutants—a loner who drove his fellow ellls wild with worry, for not only did he refuse to school normally and thereby fulfill his expected role as part of the group, but he also spent long periods depriving himself of immediate life-pleasure by engaging in relentless study, mumbling to himself in the strange, hard sounds of the languages of Earth that he was learning, and toughening himself to prolonged drought. As his youth passed, however, he gave his worried sponsors some reassurance, for on those occasions when he schooled, he played with great creativity and enjoyed life as much as any elll. Indeed, on the moment that he learned of his acceptance into the Varokian Concentrate as a student of the planet Earth, he communicated his joy to the entire school with such wild abandon that they did not regret the difficult adjustment his forthcoming absence would require, but rather enjoyed sharing his life's desire, now attainable in reality: to be an active participant when contact was made with the provincial and dangerous inhabitants of Sol's third planet.

So Conn traveled from Ellason, his watery dark world, to thirsty, crystal Varok; absorbed all that the Varokian scholars could offer his agile mind; and after he had earned the designations Generalist in Human Studies and Specialist in Engineering and Space Navigation, traveled to the Elll-Varok Observation Base on Earth's moon.

There he joined the crew of thirty ellls and five varoks who were currently entrusted by Elll-Varok (EV) Science to watch, to record, and to analyze events on Earth; to continually update the prognosis for the blue planet; and to make recommendations for or against constructive interference. The various EV crews had accumulated almost one hundred Earth-years of data when Conn arrived to make a detailed analysis of current human affairs.

Empathic being that he was, Conn felt no small pain at watching what seemed to him to be a progressive deterioration of human awareness. Before five years had passed he saw little remaining on Earth that one could call beautiful, few moments that one might call peaceful—but no one there seemed to care. Most human beings let economic pressures downgrade all other considerations to secondary importance. Conn had hoped that at least the international accords on human population control and food distribution would hold, but they did not. As a result, human beings, as well as the myriad forms of life which had been adversely affected by their activities, were well into an expected precipitous decline in numbers—a fact that the human members of the Earth largely ignored, though the decline had begun decades earlier in India and Africa. This refusal to recognize what was happening—massive die-offs—was a kind of repression that was incredible to Conn. In spite of his idiosyncrasies, he saw himself as an inseparable part of his school, as apparently humans could not. He could imagine far too well the personal costs of large-scale suffering. Meanwhile, those human beings who could obtain enough food and fuel to maintain their mental acuity lived an existence in a dulled awareness, the increasingly lowered minimal standards for air and water purity slowly squeezing thin their hope that they might escape the worsening health statistics for one more year.

When Conn was satisfied that there were no simple answers to Earth's enigma and that no species on Earth would attempt to contain the onrushing chain of natural disasters, he decided that the ells and varoks should first determine if direct contact with *Homo sapiens* would pose any serious biological problems and then, if not, should reveal themselves to offer whatever help they could.

Some indirect accidental contacts had already been made, once, when exploring a remote mountain trail in British Columbia, they had met a human—who had the presence of mind to tell the helmeted figures his name and amateur radio call sign before they made their hasty retreat. As a result, Conn had developed a working arrangement with the man, Jesse Mendleton, a mulish soul seeking tranquility in a world where very little was left. Their relationship was a continuing exercise in faith. It was as if Mendleton were a part of the crew at base now. As he continued his restless wandering, he had worked closely with Conn by radio, keeping him informed of terrestrial affairs. Conn knew that he would help arrange direct contact if he could.

When the elll had carefully reviewed the obvious alternatives and his ideas had jelled, becoming convictions, he forcefully presented to the Elll-Varok Lunar Base Directorate an old proposal: "I think we should contact *Homo sapiens* and try to persuade them to get serious about conserving their planet."

"That's nothing new," someone on the Directorate said, "We've been debating that point for many years."

"However," Conn continued, "we have been worrying too much about contaminating Earth and finding a fool-proof way of influencing its fate. We should jump in blind, take at least this one preliminary step I'm going to suggest, and see where it will lead. Let's ask Jesse Mendleton to find a human expert on the parasites and infectious organisms of man who would be willing to determine whether direct contact would seriously endanger any Ellasonian, Varokian, or Earthly forms of life."

"Can Jesse find someone like that?" Conn was asked.

"If such a person exists, he'll find him. Jesse was in and out of health laboratories and international funding agencies for twenty-five years before he finally quit and took off for the woods. I thing he has the good judgment to pick a competent microbiologist, one who also might be sympathetic with the notion of extraterrestrial life. Before we contact the person directly we could do some observations and EEG tracings and make an evaluation of Jesse's choice."

Soon after, the Directorate accepted Conn's proposal for testing the consequences of human-elllonian and human-varokian biological contact. When Mendleton called again to report some new statistics concerning the last of the North Atlantic whales, Conn explained in simple coded language what the Directorate wanted. Mendleton suggested that any microbiologist they chose should have some experience in medical immunology since they needed to study not just the risk of infectious disease, but the effectiveness of immunization and the possibility of allergic reactions; and he readily agreed to find a person capable of their demanding and potentially dangerous project.

They didn't hear from him for several weeks. Suddenly he called to say that he had found what they were looking for: "She's an idealistic young woman named Tandra Grey."

"We'll take her—if she's fertile," Conn joked, elated with the news.

"Go slowly. Look her over carefully when you come down," Mendleton said. "There's no doubt that she knows her work, but she's a dreamer, this one. That's why I think she'll go for you; might be helpful. At least she won't scare easily." He paused. "Might cause you trouble, though. She put too much of herself into politics when the World Environmental Charter was drawn up—got turned off pretty badly when she finally woke up."

The Directorate decided to send an observation team to Earth at once, and the arrangements were soon made. Conn was the obvious choice among the ellls and varoks at the lunar base for the risky task of evaluating the woman and perhaps revealing himself and the existence of the base to her. His years of study had left him the uncontested master of human custom. He had perfected his English and could effectively control the long rolling *ll*'s in his accent. He was ready.

Now, at last, the elll found himself at his goal—on the planet Earth, somewhere in the southwestern mountains of the North American continent. As he moved along, enjoying the more muted light of evening and listening to the merry grinding of cricket legs, conscious of the delicious feel of the soft pine-covered ground beneath him, he anticipated with some excitement his first close observation of a human being, the selected contact, Tandra Grey; and hoped, with more eagerness than discretion might allow, that he would win her confidence and her commitment to attempt the first direct contact between their species.

He began climbing a gently sloping hill speckled with sage and dark juniper and paused beside a tall pine to enjoy his infrared view of the bright crescent moon against the dimming sky. Though the apertures of his contact lenses were very small, they were barely adequate to dim sufficiently the brightness of Earth's daylight; he could see more detail now that the sun had set. Suddenly a grasshopper bounced out of the grass and landed on his isolation suit.

"Hi, pal. Want to go to the moon with me?" He bent down and lifted the insect to his helmet, but it hopped off into the grass and was soon lost to Conn's vision. "I'm going to have to improve my approach technique."

In spite of the disagreeable restriction imposed by his isolation suit, he moved silently and swiftly toward the brow of the hill. Pulling at his sleeve irritably, he crouched behind a gnarled juniper for a few moments, listening; then he started to move toward the back of what ought to be Tandra Grey's house, if Jesse Mendleton had described it accurately. He was less cautious now. His stride lengthened and relaxed as he neared his goal—when suddenly he tripped on something soft in the grass. His primary blood chamber paused in its undulations for a moment. All was quiet except for its annoying slush. He was about to move on when a gentle rustling noise sounded immediately to his left. Conn froze, and his fan-shaped glove leapt to the self-disintegration needle in his right sleeve. Yet even as he searched nervously for escape, his wry mind enjoyed the humor of the situation: He had almost stumbled over his quarry as she lay sleeping in the grass.

While the crickets spun rickety threads of sound in the moonlight, Conn's primary blood chamber seemed to splash more and more noisily. Finally he decided to risk easing away. He started to move backward slowly, and one of his long limbs abruptly pushed into another soft mound in the grass. Something let out a cry. This time Conn did not wait. He jumped clear and rolled away frantically to the gnarled juniper.

Inside the house the telephone began to ring. Tandra Grey sat up in her sleeping bag, and Conn had an unexpectedly pleasant impression of her fine profile and long hair silhouetted in the cooling air. She checked the child sleeping near her—the second mound he had kicked—then started toward the house, when suddenly joining the peaceful cacophony of the night creatures came the noisy rasping song of a cicada. The Grey woman turned around and began searching for it in the grass. She rummaged for something in her jacket and drew out a flashlight. Its beam of light chased into the dark after the insect. The telephone kept ringing.

A string of Elllonian invectives raced silently through Conn's mind. He was tempted to end this game and simply introduce himself, but he knew far too much of Earth's history and literature; his knowledge of human xenophobia made him cautious. Tense and frustrated, he lay in the grass while Tandra's light circled near him. "Why the hell doesn't she answer that telephone?"

The light swung away as she homed in on the cicada and knelt in the grass to stare into its large complex eyes. "Hi, pal," she said.

Conn smiled. Then the woman turned away from the insect and disappeared into the house.

Not one to let a moment's enjoyment be interrupted by work that could wait—for all his difference from the school, he was still an elll—he rolled over on his back and nestled lazily into the soft earth beneath the radiant moon. There was the constellation Alleoon, stretching like a great eel into the pine trees. Most of those stars were infrared. How many could the woman see? Certainly he would never know if he kept botching his approach to her.

He got up and crept swiftly to the house. He took a compact instrument from his belt, fitted it with an ultra-sensitive EEG pick-up, and probed the wall. Nothing. He tried again, placing the tiny detector on the window, and received a faint but distinct signal from Tandra's brain.

Several minutes passed while the gadget picked up, amplified, and sorted a variety of Tandra's microvolt patterns as she talked on the telephone: "If it rings that long, then it might be worth answering. . . ." She laughed. "I don't intend to sleep in the house at all this winter. . . . Why should I make Shawne miss what few stars there are? A little snow won't hurt her. . . . Eileen, I don't want to be rude, but why did you call? . . . Yes, I'm free tomorrow night. . . . What do I want with a party? There's no one I can think of that I'd care to party with. . . . Lonely? Not really. Empty perhaps. . . . Of course, I'd be delighted to find someone who needs nothing but *pine trees!* But I'll never find him at any of your parties. . . . I'm sorry, but they're a horrendous waste. . . . Costumes? That's even more ridiculous. I'd feel like—. . . . All right. You've got me now. I'll come. I don't deny being a hopeless romantic, but I don't like being called a snob. Tell what's-his-name that I'll dirty my hands here on hard ground with real people if *he'll* promise not to dance with me." She laughed nervously. "You'd better tell me how to get there. Is it the second or third driveway off Tanner's Road? . . . The second? . . . Then the third gate on the left? . . . I'll find it."

As Conn listened, a plan quickly formed in his mind. He left the house and made his way across the brushland behind it to a stand of pine trees. He stopped beneath a browning ponderosa and using his native throat language, spoke into his communicator: "Tallyn, stay where you are. I'll be taking a hike tonight. Find Tanner's Road on the directional Mendleton gave us. . . . Now find it on the larger sectional. . . . Okay, how do I get there? I've only got twenty-four hours, half of them will be in daylight, and I can't see a damn thing when the sun's out. . . . Twenty-five kilometres? That's more than a thousand *pallons*. I'll be scraped raw in this damnable isolation suit."

He wasn't though. In fact, he actually enjoyed the walk. For the most part, the broad canyon led him in the right direction, there were only two highways to cross, and the few fences made delightful obstacles to jump in the mild gravitational pull. On he went, hour after hour, striding easily, pausing to watch the moon and to listen when the wind whistled in the pine trees.

Just before sunrise Conn reached his destination and set about to find a place to hide. He settled into a dark corner of a storage shed, apparently rarely used, and after an intensive survey of Tandra Grey's EEG recording, slept undisturbed through the day. With the chill of night he awoke, stretched to his full length—and kicked over a shovel. After that he sat quietly and waited for the sounds of the party to begin.

Before long several cars pulled into the driveway. Then more. Human chatter rose to gay crescendo. Conn eased quietly out of the shed and crawled toward a hedge surrounding the garden, where he could hide and watch. He wondered how he would know Tandra Grey if she arrived as foolishly dressed and as totally masked as all the others.

The minutes passed slowly; his wonder became anxiety before he saw a lone woman drive a small three-wheeled vehicle into the driveway and park it where it could not be blocked by anyone else. After some minutes the woman emerged from the vehicle; to Conn's relief, it was Tandra Grey, dressed simply in a full skirt, peasant blouse, and matching kerchief. He watched her tie a black veil over her face and hesitantly make her way into the periphery of the crowd on the patio. Then, like a stealthy weasel, the elll moved behind the hedge toward the shadows at the far corner of the house, and waited. When no one was facing his direction, he quickly stood up, stepped over the hedge onto the patio, and assumed a casual slouch by the punch bowl. No one seemed to notice him amidst the versicolored jumble of feathers and capes and animal masks. He poured himself a glass of punch and looked longingly into the liquid. Where was Ellalon right now? Probably in the pool with Killah. *Re-o-o,* wouldn't that feel good? On the other hand, Killah rarely had a chance to get away from base, poor bastard. He'd like it down here. Good to be surrounded by living things again. Beats that goddam hot dust and dry rock up there. He saw the patio pool then and moved toward it.

Someone pushed past him, mumbling "Scuse me,

skin diver," and the elll spotted the Grey woman across the patio, apparently engaged in an argument. He wandered closer and listened.

"There is nothing in evolution's rulebook that says accumulated knowledge will lead man into a more perfect social order," Tandra was saying. "Distortions in human behavior are quite possible. They are occurring right now. Man's misguided emphasis on comfort and convenience is leading him straight into a blind alley."

"You mean you intend to raise that adopted baby of yours like a wild Indian?" said a large man in Arabian dress.

"I trust her God-given instincts more than I trust the demands of human society."

"You'll produce a spoiled brat and a social misfit, if you ask me," said a stout Cinderella.

"But I didn't ask you. I will teach her that she must never impose herself on anyone—that she never hurt anyone, physically or emotionally. But I will also insist that she ask herself, not others, what is the best way to live."

"That's crazy. There are proper ways, time-tested ways, of doing things—for very good reasons."

Conn could no longer remain silent. "And what are they?" he said, stepping forward.

The distinctive musical lapping tone of his voice struck Tandra's ear.

"I'm sure we all know what they are—spaceman, or whatever you are. What are you?"

Conn's varokian isolation suit was sleek and trim, as if it had been tailored to fit his lean body; only on its small, slightly squared helmet were there hints of electronic gadgetry and extraneous hardware. The suit's material, a fine, natural cloth, was randomly marked with warm, muted colors that served as excellent camouflage for Conn's long torso and limbs.

As Tandra's appraisal lingered over the nonchalant newcomer, who was apparently indifferent to the awkward angles his lanky figure made, she thought she saw him smile. But then she decided that she could not see the man's face through the reflection in his face-plate clearly enough to say. She tentatively concluded that he was someone she had not met before. Certainly she had never before heard that calm but strongly melodious, strangely accented voice. It created a whimsical image in her mind of men of Slavic tongue imitating Japanese language students speaking English. Though his syllables were slightly angular, they slid over each other in a thick, rolling progression.

"No, I don't think we know the proper ways of doing things," Conn said, ignoring the man's question. "At least, I don't, other than not hurting others, as Dr. Grey has suggested."

"Well," snorted Cinderella, "You needn't give us a lecture."

"I'm sorry. It is only that I am sincerely interested in Dr. Grey's thesis. The wisdom of genetic instinct is of a more ancient variety than the accumulated wisdom of human society."

"Then you want us to revert to our animal nature?" the Arab challenged.

With that Conn let out a hoot of laughter that sent Cinderella off in a huff, shocked the Arab into wondering what he had said, and thoroughly delighted Tandra. "But we *are* our animal nature," Conn cried. "You couldn't possibly escape that fact."

The Arab shrugged and walked away. "I don't have to stand here and be insulted," they heard him say.

Tandra stood alone with Conn. Her eyes were bright. How she had been hating that conversation. It would have gone nowhere with those people. Why couldn't she argue sensibly without getting so emotional? Why did it matter so much?

"The term *human society* is a semantic myth," Conn continued with a mock stiffness, "certainly not an absolute reference for good conduct. The phrase merely refers to the habits, good and bad, of the current swarm of *Homo sapiens*. Don't you agree, Dr. Grey?"

Tandra laughed, entering Conn's light mood. "I don't believe I know you," she said, offering her hand to him. "In fact I don't think I've ever known anyone anything *like* you. You talk as if your mouth were connected to your brain."

"I'm afraid it's connected to more than you'd like to imagine," Conn muttered, taking her hand.

"I doubt that that's possible."

Conn looked at her closely, remembering Mendleton's warning. "How possible?" he asked.

"Im-possible, after what you've just done for me. That argument could have left me stewing around all next week. Besides an understanding heart, your mouth could be hooked up to sixteen crossed eyes and great hairy teeth, and I wouldn't mind a bit."

An easy laugh tumbled out of Conn's helmet. "I'm not *that* weird."

"How weird are you? You seem to know me, but I can't guess who you are." She looked down at his large glove in her hand. "Do I know you?"

The elll hesitated. "You will, I think," he said.

An insistent melodic beat began to tease from the patio loudspeaker.

"Can you dance in that suit?" Tandra asked.

"It's designed not to slow me down."

He took her hand in his large, flat glove and balanced his punch glass on the hedge.

"We spacemen pull—eh—a mean beat, lady," Conn said as casually as he could. "Think you can keep up?"

"Try me."

They began to move rhythmically to the music, and Conn gradually coaxed the quiet, soft woman into his arms, imitating other couples that were dancing on the patio. To his delight he found that he could easily cue her responsive body with gentle nudges and tugs as he followed the beat; soon they were sensing it as one. They floated together on the thread of the sound in a harmony so complete that they lost awareness of everything but the matched and answering movement of their bodies submerged in the rhythm.

"Where did a staid lady scientist like you learn to dance like that? You speak the language of ellls."

"Are you an elll?" Tandra said. "You couldn't be a

man; your ideas match mine too well. And your dancing—it was almost meaningful."

"Almost? Don't belittle such meaning, cool chick. You may have need to understand it some day." Conn paused, suddenly tempted to take her from the party and reveal himself. She seemed ready to accept the fact of his alienness, she seemed even to invite it. Or was it his mood only that was affecting him? Then he noticed a broad grin behind her veil. "Are you laughing at me?" he asked.

"I've never been called 'cool chick' before. You have a delightful accent, but it doesn't match that outdated slang."

"The colloquialisms and slang of human languages are a hobby of mine," he said. "I enjoy using them."

"Will you tell me where you're from? I can't place the accent."

"I am from Ellason," Conn said. The rolled *ll* was a tuneful, lapping sound. "I am an elll, and my name is Conn."

At the sound of a heavy Latin beat, he pressed Tandra to his body and guided her again into the music, effectively silencing her next question. They danced with an absorbing, syncopated rhythm while her mind followed its fancies. What fun if this lanky figure with the attractive slouch were actually alien— if Ellason were somewhere far from Earth. Ellason. His *ll* had a strangely beautiful sound. She quietly tried to imitate it.

Conn's voice jolted Tandra to awareness. "Don't try to say Ellason that way. You'll get a cramp in that fat tongue of yours."

Tandra laughed. "You said you specialize in *human* languages. What other kinds of languages do you speak? Dolphin?"

"Yes, some," Conn said. "Enough to get along." No hint of jesting was in his voice. "And all the Elllonian and Varokian languages we've figured out."

"Ellason. Ellason. That's somewhere between Harnaf and Skrinkland, right?"

"Wrong. It's far beyond Varok. And I've come here

these many light years, if you'll pardon a slight exaggeration, to shop for help from sympathetic human microbiologists. Interested?"

"Who wouldn't be?" Tandra laughed.

"Your name came to our attention from two different sources. You have published some work in comparative immunology and bacteriology, yes? And you enjoy music, play flute and piano. But best of all, doll, you have beautiful brain waves. They indicate a good measure of adaptability, spiced with some stubborn willfulness, a fantastic imagination, and a sense of humor. Moreover, your low voltage patterns have a strong romantic twist that might even be compatible with the notion of extraterrestrial life."

"Daydreams put out strong voltages?" Tandra asked.

"Relatively. We've been spying on you with an EEG amplifer. I hope you don't mind."

"So! You're very careful in picking your contacts."

"Extremely."

"But you don't care much who you dance with," Tandra said.

"Now what is that supposed to mean?"

"I asked *you* to dance."

"Clever of me, wasn't it?" Conn said. "But understand well, me lass, I honestly intend—"

"Let's go find something to drink," she interrupted.

"I more than wish I could join you. Here, take this." He found the punch still balanced precariously in the hedge and handed it to her.

"Do I have to drink alone?" she asked.

" 'Fraid so, though the *lohn* bird knows I'd break this smothering disguise if I could. The filters in this helmet make breathing an effort, and I don't like to rely on lungs alone. We put up with these suits, even though none of our gèrms seem dangerous to Earth's life forms, because we don't want to take any chances of contaminating Earth."

Tandra smiled and draped an arm around Conn's waist. How could she be drawn so quickly to this man?

Conn looked down at her. "You're not living up to your reputation for cool reserve."

"I'm not reserved with people I like," Tandra said. "Tell me more about your suit. It protects you from our bacteria and viruses, too, I assume."

"Of course," he said, pulling her closer. "The isolation suits are worn as a routine precaution, though all of us at base have been immunized to your infectious diseases and carefully exposed to your normal flora."

"You're very thorough, Mr. Ellrunian."

"The adjective is *ellonian,* but call me Conn for short. Come, let's relax on yonder grass, and I'll tell you a story about us alien space-types." He led Tandra around the pool, motioned for her to be seated, then sprawled beside her.

"Once upon a time," he began, cocking his head at Tandra's grin, "on a large, floating haven of life not too far from here—a dry place, hidden within gigantic swirls of colored mists and crystals, a place called Varok by its grim, hard-working inhabitants—an aging poet, who was an astronomer by trade, tackled for the hundredth time minute wobbles, mathematical deviations, in the orbital paths of what you call Halley's Comet and the planet Pluto. At his urging, which involved a good deal of compromise by the more conservative minds on Varok, great silver vessels eventually sailed from that arid lump into the black, mindless space beyond Pluto—way beyond Pluto—and found that it was, indeed, *not* mindless. A self-heated dark body was found to exist in physical not just mathematical reality; and its waters were found to contain creatures of remarkable mental ability (if you don't mind my saying so) with a fascinating take-it-or-leave-it attitude toward most of life's bothersome details. Not even on the third planet out, which you call Earth and where life was known to exist, was there such potential for communication. The varoks worked for almost ten thousand Earth-years at the puzzle of how best to talk to these creatures, my ancestors—who preferred pressure signals even above their more extensive ultrasonic vocabulary—while man grew a bit straighter and less hairy far off on his blue paradise—until finally a compromise was reached, and the ellls (as they came to be called) agreed to invent and utter a pattern of throat sounds in order to communicate with the varoks within their audible range and air-constrained capabilities.

"Thereafter, through the millenia, as Varok weathered its storms and my warm, damp planet continued its long, silent course around the sun, an intimate partnership developed between the two species. Then, as man began to move about Earth leaving intelligible scars, the two species from further out decided to keep a closer watch on that third planet. In time, not so long ago, a magnificent laboratory home was buried beneath the wall of a small crater on the rim of Earth's moon, and the ellls and varoks settled down in some comfort to watch what happened on Earth. Needless to say, they were not disappointed; lots happened. But they didn't care much for it."

Conn stopped, glanced at Tandra, and shifted uncomfortably on the grass.

"Here," Tandra said, taking his helmeted head into her lap.

"EEG patterns don't lie after all." He nestled down happily.

"I'm not as cold as some people think. It's just that I make no pretenses. I've always been quick and definite about what I liked."

"Or what you thought you liked."

"I'll try to remember that," Tandra laughed. "Now please go on. You've touched my most romantic soft spot. How I would love to know of life beyond Earth!"

"I'll tell you all I can. After some ten decades—we operate on Greenwich Mean Time at base; saves confusion in trying to keep track of things down here—an aggressive young fool named Conn arrived at the observation base on Earth's moon and began his own review of your planet's affairs, obtaining information by radio contact with a kindly old coot on Earth named Jesse Mendleton, whom some of my fellow ellls encountered rather dramatically on one of their exploratory expeditions. As it happened, their carelessness produced an undeserved benefit, for Jesse Mendleton soon became our official contact down here, a great help in obtaining information for us: books, newspapers, tapes, anything we could get or transmit without causing a ruckus."

Tandra's magnificent brown eyes widened with amusement. "No doubt your ellls are responsible for some UFO sightings."

"Yes, some of them, I suppose," Conn said. "Our ships have a low radar cross-section, but occasionally we use ionic or electrical display decoys."

"So here you are, snooping around again," Tandra smiled. "But what exactly does Conn want with me?"

"To get you good and drunk, then capture you as my prize specimen, of course."

Tandra laughed, and her hands reached out hesitantly to touch his helmet as he continued.

"Actually, we are considering making official contact with Earth. Your affairs haven't shaken us up much until lately. But now you've outstripped, not only our predictions of your adaptability to stress, but also our wildest estimates of your unfathomable capacity for repression. You write off incredible disasters to natural causes and breathe gigantic sighs, apparently feeling quite relieved of responsibility. If we can find a way to approach Earth correctly and to prick the conscience of man enough to stimulate his capacity for self-control, we might have an outside chance of helping you put a lid on a few of the more explosive problems."

"I wish you luck," Tandra said darkly, abruptly dropping her playful mood. "Just don't forget that man's conscience is made of money. No matter what political or economic or religious philosophy we espouse—in practice, the profit motive in one form or another is the basis of all of our morality."

Conn sat up and looked at Tandra carefully. Was she angry? He couldn't tell. She was damn near as stolid as a varok.

"Where was I?" he asked. He settled back into Tandra's lap and left his long legs dangling under the hedge. "We would like your help with our microbiological studies. Before we decide whether to interfere in the affairs of Earth, we want to be very certain that there is no danger of transmitting lethal organisms between species. If you came with me, we would place you in quarantine at base with a small lab of your own for several weeks while we completed tests in comparative bacteriology and virology. After you had done an analysis of our normal flora and received our immunizations, you could begin exposure procedures and eventually leave quarantine to join us for a few months. Our life requirements are roughly similar to yours. Our natural cycle is about thirty hours, and the varoks evolved in a twenty-hour system, so we can all get along on a twenty-four-hour rhythm fairly well. There shouldn't be any major problems. Of course, it's unavoidable; you'll be something of a—a—"

"Guinea pig," Tandra said. He sounded so serious and believable. She wished that it was all true, that his story was more than a fantasy invented to amuse her.

"Yes. We would say *kaehl*. We think there is little danger for you, but we can't be sure. We have not tested the pathogenicity of our parasites on any of Earth's other species, for none are capable of giving their informed consent, as far as we know. But we have vaccines prepared for you from all of our potential pathogens. You will be given a complete report of our studies so you can judge their thoroughness, and we'll conduct any further tests that you feel are necessary. Perhaps I should ask you if you would be willing to submit to personality studies, behavior patterns and such—a psychological analysis of yourself as a representative of the human species?"

"In captivity?" Tandra searched for ways to stretch the imagination of her new acquaintance.

"Absolutely not. If the situation causes you undue stress or if you wish to leave for any reason—off you go. We can have you back home in less than thirty-six hours. We won't even cut out your tongue. No one would believe you anyway." His easy laugh delighted Tandra, but it disguised a strong desire to be believed.

"You have ten minutes to decide if you want to come with me. I'll get you another drink to help you make up your mind."

He rose quickly, ambled over to the bar, paused to exchange banter with some other guests, and returned.

Tandra was feeling relaxed and happy, and she watched him with unabashed admiration. "Don't be silly," she admonished herself. "Here's a *real* one. Do yourself a favor: don't let your daydreams get in your way."

"I wish you would unmask and join me now that your story is finished," Tandra said. "I want to know you."

"You like me then?"

"I don't often find someone I can talk to, someone who loves the things I do. I shouldn't tell you how long it's been . . . It's time I found out who you are!" She bent toward his helmet and tried to pull it free, but he caught her hands and held them together effortlessly.

"Tsk. Tsk. Rude and aggressive woman. I have already told you who I am: Conn of Ellason, an elll with two Varokian degrees. You should be honored. Look now. Sit down here beside me and look at the sky. There's the moon, right? Our observation base can't be seen from here, obviously, and neither can Ellason. But there are other stars. What constellations do you know? Tell me where they are and I'll tell you if I can see them, too."

It soon became obvious to Conn that they were seldom referring to the same stars. Lining up the limbs of fruit trees with the heavenly bodies helped, but the vodka hindered. Laughing noisily, they finally gave up, arose together from the lawn, and, dancing with unrestrained warmth, moved toward the pool.

How long has it been since I've met a man I could like so well? Tandra thought. Life is too short and love is too scarce. I won't let this one go.

They were dancing close beside the pool when she again pounced on his helmet and tried to remove it.

Conn panicked; she almost had it. He forced the locks back in place but couldn't disengage her hands.

He grabbed her about the waist and with a low hoot toppled backwards into the pool, taking her with him. Tandra screeched and struggled to free herself, but he carried her to the bottom.

There in the dimly lit water, before he released her, she looked into his face plate and saw his pleasant smile flashing gray-green and white, happily expectant, thoroughly warm—but totally alien. Her mind immediately cleared, and sent her scrambling to the surface. She pulled herself out of the water and stood stunned.

Other people?! No. They mustn't know! They might harm him.

Conn coasted toward her and gave her foot a playful tug before he sprang effortlessly onto the deck behind her.

"That was no story you told," Tandra said in a tight whisper.

"No story."

"We must go now, immediately, before anyone else suspects."

Their fall into the pool had precipitated a noisy melee of disrobing, splashing, and dunking games, and it took several minutes of being buffeted in the crowd of revelers before they were able to break free for her car.

Once they were on the road, Conn slumped awkwardly in his seat and placed a broad glove on Tandra's shoulder. (Was it a hand, fin or paw? she wondered.) "Are you warm enough?" he asked.

She was shaking, incapable of focusing on the reality that sat next to her; but she could hear the real concern in his voice. She nodded. Reality was now in his concern for her, as it had been in the touch of his sensitive body while they danced, in the understanding he had shown her, in the pleasure they had shared with stars, in the warm smile behind the face-plate.

She began to relax as he spoke, his voice rolling slowly and gently at first, then faster and more easily as he sensed that this woman, who had somehow come to mean more than just success to him, was listening intently.

"Tandra, let me be serious for just a moment. Put yourself in my place. I have decided to risk contact with you only because my evidence supports the conclusion of our informant, Jesse Mendleton, that you are the person to give us the help we need. I am in considerable danger here. Though I mean no one and no thing on Earth any harm, you should know that I am armed." He stretched out both arms toward Tandra and turned them outward slightly. There was a long, narrow pocket in each sleeve of his isolation suit. "Under no circumstances will I allow myself to be captured. I can hold off a sizable attack with the paralyzing gas in this ejector. Or, if cornered, I can activate this other hypodermic and disintegrate into pea soup so fast and so completely that no one would be able to ascertain what I was, or that I had been anything at all."

"I—I don't know what to say," Tandra stammered. "I had decided that you were a man I could—could care for—" She stopped. "But now, how can I know that you won't suddenly turn—You aren't even a man!"

"Turn into what?" Conn chuckled. "I am already a monster from outer space." He ruffled her hair. "Take me home with you. I won't do anything to compel or even to persuade you to go to moon-base with me. You can decide on the way."

"I am a fool to go and a fool not to. Your offer is too attractive if it is real, and no one—no thing—could fake being you so well."

"You can be damn sure of that," Conn said. "I'm no fake. A bit weird perhaps for an elll. They call me a loner, one of the mutants. But no fake. We'll take good care of you, Tandra."

She took his glove in her trembling grasp, and momentarily a hand and a prehensile fin tightened together.

"At the party you must have seen what small minds we have," she said. "Few men see themselves in the larger context, but I think you do—whatever your context is."

"That's an indirect way to ask more than I can tell you, Tandra. My context is very different from yours and yet very much the same. It's all one: Earth and Ellason and Anywhere Else. We live and some of us breathe and all of us need love." He paused. "You see yourself in proper perspective I assume."

"I doubt it; I'm far too cynical now. I'll find a way for my daughter, Shawne, to survive. That's all. That's my only real purpose in life."

Conn shifted uneasily. "Let me understand you, Tandra. Mendleton warned us that you had rejected politics, but I'll bet it's politics that concerns your child, probably the way she has to live, right? I understand very well; ellls are infamous for doting on their children."

Tandra nodded slightly.

"Have I caught your wave length? You sit there like a warm afternoon with not even a long, misty hair out of place. Your voice shook more during that argument at the party than your body shook when you realized I was alien. You're cool as the proverbial cucumber, but you run deep—deep and hot where Shawne is concerned." Conn felt a strong urge to expose the heat—the elllonian-like passion in this woman.

"Perhaps you're right," Tandra said. "The few friends I have might agree with your analysis, though my acquaintances would laugh at your description 'deep and hot.' I may be indifferent too often; but 'cool' never, at least not now. Can't you see how nervous I am?" She laughed. "Here, let me hold on." She reached out to touch him again. "You're the source of my fear, but you're also its best cure."

They drove the rest of the way in silence. At her house, Tandra ran in to dismiss the baby sitter and then quickly retrieved Conn from the car.

"Have you ever been to one of our homes? That contact you have, Mendleton's?"

He gave a negative shrug. "Never met the man face to face, nor any other man either."

"Then help yourself. Look around while I arrange for a leave of absence."

"Then you are going with me?"

"You haven't doubted it since we danced the second time."

2
Obliteration of Doubt

While Tandra talked on the telephone, Conn made a detailed survey of the house, set aside stacks of records and professional books, and searched the kitchen for cans of soup that would be both familiar to Tandra's child and convenient to eat aseptically with isolation suit straws.

When Tandra put down the phone, Conn was nowhere in sight. Suddenly she heard him bellow, a sound of unmistakable delight. It came from the bathroom.

"Conn?"

The elll was turning drunkenly under the infrared lamp in the ceiling. "Feels good to see again. This lamp is too bright, but it's so much better than your fluorescent lights. Come here, Tandra. Let me look at you." He took her hand and turned her slowly around. "Your skin is now a lovely shade of warm-bright," he laughed as he clasped her shoulders. "I wonder how different our vision is. We'll be able to tell better when we dim base to Elllonian light levels and I take my contacts off."

Tandra smiled and put her hands around his helmet. "I wish I could see through your faceplate," she said. "It gives me the feeling that I'm talking to a ghost. Are you really in there?"

In answer Conn wrapped his long arms around her and pulled her into a comfortable hug.

"Yes, you *are* really in there, aren't you?" She rested against him and let her apprehension drain away. They moved back into the living room.

"You know, Tandra," Conn murmured, "I haven't

had close contact with a human being before, and much that I see in human culture tells me that you should be screaming in panic or going for your gun now that you know I am alien. Please don't lose faith now. When you're safely wrapped up in one of these isolation suits on our ship, the *Lurlial,* I'll exchange this miserable suit for nature's own and you'll see just what you've got to put up with."

"Do you really intend to take all those old records?" she asked.

"I've about worn out the music library at base in my five years there," Conn said. "I'd like to try experimenting with some of these if I may—convert the bass line to ultrasonic—" Suddenly the elll stopped, his gaze rivetted on the piano, which was obscured in one corner of the room under stacks of music and several smaller instruments.

"That must be a piano," he said. He approached it slowly and touched one of the keys. "May I?"

"Go ahead. It's not fragile."

Conn ran his glove over the keys and then set about searching the case with his fingers. "Where is the mechanism?"

Tandra helped him clear the music from the piano top and lift it off.

"Play it for me," he said, as he reached into the piano to inspect the hammers.

Tandra happily played a series of chords and was engrossed in steaming through "Rustle of Spring" when a child tottered sleepily into the living room. The young girl stared at the helmeted figure bending over her adoptive mother at the piano, recognized him as a skinny version of the men she had watched exploring the moon on television, and decided to present him with her Pooh bear. She approached the elll, who was absorbed by the music, and tugged insistently at his mottled brown pant leg.

Conn acknowledged the tug, and immediately knelt down to the child's height.

Without a word, she pushed the stuffed toy into his gloves.

"Shawne," Conn said gently, "are you letting me play with him?"

"You keep 'im. He wants to go in a rock' ship."

Conn looked to Tandra for approval; then he took Shawne in his arms and gave her an affectionate hug. "All right. He can ride on top of the control panel in my ship. Would you like to take a ride, too?"

"Yes, I'll go too," Shawne said. "But you better call 'im Pooh. He eats Kleenex." She giggled, and Conn responded with a natural childish humor that completely captivated her.

Tandra watched them playing noisily on the floor. The baby accepted the stranger without question. And why not? His interest in her was obviously genuine, warm and sensitive; yet, abruptly, Tandra recognized in herself the feeling that she shouldn't trust him. *Shouldn't*. But she *did* trust him or wanted to. She could find nothing dishonest in his words or in his manner. Then why *shouldn't?* Such distrust was a denial of her faith in life itself. And wasn't Shawne now proving the rightness of trust? I'm a product of attitudes I hate, she thought. Begone, doubt! We're off to the moon with God-knows-who-or-what!

She laughed to herself and set to packing, moving from room to room, much as Conn had done, scanning everything systematically for Shawne's favorite toys, for items that would be useful in her work, and for artifacts that might interest the ellls. Gradually a small pile of things accumulated in the kitchen by the back door. "Conn, come here and tell me if we should take all this."

"All what?" he asked as he came into the kitchen carrying Tandra's sewing machine. "That little pile of toothbrushes and dolls? Don't be so conservative. We've got lots of room. I'd like to borrow this, if you don't mind. Junah and Erah would have good fun with it. It is a sewing machine, isn't it?"

"Yes, but—"

"You don't have to take that microscope or any lab equipment, just your reference books. The varoks are well equipped." He stood thinking for a moment. "I wish we could take the piano—no—we can't get the *Lurlial* in close enough. Aren't you going to take anything for yourself?"

"I would miss something to play. May I take my recorders?"

"Bring the guitar, too. I'd like to try it; in fact I'd like to try everything you've got. Bring all your tape recordings."

She went to the living room to get the musical instruments and returned to find Conn and Shawne carrying into the kitchen two watercolor originals of sailboats on Lake Michigan and a framed print of Picasso's *Don Quixote*.

"Do you mind?"

"Of course not. I'd love to have them along." She laughed as she looked at the growing pile. "What are we forgetting?"

"A watch?"

"Do you want me to take a watch? I have one somewhere. Why do I need a watch?"

"I thought human beings always needed watches."

"I refuse to be a slave to anything, especially time," Tandra said. "I think I've forgotten something."

"I know what it is, but I'm too much an elll to want to remind you. You won't need them anyway."

"Oh—clothes! What kind of clothes should I take?"

"I'm a poor one to advise you because I can't stand the things; I'm about to go mad in this isolation suit. But it's very warm and humid at base. If you're the modest type, bring a bathing suit."

"I'm not the modest type, but you must be kidding. I'll just bring a few shirts and slacks." She turned to go to her bedroom. "Now I know what we've forgotten— the turntable. Won't you need it for all those records? The needle is very old—we can't get them anymore— but it works."

"I'll make a new one for you at base," Conn said.

Thus the night slipped away unnoticed, while Conn alternately played with Shawne and interrupted Tandra's packing with questions. Finally the contents of the house had been thoroughly appraised in terms of their common interests, and they were ready. Conn radioed for his ship.

"The house is set on a hill, Tallyn; and the canyon drops forty or fifty metres—about two *pallons*—beyond, near a stand of trees. Set the *Lurlial* down in the canyon. It's plenty tight, so I'll beam you in. You should be on final approach by the time we get there with all the things we've collected. The baby is with us, so put Da-oon's isolation suit into the entrance chamber with Dr. Grey's suit. Aim carefully, wild elll. There's no room for slop." Unobtrusively Conn deactivated the small transmitter in his helmet.

"Your co-pilot has a good command of English," Tandra said. The fact for some reason upset her.

Conn's reply was pleasantly disarming: "There's no excuse for using a language unknown to someone within audible range. Tallyn understands me; he's been on the English language impressor. But he has a prejudice toward the human race that has blocked his own ability to use human languages very accurately."

They hurriedly bundled Shawne into her jacket, loaded their arms with as much as they could carry, placed Pooh ceremoniously on top of Conn's load, and made their way down the path to a clearing at the bottom of the canyon. Then they returned to the house for the rest of Tandra's boxes. Soon after a queer silvery shape appeared and hovered above them, shivering in the first morning light.

"Bull's eye," Conn said into his communicator. "Bring it on down, Tallyn. How do you like my ship, Dr. Grey?"

"It looks like a clumsy, pregnant bat wobbling up there."

"And to you it's silent like a bat no?" Conn laughed.

"No. But it is very quiet."

As the strange ship slowly settled toward the ground, Tandra's palms began to sweat. Two gray-brown figures emerged from a side hatch and started pushing the boxes of books, records, and soup into the ship, along with the rest of the paraphernalia.

While she stood with Shawne under the moon-dipped shadow of the great silver shape, Tandra found herself trembling. She knew nothing about these strangers. She yearned for something definite—for guaranteed safety, guaranteed anything. But there was no certainty to be found. Only faith, faith in life—which promises nothing.

Finally, all was stowed away in the sterilization chamber of the *Lurlial*. The two strange figures disappeared into the ship and Conn gave Tandra instructions for entering the outer hatch after he had gone inside. She was to close it behind her, and she and Shawne were to don the isolation suits.

Then Conn backed through the inner hatch and was gone. Tandra was suddenly alone with Shawne beside the grotesquely alien space ship. A deep impulse possessed her, insisting that she dig her fingers into the soil or grasp the trees before she lost them. How could she know that she would ever stand on Earth again? And Shawne. She couldn't gamble with Shawne's life this way—walking blindly into such an unknown.

"No, no. We can't go," she cried frantically as she grabbed Shawne by the arm and started to run toward the house. But the baby pulled away and turned back to the ship. The two of them could see Conn carefully placing Shawne's stuffed Pooh on top of something within the forward window panel.

"Look! Pooh gonna drive," Shawne said. "Want to go with Conn," she exclaimed, running down the hill.

Tandra hesitated, then raced after the child and caught her as she reached the outer hatch of the *Lurlial*.

"You promised bye-bye to da moon," Shawne cried, thrashing wildly against Tandra's grasp.

"Shawne, we can't go. It isn't safe."

But as she pulled the child away she looked up and saw Conn's easy slouch framed in the open hatchway.

"You can't come alone, Shawne," he said. "I think your mother has changed her mind. I'll try to come see you again sometime." His voice carried the disappointment that lay hidden behind his face-plate. He turned into the entrance of the sterilization chamber and brought out Tandra's guitar and the watercolor of sailboats on Lake Michigan.

"I'd like to keep this picture, Tandra. May I? I'll find a way to pay for it later."

"No. No!" Tandra said. "Take it."

"I'll get your Pooh, Shawne," Conn said.

Suddenly Shawne escaped again from Tandra and climbed into the *Lurlial.* "I'm going with my f'end Conn."

As Tandra lurched through the hatch to retrieve the child, her hand hit a furry spot on the inside of the ship, and several large silken blue flakes fell off into her hand. Startled, she looked above her and saw that the entrance chamber was invaded by rounded fingers of a mossy substance. Indeed, the walls were almost half covered with a thick growth of delicate leaf-life structures.

"A moss-covered space ship!?"

Mirrored in the beautiful plant growing so wildly in that incongruous place, her panic seemed ridiculous. "You can't be so wrong, can you, Shawne?" Tandra sighed. There is nothing but grief here for you now, anyway, she thought, nothing but asphalt wastelands and death in greater and greater numbers. The idea struck harder than she expected. Maybe with the ellls Shawne could have a glimpse of life without grasping, life appreciated and savoured. "All right," she said, "We'll go."

She turned around to shut the outer hatch, but Conn blocked her way. "Be sure, Tandra." If she panicked *en route,* he knew, his mission would be worse than a simple failure—the varoks would call into question his good judgment.

Tandra stood for a long moment looking into his blank helmet. "It's true isn't it, what we talked about at the party? Shawne knows better than I. Yet when you are near, I know I can trust you. I want to go, if you'll still have me."

"I'd think you were nuts if you walked into this potential trap without some fear," Conn said. His warm, firm touch found her hands and did much to soothe her. "But if we're going to take any reasonable precautions against contamination, I'll have to leave you alone again." He turned away and entered the inner hatch of the *Lurlial,* closing it behind him.

The mossy walls were very soft around the woman and her child. Tentatively, Tandra touched an irregular patch of her plant-friend, then felt the smooth inner hatch that Conn had just slammed shut. It was not metal as she had first thought; it had a neutral, strange, light feel. Suddenly the walls seemed to close in, and the oddly neutral objects around her mocked her with threats. If only Conn could have waited with them!

"Tandra, are you all right?"

"Dr. Grey?" A different, strange, thick voice came through the ship's intercom.

"I'm all right now. I see the isolation suits. I'll dress Shawne first."

"Yes, do," the new voice said. "It will take you some time to learn fine manipulations with the gloves on." The heavy, clipped voice continued. "Dr. Grey, I am Generalist in Behavioral Science Llorkin. When Conn left you in the entry hatch, your eyes grew wide and your movements were like those of an undomesticated, caged animal. If you wish, you may return to your home. You are not obligated to come with us. Once we leave Earth, it will be very inconvenient for us to return before the agreed upon six months."

His tone was aggravating.

"I am quite all right now, Generalist Llorkin."

"Hurry up and get those suits on, will you?" Conn said.

His voice rang with the satisfaction he felt. He had done it! He had won the trust of a human being! The years of careful self-cultivation had borne good fruit— fruit that promised to be especially sweet, for the woman was already his friend. "Be sure that the helmet is locked," he continued, "and that you're getting air through the filters before you come into the shower hatch. The UV lights and disinfecting spray will stay on for a minute before the inner hatch opens."

As she pulled on the light green isolation suit, Tandra felt soothed by Conn's voice. Her dark eyes flashed with anticipation. Conn was beautiful, no matter what kind of creature he might be: his quick wit, his rolling voice, his loose joints. She loved him already.

Quickly she dressed Shawne with impatient hands, then the two of them stepped into the shower hatch. It immediately sprang to life with a fine spray emerging at every angle from a hundred obscure fixtures. Tandra counted fifteen seconds—thirty seconds. She tensed with excitement. Forty-five seconds—fifty-five. Only a few seconds more and she would be with Conn. Sixty —eighty. The grin she had seen last night—it must have been a grin—one hundred seconds—was extraordinary, alien beyond doubt. One hundred twenty—one hundred fifty. Was that party just last night? One hundred eighty. Damn it! Damn it, Conn, this is taking forever! Two hundred—two hundred and twenty.

Finally, the spray quit. She held Shawne's hand, and they stood dripping for another interminable minute. Then, at last, the seals on the inner hatch began to turn.

"Conn, you have no sense of our time. The shower was on well over—"

The inner hatch flew open, stunning Tandra with a silver-green vision that choked off her words. It was more even than her imagination had painted. Within the *Lurlial's* central passageway—a softly lit cavern carved from thick living mounds of silver moss—stood Conn, tall and slender and magnificent, planted at a relaxed tilt on broad webbed feet, his body a mosaic of hexagonal tiles of gray-green velvet grouted with pale, vibrant chartreuse. His powerful arms and sensitive prehensile fins, tipped with long, partially webbed fingers, reached out to Tandra in welcome as his pleasant grin gradually spread over his face, accenting the feathered laugh lines that radiated out from his brilliant emerald green eyes. His deep brow ridge was set at a steep angle, giving him a permanent quizzical expression. And

—matching a fur-like patch that modestly enclosed his hips—a short, tousled crown of feathery black-green plumes, sprinkled sparsely with dabs of bright red and yellow and iridescent blue, carelessly softened the top of his earless head.

Tandra stood transfixed by the vision before her until Shawne ran to Conn with a burst of joy, somehow recognizing him as her former friend in the helmeted suit.

"Dere's Conn. Hi, Conn," she shouted as he scooped her up in his arms.

Unconsciously, Tandra followed her, tears of delight and relief streaming beneath her face-plate. Conn put Shawne down and grasped Tandra's gloved hands. "Welcome aboard the *Lurlial*, Tandra," he said. She buried her head in his wide chest, and released the accumulated tension of the last few hours in welcome sobs, while the elll pressed his arms around her, frustrated, as any elll would be, with the barrier her isolation suit created between them.

"I'm not that bad, then, am I?"

"You're beautiful, Conn," she said, pushing him away to arm's length so she could absorb the deep crystal of his emerald eyes and confident strength of his regular features.

"Horr-shit," he laughed. "But I'm glad that you don't find me repulsive."

They stood silently enjoying each other, preoccupied with their own delight: Conn remembering the dance of the night before, impatient for contact in the flesh, relieved that Tandra had found his visage pleasant; Tandra remembering the game of stars, impatient for more long stories of life beyond Earth, relieved that the other ellls had left them alone. She turned then to see if they were in fact alone—and found one elll shifting nervously on wide, webbed feet as he watched them.

"Tandra Grey, doctor of microbes, meet Generalist Llorkin, our resident head-shrinker," Conn mumbled.

"How do you do, Dr. Grey. I am most pleased to

make your acquaintance," Llorkin said. His stilted
English emerged thickly and with considerable difficulty, contrasting sharply with Conn's easy diction.

Though obviously an elll, Llorkin did not resemble
Conn. He was stubby and irregular, a much lighter
green, his plumes obviously clipped. He held himself
rigid, twitching in the silence following his oppressive
greeting, then shifted a pencil-shaped object to the
hand that clutched a pile of plastic sheets and awkwardly held out his left fin to Tandra. Not knowing
what else to do, she shook it.

Conn raised a fin and turned it so that its fingers
spiraled inward. "This is the common elllonian greeting, Tandra," he said. "Llorkin, there's no need for
formality here. Dr. Grey and I have already been swimming together."

Puzzled, Tandra glanced at Conn, but his only answer was a quizzical wrinkle that flashed between his
brow lines. She followed his gaze to Llorkin and noted
the psychologist's obvious embarrassment.

"Formality may not be required, Generalist Conn,
but low humor is certainly out of place at the moment.
I think that Dr. Grey should sign this immediately."

Llorkin's stubby, green fingers held out a thin, dull
sheet of plastic to Tandra. In the center was a short
paragraph laboriously hand-printed in English:

The undersigned agrees to associate with the designated company, *Elll Varok Science* at *Observation Base, Earth-Moon* for a
period of *six months* and bears said company no responsibility for
accidents, unavoidable or natural. He She It enters this agreement
and our company in full awareness, under no unnatural persuasion
or obligation, and by his her its own free will.

Signed _____

Witnesses of other species (please designate):

_____

_____

_____

_____

"Where the hell did you dig out that ancient trash, Llorkin? We don't need it here." Conn's voice had lost its lilt.

"I believe," Llorkin puffed, "that it is essential that this human female sign a statement of free will immediately. Her behavior has been erratic and emotional. I judge that her actions are unpredictable. The consequences of the implication that we have taken her by force would be severely detrimental to the establishment of a trusting and effective relationship with Earth in the future. *Uyen l'e advant . . .*"

Conn's temper flew out of control. "G. Llorkin, I will tolerate no more insults to Dr. Grey. You will continue to speak English in her presence and when within her audible range." His wide emerald eyes were narrowed to slits.

"It's all right, Conn. I don't mind signing the paper," Tandra said.

With a nervous half-grin, Llorkin handed her his pen. It was a bit large for her hand, but the conical tip slid easily over the plastic sheet leaving a dark, reddish mark.

"You may keep the pen if you like, Dr. Grey." Llorkin's tone was condescending now. "You will want to keep some records of your experiences. I apologize that our paper is synthetic. Wood pulp is a luxury the varoks have not recently afforded themselves."

"Thank you very much, Generalist Llorkin. I intend to keep a diary. Is there more of this paper available?"

"Tons of it, Tandra," Conn said with an easy chuckle that erased the tension in the air. "Ellls spend half their time scribbling and the other half melting down discarded paper and reforming it so they can scribble some more. It's no doubt a surreptitious way of satisfying some of our need for sensual pleasure."

"Generalist Conn, you belittle our species!" Llorkin protested.

"Not at all," Conn laughed. "We learned it all from the varoks."

Tandra saw Llorkin start and ineptly try to silence Conn. Was it the reference to varoks?

"I'll bet the paper has a nice feel," Tandra said, as she rubbed her gloved hand over the plastic. "I won't deny that I enjoy the sensual pleasures more often than not."

"Then you've come to the right place," Conn said.

They exchanged a glance that left them feeling open and secure with each other. Llorkin didn't know what to make of it, saw he could not share in it, and retreated with annoyance.

"Come on, Shawne, I'll show you my ship," Conn said.

"Conn?" Tandra asked, "What does *Generalist* mean? Is it a title I should use when I'm talking to someone?"

"Good grief, no, not unless you want to alert someone to his professional status or butter-up some poor, insecure so-and-so like Llorkin. The title only indicates our educational achievement. After fifteen years of required basic education on Ellason or Varok, we may specialize in a chosen subject: first as Student, then Apprentice, then as Specialist or Generalist. Specialist is equivalent to an American Ph.D. Generalist studies cover an entire field of knowledge, like physics or behavioral science or biology. Then there are those rare scholars who are beginning to learn a bit about things: the Masters. They are experts in their field of knowledge, capable of integrating what they know over wide disciplines; they actually deserve their distinction. We have two Masters running the base, an elll and a varok. Great beings."

"Conn, what are varoks?"

"They're not easy to define, Tan, and I don't want to prejudice your first impression. For now we'll say they're technocrats of restraint. This ship is a good example of their talents."

"And you? What are you, Conn, besides a master diplomat?"

"It doesn't matter what I am," Conn said. "You will soon meet these others. They will mean far more to you."

"I don't think that's possible."

An enormous tear rose like a new sun from the deep green rim of Conn's right eye. "You make me cherish my lonerliness," he said.

" 'Lonerliness'? That's the first mistake I've heard—"

"It's no mistake. You'll soon know what I mean."

"You have funny hands, Conn, isn't they?" Shawne lisped. "They're all green."

"They're real good for swimming, Shawne. I'll teach you to swim at base, okay?"

"What do I do when we get to base, Conn? Just comparative microbiology? Is that all you really want me for?" Tandra asked.

"I think you'll be useful to us in many ways," Conn said. "If direct contact proves to be reasonably safe, we can then decide how to make the best use of you: how to carve out the best steaks from your legs, whether your arms should be fried or roasted—"

"Conn!"

He couldn't see her face through the isolation helmet she wore, but her hands admonished him to be serious, and he tried.

"There are several ways you might help us after the first obvious problems of contact are solved. No one knows what you'll be asked to do eventually. But we have to begin somewhere, somehow. There is no clear path. The varoks can't watch Earth much longer and just let it go. As for the ellls—I think we can only look at something for so long before we must touch it, know it at first hand—even human beings, as repulsive as they may be. All but Shawne, of course." He bounced the child up to his shoulder, where she sat happily inspecting him.

"You're pretty, Conn. You have soft things all over," Shawne said.

"Those are my touch plates," he answered. "You can feel them when you get that suit off. After your quarantine we'll snuggle up and look at pictures of some weird friends of mine."

Conn swung the two-year-old down into his arms, pressed his long, straight nose flat against her face-plate, and wrapped his tongue around it, inciting Shawne to screeches of delight. Then he balanced her side-saddle on his hip and the three of them sank to the floor oblivious to everything but the closing ring of emotion that was pulling them together.

3
Early Commitment

Too soon they became aware of the growing light outside. "Tallyn will be ready to take off in a few minutes," Conn said, rising to his feet. "I'd better take you to your cabin. This hatch over here leads to a crawlway, Tandra." He strode to a small hatch in the wall adjacent to the larger entry-hatch. "Gives us access to the engines. The whole tail of the bat in back of us is stuffed with propulsion hardware. We entered the main hatch, which is about in the middle of the left underbelly. There is cargo space below this deck and life-support equipment, navigation gear, food, and waste processing above our heads. Here on the ceiling you can see a hatch. There's not much need to get in there except for maintenance. This is the only passageway, so you can't get lost."

"What is the hull made of?" Tandra asked. "It's not metal."

"It's a varokian low-density poly-phase material. Has a very low radar cross-section, for obvious reasons. Only the moss trimmings come from Ellason."

Conn walked on down the passageway and absent-mindedly plucked and nibbled a handful of the ubiquitous, thick silver moss which was draped haphazardly on the walls. "These doors give access to sleeping cabins, and at the end of the hall down here you can see the entrance to the control room."

Just then another elll passed them, his sharply-muscled body tossing his long tousled plumes into a rhythmic swing. He went behind the transparent barrier of the control room where yet a third elll was seated in a large couch surrounded by panels of controls and read-

outs and what-not. The seated elll turned and grinned
at Tandra. She saw his long, pale, golden-tipped
plumes framing a face wrinkled by many years of
laughter, a strong contrast to the other's knotty, wild
appearance, which was accented by his coarse features
and great feathered brows.

"That is Aen and Tallyn in there, Aen is the older
one. You'll meet them once we're on our way. We com-
puterize our flights, but we have a full measure of man-
ual option. The nose of the bat surrounds much of
this entire area and is nothing but heat shield. Turn
around now and I'll follow you back."

Tandra smiled generously at Aen; he looked so incongruous sitting there like a delighted child in the
maze of such stark ingenuity. Varokian ingenuity, she
realized suddenly. Yes. Conn had said that only the
moss was from Ellason. This was a varokian ship. If
the moss was an indication, gray composite and banks
of dials were of no inherent interest to ellls.

Conn confirmed her perception as they headed back
through the ship. The varoks, he explained, had built
the *Lurlial* as a working vehicle for planetary exploration after consulting with the few ellls interested in its
design—hence the moss-lined passageways. Against
considerable varokian objection to the added expense,
the ellls had insisted on furnishing the modest craft as
alive and comfortably wet as possible; for, though they
rarely made the long voyage to Ellason in this ship,
they believed in maximizing all experiences, both long
and short, and never allowed themselves to suffer unnecessary drought even while pursuing the serious and
sometimes dangerous business of scientific observation
of other planets.

Conn rapped his soft knuckles on a door near the
control room. "This is Llorkin and Aen's cabin. You
and Shawne can sleep here across the hall, unless I can
persuade you to crawl into my water with me."

"Your what?"

"You'd drown, and I'd dry up if I slept with you,
so we'd better forget it. Each to his own. But call me
if anything worries you."

Conn's light touch opened another door in the long corridor, and they entered a colorful room carpeted with something red and plush. The room was furnished with a compact desk near the right wall and with two large oblong basins recessed into the floor against the left wall. Tandra leaned over one of them and peered through its translucent cover at its deep red lining, guessing that its design was not varokian.

"Here. Let me retract the seal," Conn said.

As he pushed the cover of the bowl into the wall, Shawne noticed the plumbing. "Momma! A fur bathtub!"

"Fur? Where would we get fur? It's a living plant, Shawne, like that in the hall. It not only gives us oxygen, but it is delicious to eat and soft to lie on. Would you prefer hot water or blankets, ladies?"

"We'll take blankets, thank you. You sleep in this, in water, Conn?"

"I can't think of a cossier way to sleep. You'll like it too, even with a blanket. It's called an *uuyvanoon.*"

"Cozier," Tandra corrected. Then she tried pronouncing the elllonian word. "U—uy—way—I'll call it a sleeping tub."

"Sleeping tub! You couldn't think of a less romantic name, could you? And *pregnant bat* for my beautiful ship! You're obviously not taking things seriously enough around here."

"I'm sorry," Tandra started to say, but Conn put a finger on her face-plate.

"Please don't take things seriously around here."

As if in a gentle dream, Tandra followed Shawne and Conn down the soft gray passageway of the ship, watched while the elll demonstrated the ingenious waste disposal system, and wondered again at his frequent reference to varokian design.

"Conn," she asked as she looked into the small galley and saw the cans of soup drenched with disinfectant, "Why can't you tell me more about the varoks?"

"Because they're weird, difficult mutants from a wild, poor excuse for a planet," Conn laughed. "They're even uglier than the human beast. You'll meet one soon enough, no doubt. Don't worry about them. Let's get Shawne to bed now; then I have to help Tallyn."

She followed Conn back to the red room and watched while he placed Shawne into one of the basins and connected her restraints.

"Sleep well, New Life," he said, stroking the baby's back. *"Uleoon,* Tandra. Next stop, EV moon base. No more panics allowed. You'll be alone now again. Will you be all right?"

Tandra nodded, but as the elll swung out the door, she sighed deeply to ease the apprehension his absence so quickly generated. She looked at Shawne, suddenly concerned that the child might be more frightened than had been apparent, but she was asleep already.

Tandra looked around uncertainly. Then she took a stack of plastic sheets from the desk, strapped herself into one of the large basins to await lift-off, and decided to describe her first impressions of the ellls. She propped her hand under her helmet, leaned on her elbow, made an abortive attempt to chew the pen, and then began to write—and found herself deftly avoiding a description of Conn, transcribing instead a wave of feeling.

"I was afraid Shawne would never know a day like yesterday! The world was bathed in sunlight and crowned with blue again. No matter how alien, any knowing perception could have found Earth's beauty: any sight would have delighted in the slowly waving, sparkling dance of the pines; any ears would have captured its endless sigh; any touch would have felt the gentle, warmed wind; any smell would have savored the wind's hint of rich, red earth and sun-baked pine needles.

"And on such a day Conn came to me! What if I had not had Shawne to pull me back! Until I tried to run from this ship I had no idea how far my faith in life had been eroded away.

"Six months I'll be on the moon. I wonder if the massive die-offs will have peaked by then. Every hour is precious now. And I almost wasted this chance to know Conn.

"I trust him entirely, even love him, but I wish he wouldn't be so obtuse concerning varoks. Their technological capability is awesome and stark—unlike the ells in many respects. I can only assume their purposes with me are as he has described."

Suddenly, Tandra became aware of slow steps shuffling through the mossy carpet toward Shawne's sleeping bowl.

"She's a very young child," a rumbling voice mused. The voice was unmistakably elllonian, but deeper than Conn's. It emerged roughly from the ancient, rotund ell Tandra had seen in the control room. "I am Aen, Specialist in Electronics, one of the old-timers in Earth-studies." He moved toward Tandra, his round belly spilling generously over his hip plumes and one wrinkled gray-green fin rolled into a fist. Gently he wrapped her hand around his fist. "Welcome to the *Lurlial*, to elllonian friendship," he said. "You don't shrink at our touch. We will not forget that." He turned toward the door with no further comment and nodded at the stocky green figure that had come to stand there, "This is Tallyn," Aen said.

The feathers radiating from Tallyn's eyes pinched together into heavy, long arrows as he said, "We leave now. I advise reclining in *uuyvanoon* and fasten belts. Normally, we leave fast. Our g-tolerance is much greater than yours. We were delayed by minor problems so we accelerate near your maximum g."

Abruptly the ells disappeared through the door and very soon Tandra found herself watching the Earth beneath her gradually, then suddenly, fall away. For a moment she was pressed hard into the side of the firmly conforming basin, but when the force of the acceleration released her, she was able to look down through her window again. The African continent floated below like a great brown and green island sugared with the brightness of clouds.

Sleep overtook her then.

*　*　*

Much later, as the *Lurlial* sped into the void between Earth and her moon, she was awakened by the noise of Shawne and Aen playing. She sat up to watch them, but her attention was diverted by a rolling melody coming from the ship's intercom.

It was Tallyn and Conn, she knew. Conn's mellow tenor joined the other's massive throat-bassoon, and they sang in sliding, angular Elllonian syllables, which fit like pieces of a puzzle into their tight harmony and haunting rhythm:

> U aloon, acuh a l'Ran
> Uyan l lea, uyan l leoon, aeyull! Aeyull!
> Al Ran oonl adl. Pallte El'sonl?
> U aloon, acuh a l'Ran,
> Uyan leell, uyan leoo, acuh.
> U aloon, acuh a l'Ran.*

Tandra made her way awkwardly down the hall and braced herself in the weightlessness behind the two ellls as they sang. When they sensed her presence, they began a new song in English, with a musical sound not so well integrated with the harder English syllables but still soft and wild:

> Do mists grow pale when I am gone?
>   Yes, One Alone,
>   The school knows pain.
> Away! Alone! Dark wet and warm,
> Deep red and deeper, pull me down.
>   You see, Alone?
>   The school knows pain.
> You say naught, Giant of the Sky,
> So what will guide me home again
> To crush me still against the shore?

* Go water being, alone to the bright blue star.
Beyond my mating, beyond my love. Cry grief! Cry grief!
Are Earth's waters filled with exquisite ellls?
Go water being, alone to the bright blue star,
Beyond mates, beyond good life, alone.
Go water being, alone to Earth.

    Yes, One Alone,
      The school knows pain.
O mighty child of empty space,
Alone with self's own life to give,
Glow warm, fine waters, crush me close.
Dark Giant, bind me firm again.
      You see, Alone?
      The school knows pain.
Drown me deep beneath bright mists.

Tandra placed her hand on Conn's shoulder.

"You see, Tall, old fish!" Conn hooted, pulling Tandra into his lap. "This soft, bright creature is mad for me."

"Then she mad for us all, no doubt. Irresistible species, we."

"No," Conn said. "She brings out the loner in me."

"What is this meaning, Conn?" Tallyn grunted. "Take care."

"Not this elll," Conn said. "I'm swimming deep, and I've got to see where the tide will lead. Did you like our songs?" he asked Tandra.

"They have a beautiful sound. Ellason, the 'Dark Giant.' It's far out, isn't it, Conn?"

"I would like to tell you all about Ellason, Tan, but you know I can't. Perhaps I will take you there someday. You've apparently read some speculative infrared astronomy and made a good guess. Don't probe further."

"Security-conscious aliens," Tandra said with a smile.

"Would not you be cautious if us?" Tallyn asked sharply.

"I understand," she said.

Tallyn sat silently as Conn and Tandra went on talking, appalled by their display of affectionate rapport. He knew that though Conn pursued life's pleasures with happy abandon, the elll was usually a more cautious and astute observer in new situations. Tallyn regarded him as inordinately tolerant of the human being.

Moments of selfless or rational human behavior in man's history were lost in Tallyn's mind beneath the knowledge of man's political and natural atrocities. For Tallyn, Tandra was a product of centuries of brutal warfare, of a senseless history of possessors and tormentors and enslavers, whose progeny had recently learned to brutalize their entire planet as well as themselves.

Tallyn had long before concluded that human beings were unspeakably cruel, for they were apparently intelligent, at least potentially intelligent enough to save their world's life. He almost hoped that they would suffer the same hideous cultural and biological torture that the varoks had suffered hundreds of thousands of years ago. The varoks didn't deserve it nearly so much as these, Tallyn had thought.

How could Conn relate to such a being as Tandra Grey? Like all humans, she must care nothing for life. How could she bear consciousness, knowing, as she must, that many of her kind were suffering from malnutrition or were choking to death, their lungs blackened and eroded by the production processes of an extravagant culture?

Yet, in spite of his prejudices, he could not feel altogether hostile toward this happy human creature and her child. The baby was a magnificent new life, not beautiful, of course, but accepting. And her mother—even she had accepted them without question; any elll would love her for that. But Conn's behavior troubled him. Conn was oddly, personally involved with the woman. His unusual, constant reserve—which had always formed a container for his life-loving enthusiasm, even when schooling with other ellls—had apparently dissolved. He seemed vulnerable.

Conn leaned back in the pilot's couch of the *Lurlial* against a cushion of nothing and, annoyed at the persistent weightlessness, pulled his lap restraint tighter. He closed his eyes, longing for the weight and warmth of deep water, for the constant murmur of pressure-talk against the hexagonal meshwork of his body, for an inviting sonar signal from another elll looking for game of sound-dodge in the large pool at base. "Tandra, where are you?" he said, suddenly realizing she was no longer in his lap.

"Just floating around watching the moon go by," she said from behind him.

"Is Shawne asleep?"

"No, Aen is trying to teach her astronomy or elllonian astrology. I'm not sure which. But he's not getting very far. There are too many infrared stars in your sky that we can't see."

"So the infrared sky is *our* sky?" Conn laughed. "Then I suppose the stars that radiate in your visible range are *your* stars. What about the ones that overlap?" He undid his lap restraint and leaned forward as he floated free of his couch. "You wouldn't want to give a poor old elll one of those famous human backrubs, would you, Tan?"

Tallyn watched with discomfort. There was something unreal—something dangerously wrong—about their ease.

"Love to," Tandra said. She spread her hands on his back and kneaded the firm, deep muscles, realizing only dimly that they hinted at power unknown to men.

"That feels good," he murmured, "but I'm dry as a bone. I need a wet-sweater. Guess I'm getting old."

"What do you mean, old? Aen perhaps, but not you."

Conn explained that though there was no biologically meaningful time equivalent on Ellason, it could be said that he was forty-two Earth-years old. With ellls reaching their peak mental capacity usually around thirty-five and complete environmental integration around fifty (the life-span being some one hundred and seventy Earth-years), he actually was in his prime, though relatively young, it was true, to be in a position of responsibility.

He did not add that in spite of his youth, he had acquired a reputation for unfailing accuracy in whatever he attempted during the five years that he had been at base. The varoks particularly admired his independent reserve when he participated in what they too often regarded as elllonian foolishness.

As he relaxed under Tandra's hands, Conn wondered what life on Ellason would be like now if the varoks had not discovered his planet and its green aquatic peoples when they did, some one hundred thousand Earth-years ago. Ellason had still been largely agrarian at that time, and its most complex species, among them the ellls, lived simple tranquil lives, schooling together with no intent other than that of enjoying each other's company and the impressions that impinged on their many senses from the depths of the enormous, warm oceans. Many of the more inventive ellls found their lives fulfilled by the single additional pleasure of watching their underwater gardens flourish. Inevitably, however, their technological competence grew with their knowledge, which was treasured almost exclusively for what it contributed to their awareness. They ignored more inventions than they used, concentrating their production primarily on gardening tools, toys, and musical devices, which eventually reached a high degree of electronic sophistication. For the most part, the ellls were simply too busy enjoying life and upgrading their sensuous experience to bother developing time-saving gadgets.

But some millenia after the ellls won dominance over their natural enemies and competitors, ominous signs began to appear. The oceans' apparently inexhaustible bounty was exploited without planning. Food supplies became critical in some areas. And though medical advances had already extended the ellls' lifespan to beyond one hundred Earth-years and though schools too often had become large and unwieldy, showing signs of neurotic stress, there was no thought of controlling reproduction.

The alien varoks, visiting from their distant planet, noted these symptoms with alarm. With an urgency rare for them, they attempted to win the confidence of the amazed green beings of Ellason, who had not bothered to master space flight and had considered themselves the only intelligent life in their corner of the universe. In Conn's opinion, they won that confidence not just because they showed considerable honest respect for the ellls, who were apparently a simpler species and could have been regarded as inferior—and who were absolutely vulnerable—but also because they distributed millions of sonar translations of Rikh's book, *Mutilation—Price of Survival,* a horrifyingly graphic account of varokian natural history.

From this book, the ellls learned of possibilities of disaster they had never imagined, and learned why the varoks remained always somewhat guarded and inscrutable. In varokian history, the creatures called varoks had been choking on their own cultural excrement for some time when the bio-mathematical reality of rampant procreation suddenly outstripped their intelligence and adaptability. Obviously and suddenly, the wrenching horror of mutation after hideous mutation struck at them until the varoks completely lost their familiar identity. The Mutilation they called it. The more fortunate millions had quickly gone mad or starved or died in infancy. But, finally, out of the horror, nature had carved an efficient though less beautiful and inordinately fragile being that could survive in the wastes of Varok. Hence the varoks' deep concern when they saw Ellason treading an unplanned path toward disaster and their profound inability, once the path had been averted, to learn to play with the joyful abandon of the ellls, who had known neither the terror of near-extinction nor even the sorrow of a biological crisis.

Ellason had never been as structured politically as Earth, Conn knew. That made the varoks' job a great deal easier.

He was lulled nearly to sleep by Tandra's firm massage. "Are you structured politically, Tandra?" he murmured.

"Hardly," she said, giving him an extra dig with the heel of her hand. "I'm much too opinionated to be effective in politics."

Conn turned to look at her. "You know that you may *have* to be someday, don't you? Isn't that assumed in your contact with us?"

Tallyn spoke: "I suggest we consider moon orbit. Ship will go alone at some hazard."

"Get Aen to help you take it in. I'm busy."

"This can wait. The pool is soon. Aen is with the child, as you know, and Llorkin is writing yet."

"*Damn!* To hell with the pool."

Tallyn looked shocked.

"Okay, let's put this crate into orbit."

The exchange puzzled Tandra, but she remained silent as Conn swung his ship around the moon in a wide looping arc and began pointing out places he had explored by land on periodic trips to check equipment and take rock samples. There were rolling hills and stark boulder piles of singular beauty, selenological formations that had fed fascinating numerical food into the varoks' data banks, and an assortment of craters in which discoveries were made that had offered choice stories for the logs of Elll-Varok moon base.

"There's the Ocean of Storms and the d'Alembert Mountains looking dry and miserable as usual," Conn said. "We'll be braking into lunar orbit in a few minutes." He smiled up at Tandra. "Buried in those dusty crags is a lush oasis waiting warm and wet for us. I just wish we didn't have to wait so long before sharing the pool. It's strange: I'm drawn to you the way I should be drawn to it, after being away so long. I wonder if this is what happened to Earth's canine species, why they left the pack and attached themselves to men?"

The elll sighed deeply and reached out to the woman with a longing his soul had never known before. "Love me, Tan. Be my brother, my mother, my soul-mate, my cousin—all the things ellls find in the school. I'm a little frightened of myself. I need you, and I can't know why."

Tandra smoothed his disorderly plumes with a gentle hand. "I have found much the same in you, and I need you in the same way. I can't help but love you, Conn."

They were silent as they watched the moon.

Then it was time for Tandra to return to her *uuyva-noon* for the landing. Some minutes later Conn's voice boomed from the intercom. "We're coming in now, Tan. Aen, take the emergency post. Tallyn's up here. Where the hell's Llorkin? Tandra, you might be able to see the base from your window."

Tandra searched the moonscape futilely until a hidden entrance, sensing the approach of the *Lurlial,* yawned open to receive the ship, momentarily revealing the base set under the terraced slopes of a large crater. After some minutes of settling and maneuvering, the landing and docking of the *Lurlial* were accomplished, and the ship lay at rest in the warm red glow of an enormous pressurized hangar beneath the dry rugged wastes of the d'Alembert Mountains on the western edge of the moon.

4
Behind the Window

Tandra stepped out of the *Lurlial* into the steamy red glow of the hangar at EV Earth-moon base. She shuddered involuntarily with the sensation of being swallowed by a great cavernous mouth. The hangar's high, arched palate loomed ominously behind giant braces, and the *Lurlial* and the other vehicles—a long, cruiser-like craft and a smaller conveyance—glowed ruddy silver and brown against the walls like irregular teeth. It was clear to her that the hangar was a varokian design.

Conn followed her with Shawne perched like a tiny brown elf on his hip. They hurried toward an entrance panel inscribed ꟼꕉ᠊, beneath which hung a strip carefully lettered "Quarantine."

"You can take your isolation suits off in the outer shower chamber and leave them there. We'll unload your things and send them through the same shower. When you feel presentable you can open the panels on the opposite wall and meet the school. No doubt Killah will want to start pumping you full of vaccines right away. Hey!" he whispered, trying to look through her face-plate for a clue to her quiet stiffness. "Not another panic. Come here." He set Shawne down and pulled Tandra into his arms, molding his body to hers in a concentrated effort to give her all the security he could.

"There will be walls between us for a long time, won't there?" Tandra said. "Stay near us, Conn."

"Don't worry. You can't understand yet what you've done to me. I'll be as close as I can get."

A new voice spoke: "You are welcome here as one of us, Dr. Grey."

Tandra turned from Conn and saw a dark, mossy

green bulk of elll accented by plumes turned to muted gold with age, a solid figure of quiet dignity. "I am Artellian, the base director." His voice was firm and resonant. "Tallyn, good trip." He nodded to the grim engineer as he approached. Then he clasped Aen's shoulders with affection. "The school is ready for the adjustment as soon as we greet Dr. Grey."

He gave her a winning, apologetic smile, then ushered her and Shawne into the quarantine room shower.

Conn turned and faced the Master elll, his fin spiraled up in greeting, and now that Tandra was out of audible range he reverted to Elllonian, the ellls' throat language. The soft syllables tumbled over each other as he explained to Artellian that all had gone well and that he foresaw no problems in communication or cooperation with the human microbiologist, Tandra Grey.

"Apparently," Artellian grinned, "if I know anything about human response."

Tallyn's brow deepened as he stood by and listened to Conn's cool report. He was about to make a blunt comment when Llorkin came rolling and steaming toward them from the ship.

"Director Artellian, the human being has signed the release papers. However, I would suggest that you post a competent watch, certainly not Generalist Conn, on the quarantine chambers. I regard Dr. Grey as a psychological risk."

Conn answered Artellian's quizzical glance with a shrug. "Generalist Llorkin and I don't agree on Tandra's stability. She is adaptable, tolerant, thoroughly capable of her assignment here. I will personally take responsibility for any problems she might cause. I foresee none."

"You leave out most of story, Conn," Tallyn said pointedly in English.

Conn's eyes narrowed in annoyance. "It is enough to say that I have been able to establish significant rapport with Dr. Grey. Other members of this crew could exercise more tolerance until we all know her better. I believe she will integrate quite well."

"Integrate?" Artellian nodded, his lips pursed in an

understanding smile. "Then she is willing to speak the true language of ellls? I didn't think it possible." He sensed that Conn was not willing to reveal all that had transpired between himself and the woman, but he let it drop, respecting as he always did the young loner's idiosyncrasies. "I think we should be going inside now," he said. "I want to be present to welcome Dr. Grey when she opens the panels of the quarantine room."

Shawne responded with curiosity and delight, but Tandra's first vision from the quarantine room of a windowful of tall, shifting, alive green beings peering at her, almost unnerved her. She searched frantically for Conn; found with considerable relief his loving, crooked grin; and thanks to his witty introductions, soon lost her self-consciousness at being viewed like a specimen in a cage. She didn't completely relax, however, until she felt with her hands the tough, transparent composite that walled her away from the ellls. Then she actually enjoyed meeting the two dozen or more ebullient, irrepressible characters.

Finally, the elll called Killah stepped forward. He was not as tall, not as thin, not as un-glued as Conn, and his tousled crown plumes which framed his sharp features like bangs—one might call them feathers, but that would not be quite accurate—were not as wild as Conn's.

"This is our medical practitioner, Tan," Conn said, "a quack by nature, but an artist of considerable talent, Killah, Generalist of the Pathological Life Sciences. He is not likely to waste his precious time on amenities."

"I see no point in it, Dr. Grey," Killah said. "You must be as eager as we are to have the formalities done, so that we can begin serious study together."

"It's encouraging to hear you call these immunizations formalities."

"I hope that they are. Most of your pathogens, like ours, are highly specialized organisms, designed to parasitize only certain species. Our germs have become increasingly benign, as have most of yours, since there is no evolutionary advantage in killing off a host species. I doubt if they are interested in conquering whole new physiological systems."

As Killah talked, peering at Tandra through the glass with a cocked half-grin, Conn sensed a warm professional congeniality grow between them, though Tandra's fine smooth face, looking pleasant and calm as usual, revealed little response to Killah's increasing intensity. A strange feeling, new to him, gripped Conn: he realized that he could lose his favored status with her. But the thought was profoundly alien to his assumptions, and his elllonian mind—fully as capable of repression, distortion, and fabrication as human mentality—fixed itself on the idea that her ability to relate to aliens was, after all, of academic interest.

"Dr. Grey," Killah said, "this is Ellalon, Apprentice of Pathological Sciences."

The smaller elll beside Killah gave Tandra a bright smile. Her delicately chiseled green features were accented by long, pale-blue crown plumes meticulously clipped and shaped into a smooth downward curve. Tandra decided that this elll, like all the others sporting blue plumes, was subtly but definitely, and disturbingly, female—though her sex, shrouded in a stylishly clipped bikini of the curious, soft elllonian plumes, was betrayed only by wide hips set on short, smoothly molded legs.

"Hello Shawne," Ellalon called. "Come here, I've got something for you."

Through an ultraviolet hatch she pushed a small plush model of a Varokian *kaehl*—a squat, little animal, hairy and pink, with black eyes, a large red nose, and a flabby pocket containing soft pink eggs.

With a splendid satisfaction, the ellls watched Shawne mother the soft toy. Then abruptly they turned their attention to one another as if they suddenly remembered that there was something they had been waiting to do; and they disappeared down the hall—all but Killah, Ellalon, and Conn.

"After the adjustment our work will begin, Dr. Grey," Killah said. "Ellalon, do not neglect Conn. See to his adjustment."

The three ellls laughed heartily, and unceremoniously hurried down the hall after the others.

Tandra was perplexed at finding herself alone so suddenly. Were ellls always so erratic and abrupt? If she were there for a serious purpose, the result of much planning, as presumably she was, where had they gone? Were they all as unserious as Conn? And where were the varoks? Why had she not met one? Was the ellls' appearance of technical and intellectual competence an illusion? Perhaps they were just the lap logs of the varoks—whatever varoks were. The varoks must be very strange, or else the ellls would not be so secretive about them.

A vivid image grew in her mind: beings with very large brains and delicate prehensile appendages of some kind; with small bodies perhaps covered by a tough casing that boils and foams to protect them in the acrid atmosphere of their home (which she guessed must be associated with Jupiter). They must be huge elaborations of unicellular organisms similar to those that first populated Earth, like huge prehensile amoebae with eyes that—"Oh, stop it!"

"Shawne, where are you?"

The child was already engrossed in showing the toy *kaehl* some large pictures that she had found on a low shelf.

"Look at these things," Shawne laughed. "They glow funny."

With that Tandra relaxed, and she turned to explore the quarantine room in which they were to spend their first six weeks with the aliens.

It was furnished with two deep-red, shaggy synthetic rugs; an over-stuffed chair near a large low bed-pad on the wall opposite the window, both bed and chair covered with an incredibly soft, oddly tough, beige material; a desk and a closet on the left wall facing the window, both fitted with compartments and shelves of all sizes and shapes; and a small bed for Shawne next to the desk, the bed covered with three climb-in pillows shaped like elegant flowers. Someone had gone to considerable trouble to provide a comfortable and interesting apartment for their human guests. The wall behind the desk was lined with books and a control panel which, she saw from its labels, allowed the quarantined visitors access to the base's intercom, its long-distance communications, and its entertainment. Beneath the window and along the opposite wall were long work benches and cabinets, an incubator, a small sterilizer, and a telephone-booth-sized complex of fine instruments for which the word *microscope,* Tandra realized, was hardly adequate. Apparently the ellls expected her to do some real work.

She searched the shelves for volumes that might tell her more about the varoks, who seemed silently and mysteriously to dominate all that was about her. Yes, one entire shelf was devoted to them; but, oddly enough, there was nothing about their physiology or anatomy. Well, she would have to wait to see what they looked like. Meanwhile, she might as well learn something about their culture. No. Psychology would be more practical. But one title caught her attention. She picked up Rikh's *Mutilation: Price of Survival.*

As she began to look through the strange book, Tallyn and Aen tapped on the large window of the quarantine room. In Aen's knobby, webbed fin sat a model of a plump, football-shaped animal with large webbed feet and stubby wings, all of which completely dominated its ridiculously small bill-less head. It was colored with many shades of deep red and pink. Shawne ran to the window and gazed longingly at it.

Aen started to shove it into the ultraviolet sterilization drawer that acted as a material exchange route to the quarantine room, but Tallyn stopped him.

"Wait. Is live model. UV might harm it."

"I'm no botanist. Would it?"

Tandra came to the window to examine the object. Aen set it down and pressed a hidden switch. The toy lumbered about the shelf outside the window flapping its wings and emitting a high pitched squeal that seared Tandra's brain.

"*O-o-o!* Shut it off," she said. "It—it's a delightful toy, but *o-o* my poor ears!"

"You don't like that?" Aen asked, disappointed. "I thought that it would be within your audible range if I lowered the sound."

"Yes, it is, but it's too high to be comfortable. It would be better if it were much higher so we couldn't hear it at all."

"Ah, now that would be too bad if it had no voice for Shawne. Our tads love the hum. It's a good imitation of the real *lohn* call, too. Maybe if we lower it some more?"

"Okay, but lower it much more, please," Tandra said. "It looks very soft. That's not the same moss that lines the sleeping pools on the *Lurlial*, is it?"

"Yes, yes," Aen said with enthusiasm. "The tads eat it for snack. It should be good food for Shawne, too. The more they eat, the faster it grows. But you must wet it thoroughly every twelve hours."

"Oh, Aen, I'm sorry. I can't take that in here, at least not yet. We should avoid contact with objects that can't be sterilized until we are sure that the immunizations are taking."

Tallyn grunted.

"Well, then. I'll fix this for you, Shawne, and save it for later," Aen said. "Meanwhile, you can have this, eh?" He uncovered a small model of an ellonian girl with long blue plumes that framed the delicate face and indicated delightful laugh lines, exaggerating the large emerald eyes. "This should stand a good bath, Tandra," he said as he pushed the doll into the narrow tank of disinfectant that formed a second bridge between the base and the quarantine room. He watched with delight as Shawne scooped it up and settled down on the floor to groom and dry it.

"I see you reading," Tallyn said, glancing at the book Tandra held in her hand. "What?"

"The title intrigued me," Tandra said.

"Rikh's book. Yes, you must read. Carefully. And learn. You ruin Earth for all. Resources, then life gone at once. Why choose so much death?"

She saw that his question was serious.

"Because natural disasters, so-called, make good scapegoats. Men don't see what they don't *want* to see. Now it is too late even for the most unpopular decisions."

"Too late years ago. We heard talk. Too much talk. Many species already gone. Who cares? Every day. And who cares? Can see no change in wasteful living."

"You're entirely right, Tallyn. Not enough care."

"Is human race worth saving? Man earned right to survive? *Agh*. Read history, eh? Read own history. And, if continue with Conn . . ." The English words momentarily failed him. "If know what you do to Earth, don't read Rikh. Read of ellls. Learn of Conn. He is * elll;* learn of Ellason and ellls. Do not destroy him. Do not lead him to yourself so."

He turned quickly away.

Tandra looked to Aen. What had she done to anger Tallyn? But Aen had missed the exchange: he had become engrossed with Shawne. She watched for a while, then irresolutely turned to her book.

She was immensely relieved when Killah appeared. "Now then, Dr. Grey," he said, "we are ready. Do you or the baby tend to have allergic reactions?"

"Yes. We should be very cautious with Shawne."

Aen excused himself, Shawne continued playing with her new toy, and Tandra and Killah set to work. They decided to try some scratch tests before proceeding with the more hazardous intradermal and intramuscular inoculations.

Killah pushed through the ultraviolet hatch a small box containing a set of sterile packets. In each packet were two small needles filled with a nonviable elllonian vaccine.

"There is a marking pen in the tool drawer to your right," Killah said. "Mark squares however you like, and I'll keep a diagram of where you apply each vaccine."

Tandra found the pen and drew a grid on her left forearm, then on Shawne's.

"There are gloves and sterile tongs available," Killah said. "All used contaminated items go into the trap door on your left. It opens with a foot pedal."

Tandra found the tools she needed, set them out, and opened the first packet. Carefully she grasped a needle in the tongs and gently scratched the alien antigen into the top layers of her skin within the upper left square drawn on her forearm. Killah marked the corresponding square on his diagram: "Sonarplate Apraxia—elll. RNA agent" and repeated the label in elllonian box letters.

"Double-check the labels, Dr. Grey," he said. "Can you read my writing through the window?"

"Yes, I see it." She looked down at her arm and waited.

"There are no known human toxins in any of these vaccines, Tandra," Killah said, perceiving her concern. "We've checked chemical structures and modified those few that were even remotely similar to molecules toxic to humans."

"I don't mind experimenting on myself. It's Shawne."

"Yes, why don't you wait? Test Shawne after you've done all the scratch tests on yourself."

Tandra agreed and applied the other eight vaccines to her arm.

"We'll watch you for a few moments and then take readings every four hours," Killah said.

"Fine. If we have no reactions to these tests, we might as well do the intradermal vaccinations and then recheck for sensitization."

So it was that Tandra began her work with the ellls. The days that followed were so full that she soon forgot Tallyn's anger. She and Killah isolated and cultured and counted and tested innumerable bacterial and viral strains, looking for loopholes in their concerted effort to avoid biological catastrophe. It was soon evident that they needed the facilities of a large institute and an army of bacteriologists to do the work they outlined for her six-months stay. Tandra's frustration was considerable: she knew that, ideally, each alien organism's chemical and biological reaction to all known earthly organisms should be thoroughly studied and she realized at the same time that the study of alien contact by just *one* organism could be more than one man's life-work. She and Killah would be able to make only the grossest first approximations with the more dangerous pathogens of human beings, ellls, and varoks. The prospect of such an enterprise was overwhelming, as was the responsibility it implied, but Tandra relished it and the secure feeling of usefulness it gave her.

One result of all this activity was that it kept her mind occupied. After her initial concern, she wondered little about the varoks, their unspoken presence in the fabric of the base and its routine, and their strange absence from her window.

While the work at base continued and the ellls eagerly anticipated Tandra's release from quarantine, an occasional three-centimeter signal leaped from the moon base and rode through space for thirty minutes on its way to boost Conn's hero ratings on Varok, then sped on for seventeen hours past the outer planets into the black void where Ellason lurked. There it stirred up in the ellls only a mild interest in their cousin's experiences with the human being before it returned to its home at EV base with a brief message of encouragement and approval—inadvertently exciting, for a moment, a few radio astronomers on Earth. The ellls at base read and reread these messages from their home planet and grew homesick and found solace in their sleeping bowls or in the large pool deep inside the base.

Conn, for his part, ate all of his meals with Tandra and Shawne at the window of the quarantine room. At first they stretched their dinner hours into extensive periods that almost overlapped, enduring with impatience the impenetrable wall of clear synthetic that separated them. Conn talked for many hours of warm deep Ellason enclosed by the swirling colorful mists of Alahranon. He described ellls he had known and told Tandra of things that he loved: the touch of *llaoon* grass on his plumes; the gentle thumping of pressure signals from every direction as the ellls schooled, each telling a different story or carrying a different message; the shrill chatter of the tads as they experimented in social integration and learned to school; the cool, living touch of moss when he donned a wet-sweater over his water-starved body too long exposed to air; the intense, climactic moments of adjustment when an elll returned after being absent from the school, when the pressure signals mounted and joined with the sonar chorus to finally drown one's individual awareness in the overwhelming presence of one's fellow ellls. And he wondered what it was in Tandra that made him talk so much.

Tandra enjoyed listening to him, though she found she usually offered little of herself, other than an unquestioning devotion. The exceptions occurred when Conn showed some willingness to pursue larger philosophical questions or, better yet, to discuss the pitiful dilemma of the planet Earth and her rapacious species, *Homo sapiens*. Then her eyes would flash and her dark hair would fly with frustration. To the observant Killah these exchanges were a waste of energy and time. Why didn't she and Conn wait until they could really mingle and understand each other, not just throw words back and forth?

Meanwhile, Tandra's attempt to keep a diary of her impressions were interrupted again and again not only because of the endless rows of cultures and microscopic samples, but also because of Conn's and Killah's and twenty-eight other garrulous ellls' relentless demands on her attention. Three weeks in quarantine passed before she was able to add to the little writing she had done on the *Lurlial:*

"I have grown to love the ellls very much—all of them—even poor, bumbling, obnoxious Llorkin. They are such open, accepting beings; I feel that I know them already—a good thing, for I spend what little time I have reading varokian books."

She started to write more about the ellls, or at least Conn, but her pen stopped. There seemed to be no words for them, for him. They were soft with a warm muted-green understanding that eased her mind and gave her pleasure; and Conn, he was like an intimate extension of herself, like a home of unquestioning acceptance.

When her pen moved again, it strayed into words she usually did not allow herself to say:

"The magnificent EV microscope (I have finally mastered it) must have been manufactured by varoks. The inscription on its base in a flowing script quite different from the boxy elllonian symbols. I am very curious to know more about the varoks. Though they are 'hideous mutants' (to quote Killah), they must have remarkable skills and possess a good measure of intelligence, perhaps beyond the human. Killah says they will be pleased with our results, but I wonder. What do they really want with me? And why do they watch Earth at such expense? What are they waiting for? With their capability they could do much to help if they wanted to. The truth is I am not certain help is what they intend."

What if they assume control of the lives of other beings, as men do, Tandra thought. Then it was logical that they would wait until the great masses of men died off so that they could more easily direct the fate of Earth themselves. The varoks were unquestionably brilliant enough to betray the ellls and use them for such devious purposes. It was too much to hope that another intelligent species besides ellls should be so unlike man as to forego the power they must possess.

She was marshalling her thoughts to continue writing when Conn tapped on the window, startling her. He was there, as usual, to spend some time with her.

"I'm sorry," Conn said. "I should have sounded my approach. What are you writing?"

"Just some notes to myself." She got up and pressed

her hands against the window. The gesture had become a habit. The window substituted for the security Conn's touch had given her at first. She loved Conn no less; it was just good to feel the window there, knowing it held out everything that threatened her: the germs still unstudied, the varoks—the ellls. No. Certainly not the ellls. She looked at Conn and hesitated before she spoke again. "Why haven't I met any varoks yet?"

Conn choked loudly with a burst of amusement. "Finally you ask! Tandra, you're the damnedest enigma! How can you be so competent with those bugs of yours and so blind and assuming about so many other things? I thought you would never ask about the varoks. Most of them are out on expedition. Orram is with them. With him gone, Llorkin was able to insist that you meet no varoks so he could sort out your psychological response to ellls first. Personally, I think that your reaction to varoks will be infinitely more interesting.

"I should tell you about Orram sometime—Master Oran Ramahlak, Director of Scientific Operations. He would have been here to greet you in spite of Llorkin, but they had trouble with their land craft. The *Arlaht* is an old moon buggy—been working amost a century —and she can hover or clamber around damn near anywhere without leaving a messy trail to upset your moon watchers, but she's got a neurotic power package. They should have taken the *Nalkah*. I'm afraid they won't be back until after you leave quarantine."

Tandra said nothing, and their talk wandered elsewhere.

The Master varok, Oran Ramahlak, turned away from the controls of the land craft, *Arlaht,* as it ambled through the lunar dust, and spoke to the young varok behind him. "Vohn, plant geophonic probes on this plateau and call base. Tell Director Artellian that we should reach base three days prior to our last estimate."

Orram left his couch and motioned to Vohn as he spoke without sound.

"Yes, you look tired M. Ramahlak," Vohn said. "I will guide us from Shröter's Valley and then call Erah to the controls. We will complete the navigation to base so that you may remain with Junah."

"You misread me, Vohn. My time with Junah will be brief. I will return to the controls after I have rested. Call me if any new indication of trouble develops."

Orram made his way back to a small resting cabin as the craft continued to maneuver through the rocky lunar terrain.

Junah was waiting for him. She was entirely composed, as one might expect a varok to be, but a bit less decided than most. Her eyes were not firm, but they were even more beautiful for their dreaming quality.

"You are my need at this moment," Orram said.

"Your touch is welcome," she replied.

"Soon I must sleep," he said. "I have worked too long in the sun. My exposure suit was barely adequate. But it is finished now, and we will arrive at base within fifty-two hours unless more trouble develops. Are you satisfied with the samples we have taken?"

Silently, Junah told him of her satisfaction. She was chief geologist at moon base and, though a Generalist of Planetary Earth Sciences, she preferred to confine her studies to mineralogy. "The samples are adequate for a detailed analysis of the Aristarchus complex," she said as she undressed and extended her forearm to Orram.

"You understand that I need only to relax," he said.

"Yes, M. Ramahlak. Your mind is your own. I will not invade your privacy."

He clasped her to his feverish body and, after the first shock of contact, enjoyed its coolness; but a persistent longing reached out to him from the varokian female and disturbed him, for he could not satisfy it.

Shortly before her quarantine ended, Tandra made one more entry in her diary. It was to be her last.

"The period of quarantine has been hardest on Shawne. She soon learned that she could not leave this room nor could she follow her favorite friend, Conn, when he disappeared down the hall. The assortment of toys has grown at an alarming rate; for our elllonian friends, belonging to a species which shamelessly claims to pamper and adore their own children, have continued to bring her bright ingenious building toys and elegant dolls.

"At first Killah carefully supervised the sterilization of the toys, but as the time approached to introduce us to the microorganisms which constitute the normal bodily flora of the ellls and varoks, he relaxed his vigilance. Finally, we both approved Aen's jumping, mossy *lohn* bird as an appropriately humorous first contact between the life forms of Earth and Ellason. Killah said that our constitution is much too alkaline for his poor bugs to survive in, on, or under; none of the alien normal flora or fauna has shown any interest in us at all.

"Yesterday he asked me to look over the last of our preliminary findings and said, 'Two more days to verify your good health under the onslaught of two weeks of filthy toys and rotten food, and we can let you out of there to meet us in the flesh.'

" '*In the flesh.*' Why are those such fearful words? Sometimes I wish I could stay here, observing them from behind glass. I must be afraid that the ellls will evaporate into a dream, and I will wake up too soon. But more likely I am simply afraid of direct exposure to potential pathogens.

"As for the varoks, I am plagued by the vision of them as blank-eyed, organic protozoan forms endowed with a mentality equal to that of man at his worst." She couldn't deny, as she could in regard to the ellls, that she was afraid of the varoks, of power and intelligence in an unknown, perhaps hideous, form—afraid of their unspoken purposes with her. "In any case I wish that the varoks would return while I still have the window."

Suddenly she felt something watching her, a presence she had not experienced before. It was very near, all around her! She looked up in terror and her vision became insanely narrow: all she saw was two brilliant blue-black eyes, deep and demanding, fixing her with an intense awareness. She drew back. The eyes were set into a face stolid and severe, a face of smooth, angled planes, as if chiseled from granite. It was totally unlined, she realized, by the wear imposed by emotion. As she stared, her vision cleared and broadened. She realized that the eyes were behind the intact quarantine window and that they belonged to a countenance that was firm but kind. Her terror subsided, though she was still conscious of nothing but this new presence.

Her fascinated stare left the eyes and moved down the dark figure. As tall and lean as Conn. Dressed. Trim and brown, apparently human—exquisitely human. Then I am not the elll's first human contact, she thought. Perhaps this was Conn's friend, Jesse Mendleton.

"Orram, you bastard," Conn hollered as he ran up the hall toward them. "You're six weeks too late."

Tandra, holding her breath, watched the seamless face crack slightly, narrowing its eyes into what had to be a grin. "I thought I was just in time," she heard it say with careful rasping tones. The dark granite figure turned toward Conn, and Tandra saw a distinctively non-human organ, a disk-shaped patch, lying behind and below its ear. The Master varok!

His resemblance to man was shattering! Conn suddenly looked naked and bestial standing next to the fully-clothed figure. As she watched the man-like being, a more profound fear than her fantasies of protozoan monsters possessed her. The varoks resembled man *too* closely; they would be capable of all that men were capable of, and more: they could master and subvert to their control anything of value to them, including the lives of men and of ellls. Tandra felt hopelessly inadequate. Suddenly Orram turned toward her.

"Dr. Grey, you and Killah have done a thorough job. I am perfectly satisfied with your results. Are you willing to risk direct contact with us?"

She spoke slowly.

"I feel that the risks are very small, Master Ramahlak, in regards to contamination."

"Call him Orram," Conn chuckled, "and relax. You look as if you've seen the proverbial ghost. Normally, Orram, this human specimen radiates somewhere near medium warm, like what you might call deep brown—not the frightened cold darkness apparent right now, like what you might call toilet-bowl white. It sets off your blood-shot eyeballs though, Tan. Come on, let's get you out of there so I can feel what you're like again."

He approached the sealed double doors of the quarantine room and pulled them open. "Llorkin's going to split a gasket when he learns that he missed this scene."

He reached for Tandra's hand and found that it was trembling, so he pressed it against his chest, where she could feel the excited movement of his primary blood chamber as he led her out of the room.

Orram watched while Conn explored Tandra's delicately exotic face with an affectionate, becalming touch. The varok was fascinated by Conn's obvious sensitivity to the frightened human female. She appeared to feel as vulnerable as a raw wound. She seemed hesitant to breathe.

Slowly, the feeling of being exposed left Tandra. She ran her fingers slowly over the traces of feathery down on the back of Conn's fin onto the thin, partial webs between his fingers, absorbing the feel of his soft, mossy, tiled green skin.

Conn presented her hand to Orram. Tandra chilled at the contrasting feel of the varok's bony, humanoid grasp.

At that moment Shawne discovered that the door to her prison was open. Racing against her expectation that it would shut her in again, she bounced, jello-fashion, out of the quarantine room past the three adults and down the hall, galloping stiff-legged in the manner of two-year-olds as fast as her legs would pump her along in the mild gravity.

The burst of exuberance left the varok almost smiling and the human being and the elll laughing. They turned to follow the child. As they passed an intercom,

Orram hesitated for a moment, said, "We are coming," and then walked on beside Conn and Tandra.

"Already?" Conn asked, ignoring Tandra's curiosity.

"Why not?" Orram said.

5
Reflections in Ruby Water

Conn's velvety green body flashed with its hexagonal patterns and dabs of color as he strode loosely beside Tandra, one long arm balanced precariously on her small shoulder. In contrast, Orram's straight, plain, brown figure glided straight and even on Tandra's left, his appearance highlighted only by a glint of silver in his dark auburn hair.

The varok's polished face was a mirror of his perfectly balanced torso and smooth limbs; no evidence of the excitement and curiosity that dominated Conn's mood marred his composure when his eyes fastened on Tandra. He found her smooth control and serenity, which matched his own rather remarkably, to be a pleasant surprise. He had expected the human female to be more talkative and jumpy. He slowed his step very slightly so he could better watch the red glow from the hallway's hidden lights dance in the sheen of her long, black hair. His eyes moved slowly over her light frame. Muted striped slacks and plain white shirt, light undergarments. Good. Comfortable, probably not concerned with form and trappings. Thoroughly self-restrained, yet allowing her body to swing in an unconscious, sensual way that no varokian woman could affect. Little wonder the ellls loved her. It seems we have here a mix, he thought, a compromise between the wild extremes of elllonian indulgence and the equally wild extremes of varokian denial.

Suddenly Llorkin came storming down the hall toward them. Before the enraged psychologist could speak, Orram raised a hand to stop him. "I have authorized both Dr. Grey's release and our meeting," he said in a cool, rough monotone. "I regret that the circumstances were unfavorable for your observation, but you will have a complete written report of our first contact from Conn, Dr. Grey, and myself within twenty-four hours. Now, won't you join us? I believe that dinner is being served around the pool tonight."

The excitable elll stamped and fluttered for a moment, but there was nothing he could do or say in the wake of Orram's pronouncement. "Well, yes, thank you. Thank you for your—uh—help. Yes. Thank you. I will eat now, too. Thank you," he said, laughing musically at his own befuddlement.

Tandra wondered if it were possible to dislike an elll for any length of time.

As they turned toward the large swinging doors on their left, Conn and Orram stepped back to let a boisterous gang of young ellls enter ahead of them. Then they took Tandra by the arms, approached the doors, and ceremoniously opened them wide.

She stood in the doorway, enthralled by a misty red vision alive with twenty-eight gray-green figures lounging around a large moss-lined pool of clear, deep, ruby water. A few silver-crowned varoks stood like sentries against the walls. The pool was surrounded by a soft deck etched with fine random patterns of maroon and delicate pink moss, apparently the same edible plant that graced the *lohn* bird and the sleeping bowls of the *Lurlial*. A high, light, rose-hued ceiling, walls hung with brown robes and blue moss wet-sweaters on hooks, a shower stall on one end, and several large low tables set around the pool gave the steamy room the appearance of a luxurious bath house. The sight dispelled any sense of foreboding Tandra had.

As she stepped into the vibrant, moist atmosphere, the ellls burst into a cacophony of whistles and shouts that gradually ordered itself into a wild, rhythmic song:

Bayon kahla! Bayon! Bayon!
Va ya lel be. Leoo be. Leoon be.
Bayon kahla! Bayon! Bayon!
Can sensoe. Vabrin vano eyahka.

Leoo be. Leoon be. Va ya lel be.
Yao ba lel be. Leon be. Leoo be.
Ssro ek savolla sava be.
Bayon akl. Leoo lel lak lokbe.
Vabrin senseo. Bak can eyah o.
Yav ne be ba lel yavalla.
Leoo k fahno k broon yavalla.
Bayon! Bayon! Bayon! Bayon!
Ssro ek savolla save be.
Savoll uom be akl yavalla.
Leoo k leoon be. Yavt ba lel be.
Bayon! Bayon! Bayon! Bayon!

Conn translated line by line:

Welcome stranger! Welcome! Welcome!
Come to life now. Live now. Love now.
Welcome stranger! Welcome! Welcome!
Work will wait. Science knows forever.
Live now. Love now. Come to life now.
Join in life now. Love now. Live now.
Strip the strangerness away now.
Welcome friend! Live life full rich now.
Science waits. Let work itself do.
Join us now in life together.
Live and breathe and sound together.
Welcome! Welcome! Welcome! Welcome!
Strip the strangerness away now.
Stranger gone! Now friends together.
Live and love now. Joined in life now.
Welcome! Welcome! Welcome! Welcome!

He took Tandra's hand and led her into the din to
greet the enthusiastic crew. Slowly they circled the
large pool, nodding and twisting their hands in greeting. On the far side of the room they found Shawne
sitting in Aen's lap, clapping heartily on and off the
driving beat. Finally, the song drifted into a chant of
welcome, steady and insistent: *"Bayon! Bayon!"*

"Expect to get wet," Orram shouted to Tandra, as

Conn took her by the elbows and firmly pushed her toward the pool.

"Conn, stop. What are you doing?"

"Initiation into elllonian friendship. We love you, Tan. I know it's mutual, so in we go."

The ellls hollered with delight as Conn clamped his arms around her waist and took her into the wine-red water. Tandra came up smiling, hesitated a moment, then released herself to spontaneity while the ellls cheered her on. She was no longer subject to the rules and customs of men; she would be the natural animal she was meant to be, just as the ellls were. Their absolute lack of self-consciousness gave her that gift. With no further thought, she threw her shoes, slacks, and sweater out of the pool, then swam through the clear, deep-lighted water while Conn dove under and over her, occasionally mimicking her stroke. Winded at last she paused, and the entire elllonian crew dove in to roll and tumble and leap through the water like intoxicated porpoises. All but Aen. Carefully, he lowered himself into the pool with Shawne on his shoulders and swam slowly about, keeping her face well above the slow-motion ripples generated by his friends.

Outside the general commotion, the five varoks of the crew stepped out of their simple clothes and more sedately joined the watery fracas. They stayed far apart, touching no one, and the ellls gave them wide berth. Since they stayed in the water for only a short period of time, Tandra was able to study them well from her vantage point in the middle of the pool. Beneath their outer clothing of light pullovers and loin wraps or many-pocketed coveralls, the two varokian females wore plain tanksuits that revealed large buttocks and small, rounded breasts. The three males wore firm shorts of a brown so close in color to that of their skin that at first Tandra thought they were naked. A gentle hump suggested the presence of genitals, in striking contrast to the smooth neuter appearance of the ellls. The skin of the varoks was a delicate deep brown, and their hair, covering only their scalps and trailing long or short as their whim dictated in frosted streaks of red-brown and silver, neatly framed the conspicuous round plates behind their ears.

As she watched them, Tandra began to imagine the power they must possess. What did they intend with Earth? They were too self-assured, too purposeful a people to leave Earth entirely to herself. Where did she really fit into their intentions?

Suddenly Conn sprang from the bottom of the pool, surged up past Tandra, and tossed her high into the air. She came down with a shriek and dove deep into the water in search of Conn's long legs. Her hands locked on his ankles, but his strong webbed feet thrashed easily, pulling her along underwater with exhilarating speed. Finally, she let him go to rise for a breath and saw, extended along his back, a long narrow fin rippling with powerful strokes.

"No wonder you swim like a fish," Tandra laughed when Conn surfaced with her. "I didn't know you were so well equipped."

"Equipped?"

"I didn't know you had a back fin."

"It's hydraulically engineered. Can't stand dry air. I wish you would read about us ellls in detail, Tan."

"I will. I promise. I'll have plenty of time now, and that is top priority: elllonian physiology and," she emphasized with a smile, "psychology."

"Hah!" Conn snorted. "You'll head right back to the varokian shelves."

Just then the small, blue-green figure of Ellalon brushed past Conn and turned, grabbing his shoulders and forcing him deep under the surface. When he didn't return, Tandra worked her way through the playful mob in the pool until she found Aen and Shawne. The baby had had enough of watery play and was sitting on the mossy deck absent-mindedly nibbling its tiny, leafy structures while she watched the ellls. As Tandra neared the pool's edge, Orram strode toward her holding a cowl-necked tunic made of thick, absorbent blue material. The sight of him revived Tandra's fantasy of sinister power; a spasm of fear churned in her stomach. In spite of it, she took the varok's hand, climbed out of the pool, and put on the soft robe.

"Come, meet the other varoks," Orram said.

He led her first to Vohn, the communications engineer, whose young face was set with determination and competence.

Beside him stood a strong young woman who looked straight into Tandra's eyes—and, it seemed, through them.

"This is Erah, a geologist with a passion for moons."

"You are most welcome here," Erah said in a deliberate, softly roughened voice.

The varokian astronomer, Ahl, his face deep brown with age and his hair turned entirely to silver, approached them with hands held poised at his sides. "Welcome," he said. "Come spend some time at the telescope. No clouds to obscure vision. Marvelous."

"Thank you," Tandra murmured. She didn't know what to say. Their precise mannerisms left her feeling awkward; they seemed to confirm her fears. She stopped herself. She wasn't being fair. Resolutely, she took Orram's arm.

A glint of kindness narrowed his eyes. "Let us take our places at the table," he said. "Master Artellian is leaving the pool."

As they turned toward the tables, the second varokian woman came toward them. Long and intense was her look at Tandra's hand on Orram's arm. "May I join your table, Master Ramahlak?"

Tandra thought she noted a hint of surprise in Orram's eyes, but his tone betrayed nothing but bland acceptance. "Of course," he said. "Dr. Grey, this is Generalist Junah, our chief geologist."

From deep within her intensely placid, even face, framed severely with smooth silver and blond hair, Junah looked at Tandra analytically but not coldly, then shifted her search to Orram's expression. Tandra followed her quiet gaze and felt a tense, ill-defined questioning surge between the three of them. As quickly as it had come, the tension dissipated, leaving questions unanswered, the answer indeterminate.

When the golden-fringed Artellian left the pool, his crew gradually followed his example, laughing and teasing merrily as they tossed their heads and shook their hips, sending droplets flying in all directions from their brilliant bikini plumes. Some took moss wet-sweaters from the wall hooks and pulled them over their heads before finding their seats on the deck around the low tables. Soon the gentle, rolling chatter of the ellls filled the room pleasantly, and the surface of the pool quieted to small waves until, with a boiling roll, the water was thrown back by two young ellls who emerged, squealed loudly when they discovered that the pool was empty, and clambered quickly to the tables amidst hoots of joy—which suddenly rose to a new crescendo when Conn, too, broke the surface, Ellalon immediately following him to sit happily at a far table with the varoks, who sat incredibly still and waited.

"Conn, where the hell you been?" shouted Tallyn. "We have dessert already."

"No place that you haven't been, wise guy," Conn retorted.

"Well, least I know what do once there. You don't get practice enough to know which end is up."

The ellls whistled and laughed like rowdy boys, but Conn only shrugged, cocked his brow good-naturedly, and sauntered over to the wall to don a blue wetsweater.

"Hey, you don't need sweater, *aloon*," Tallyn heckled. "Must you drive all girls mad?"

"I would if I could," Conn hollered, and everyone hooted as he sank to the moss carpet between Tandra and Shawne.

Tandra couldn't restrain her curiosity, though she knew better than to expect an answer from Conn. "What in the world is going on?"

She was surprised at the serious tone in his voice. "You should have been doing some elllonian homework, Tan. We're not 'in the world'. Remember?"

"All right. I've already promised."

"Keep that promise. Please." He smiled. "Now try some of this garbage. I think you'll find this dried *oeln* fish more tasty than the sterilized *brilln* brains you've been eating."

They ate with relish the savory elllonian food and simple varokian staples, laughing and enjoying their new companionship, talking more for pleasure than for information.

Junah sat quietly beside Orram and said nothing. Tandra wondered if the varokian woman's silent attention was annoying to him. He showed no indication of either accepting or rejecting her presence. Stoic souls, Tandra thought. *Whoo-pee,* my brain is thick. The punch was undoubtedly fermented.

"Tallyn," she called to the rough, jolly, green reveler at the next table, "Conn said they call you the Thick Serb. Why would a man from God-knows-where ever be called that?"

"Agh, human, you would pry ancient alien secrets from us?" Tallyn grunted with a laugh.

"Ask him how he lost all his tail feathers," Killah shouted from the far table.

"All right. How did you lose all your tail feathers?"

Tallyn stood up slowly, his head bent and his mouth full. "Now my warm, bright being," he said, swallowing noisily, "it was too soon I discovered joys of Serbian vodka and, too late, its perils. Now, I am having fine time discussing politics in pleasant English-style pub until someone wants me off costume—"

"Yugoslavia!? What were you doing in Yugoslavia?"

"That is a fine, fine place. The beaches, you see—"

"Don't change the subject. It was a fair challenge. Tell all, Thick Serb," Killah said, clapping his hands insistently.

"Big fellow didn't appreciate my religious views," Tallyn continued. "He thought force of argument could be made by physical impression."

"You mean he was about to smash your face-plate for offering to pay the bill in *pallonions* and for imitating his accent when he insisted on hard cash," Conn hollered.

"Now— I suppose I had some unconscious imitation . . . Regrettable error. Stunted my English since."

"Regrettable, hell," Conn roared. "Tallyn here came racing back to the *Lurlial* at full tilt with fifteen bellowing Serbians and three dogs hanging onto his tail feathers. If they hadn't been so drunk we might have been in serious trouble."

"I remained properly suited all time," Tallyn snorted. "No one saw my green."

"But who authorized you to visit pubs, eh?" Killah asked. "And who set the *Lurlial* down so close to that village? I think you were all on *dankah*."

"At least the *Lurlial* set a new speed record for takeoffs," Conn said.

Time forgot its race with life beside the steamy, red, crystal pool; and for a long while the meal continued at a leisurely tempo, accompanied by the musical chatter of the ellls and the sparse, rasping talk of the varoks. Together they nibbled down the heaps of *arl* and *brilln* and *challall* weeds on their tables until there were none left and their palates missed the continual barrage of elegant tastes. Then some of the crew were prodded and teased until they made another trip to the food center to refill the pitchers and trays.

"C'mere," Conn mumbled through his last mouthful. "Let's go make vibrations, Tan."

He pulled her to her feet and towed her to a bank of controls set into the far wall. Soon she became aware of a familiar melody drifting diffusely into the room. As the volume increased she felt engulfed in sound; the beat throbbed in her bones.

"Give an elll a complex, hard beat and a good melody, and he'll go wild anywhere, even in this damnable light gravity," Conn hollered. "Let's see what we can do."

He threw himself with abandon into a jerking, syncopated dance that tossed his body slowly and oddly back and forth in the moon's easy grasp. Tandra followed his example and was soon so lost in the joy of sound and floating movement that she was hardly aware that many ellls had joined them in creating a complex of rhythmical body patterns that were equally good in or out of the water.

Orram sat watching Tandra and Conn, talking sparsely with the other varoks, according to their custom. He was not surprised when his patch found a call from Junah.

"The human being looks very much like us, doesn't she, Junah?" he asked. "Is it disturbing for you to see elllonian qualities in her, too? I am fascinated; but you must develop your own relationship with her. We varoks make her uncomfortable, I believe. You may ignore her if you choose."

"I want to know her *with you,* Orram."

The varok met her gaze and searched her mood. No emotion crossed his face as he said, "It is not possible yet, Junah. I am driven alone."

"You have not judged her suitable, M. Ramahlak, for all the tasks in mind?" Junah said, searching for contact by a different approach.

"Not yet. I do not want to offend her, nor to trust her with maximal responsibility until we are sure of her attitudes and her qualifications. Meanwhile there are many unanswered biological questions that she can help us answer."

The varoks were silent then as they watched the ellls and the human being. The beat of the music changed and continued and changed again and the ellls stopped dancing only to redampen their dry throats with red punch. Finally, a polka emerged from the walls and threw them wildly around the pool. When it ended, Aen mercifully changed the tapes and bathed the exhausted dancers in a flowing varokian melody.

"Oh, Conn, Conn, my marvelous big lizard," Tandra gasped, sprawling beside him on the deck. "I'd forgotten what it's like to dance with you. What a glorious sensation! Tell me what you did to my records to make them sound like that. It's so penetrating!"

"I'm surprised you noticed much difference. Hey, get off my flipper. Our audible range doesn't extend downward very far, so we miss much of that great beat. Stop it, woman! Electronically speaking, we tore the band apart and rechanneled the bass notes—Dr. Grey, for shame—and the most rhythmic parts into a sonar generator. Goddam you. There!" He pinned her down with his legs, putting an end to her teasing. "Then it's terrific under water, though we can still pick up the sound in air."

He released her and she enclosed his broad chest in her arms and stroked his sides, burying her face under his chin. Here was not only home, but joy-in-life personified; she was oblivious to everything else.

Gently Conn pushed her hands away and eased her head down further on his chest. "There," he said. "Homework, my little beast. Old Conn can't take too much all at once. I'm loaded with hedonic glands along my sides and under my chin, and I do tend to be a bit modest with so many varoks watching."

Tandra sat up with a start, sending the room spinning around her for a moment. "*O-o-o-o,* I drank too much punch. It tasted much too good to be healthy. Hedonic glands! And lots of them! I think you should be my *pet* lizard."

Conn grinned. "I'll be your pet lizard, Tan, but *not* right now." He touched her lips with his as he got up. "Not a bad sign of affection, but I prefer a nudge under the chin. I'm leaving in self-defense."

He joined Ellalon and a group of astronomers who were playing a slow-motion version of volleyball, using the edge of the pool as a net or goal, Tandra couldn't tell which. Shawne was merrily trying to chase the ball when it went astray of the game, and the ellls urged her on with warm enthusiasm, laughing pleasantly at her antics in the moon's light gravity.

Tandra happily drank in the scene around her: energetic gray-green bodies splashing and running, silver-brown images of varoks mingling again with their green colleagues, red water, pink ceiling; Orram's black moccasins walking toward her on red plush moss. Where would they eventually walk on Earth? And to what purpose? She shivered.

"Aen will put Shawne into bed soon," Orram said.

"It looks as if she is now going after more Elllonian moths and varokian sweet cakes. Let us go to the garden. The party will end soon. It is late."

Junah watched from a distance.

The garden occupied the full length of the underground compound along the innermost wall of the base immediately in back of the pool room. Orram led Tandra into its rich, moist atmosphere between rows of feathery moss beds and tall, succulent plants and deep tanks filled with tufts and strings of squared or angular shapes growing under the warm, red glow of infrared light sources. There were *ahlrialka* trees and other Varokian fruit trees sporting brilliant oval fruits: some large and ruddy purple, some tiny and fresh blue, others plump and pale and furry. On one wall was a large tank containing leafy blue aquatic plants and large, flat irridescent pink creatures that stared with bright green eyes set decoratively around their periphery. Next to the tank was a tall moth colony, vibrating with color, and above all was a maze of reflecting devices designed to trap just enough sunlight for maximum growth of the varokian plants.

"You can't grow all of your food, can you?" Tandra asked.

"Yes, we can, but only because Ellasonian mosses supply most of our food requirements. Ellason specializes in moss as your planet specializes in insects. What stores of preserved food we have must last a very long time; space vehicles travel rarely from Varok. And, of course, we must always maintain a reserve for evacuation."

"You are such a spartan people; yet you don't deny the ellls the comfort of so much water. I don't know whether to ask how you do it or why."

"The how is not difficult. Little moisture is lost in this sealed den of ours; it is continually reprocessed. And the why—perhaps it is a symbiotic relationship we varoks have with ellls, as they have with the moss that cushions and feeds them. Perhaps we need them to remind us why we live at all."

Orram turned into a door near the far end of the

garden. "We will call this the recreation lounge, though such a term has no real meaning to either ellls or varoks." The room was a comfortable place, softly lit and furnished with smaller, sprawling versions of the *Lurlial's* sleeping bowls, conveniently flanked with storage shelves and working space. The walls were packed with a variety of boxy shapes that must have been books or tapes or containers for recorded information of some type. Three intricately marked and pocketed game tables were strategically placed in corners about the room, and on a work bench in the fourth corner, surrounded by piles of Conn's wires and rectifiers and tubes and speakers and Tandra's watercolor of boats on Lake Michigan, sat Shawne's Pooh bear. On the far side of the room, wide curving stairs dripping with white moss led upward and out of sight.

"Those stairs lead to the observation deck," Orram said. "Solitude is respected there. Even some of the ellls need to be alone at times. It is not occupied now. Come and see. It is the lunar sunset."

Tandra followed Orram through the recreation room and up the stairs, where she suddenly came upon a large, curved, transparent wall and the incredible, stark view beyond it. The moon's entangled pits and craters threw long shadows over each other in the knobby terrain, and far beyond the bowls of dust the irregular mounded peaks of the d'Alembert Mountains lay silhouetted on the rim of Earth.

After many long, vibrating minutes that left Tandra unsure whether to hate or fear or love this varok, she turned to him and said, "How can I thank you for bringing me here, for letting me know—the ellls." She sat beside Orram on one of the long couches facing the window and concentrated on the view, trying to burn it into her mind so that she could carry it with her always—a precious but fragile painting: so very plain and intense and harsh a painting—so very dead—so stark and lonely—like the varoks—smooth and dangerous—and yet unweird, ungreen . . .

When her head rolled against his arm, Orram looked down at her face and watched the glow of her smooth, brown skin accent the bridge of her small nose and the easy turn of her chin. Daring to lower the gate of his being so that he might know this human being better than his nature would normally let him, he moved closer to her and slumped unaccustomably into the couch. Her head nestled unconsciously against his shoulder; and, though disturbed by her closeness, he cherished it and was amazed at himself. Then he too slept.

6
Who Speaks for Man?

As the moon turned slowly away from the sun, and the d'Alembert Mountains frowned, growing imperceptibly dimmer, the sun-filter in the large window of the observation deck gradually started to clear, and the lights in the garden began their two-weeks' work releasing solar energy.

Tandra stirred and reached over her head to clutch her pillow, but she missed the expected softness and came awake with the realization that her head was cradled in Orram's lap. He did not move. Apparently he was asleep. For a moment a feeling of vulnerability overwhelmed her as she stared out of the window at the rim of Earth still visible as a bright silver beyond the darkly silhouetted mountains. Then slowly, so as not to wake the varok, she turned her face upwards and dared to look into his eyes.

Her gaze met his. "I must have slept for some time. Why didn't you wake me?"

"I would have moved if I had wanted to," Orram said. "I fell asleep soon after you did."

Tandra sat up and looked at the short silver and auburn strands framing his hard, brown face. "Your hair is very beautiful," she said uneasily. A smile shone deeply from within Orram's eyes. Impulsively, Tandra touched the patches behind his ears and the varok's smile spread slowly across his face to his lips. Tandra watched the rare phenomenon with delight, and when their eyes finally met again, she and Orram laughed aloud together.

"M. Ramahlak," Tandra said, "except for those

patches behind your ears, you would easily be taken for a man anywhere on Earth. How are you different from us? Are the patches sensory organs of some kind?"

"Yes," he answered, "but we rarely talk about them because their function is a personal one for us. At very short range they detect and amplify low frequency electromagnetic signals. I cannot explain the patches to you in any detail, for their full potential cannot be made known to human beings yet. You see, this sense could be easily misunderstood and evoke unnecessary fear in those who do not possess it or understand its limitations. You are correct in assuming that it is the most obvious difference between our species."

He stopped talking and searched Tandra's eyes, hoping to receive and define her mood. How beautiful. Brown and dark and clear. And her mood? Obvious. His patches found little tension now, some fear, but more curiosity, perhaps some respect. How easy she was to read. If only he could understand himself so well. Strange, he thought, that I am not repulsed by this woman's touch.

"What did you say?" Tandra asked.

"Dr. Grey," Orram said, "we anticipated problems in relating effectively with you. But I am afraid our real problems could lie in the other direction. I am glad that you have not yet studied varokian psychology. Your ignorance may have saved us both from useless and time-consuming psychological precautions."

"But I *have* studied varokian psychology, M. Ramahlak," Tandra said.

"Then you did not understand the varokian abhorrence of touch?"

"Yes, I believe I understand it. A series of mutations occurred during the period of stressful overcrowding on Varok which resulted in the appearance of highly sensitive tactile organs in some of your ancestors. Those mutants could not stand the constant jostling and superstimulation of your urban centers, so they moved out to the wastes and eventually learned to survive independently there. As a result, they and their offspring avoided the plagues and famines of Varok; they were the ones who saved your species from extinction. But they had stopped mating, except when they decided to have children; they commonly went to great extremes to avoid contact with others. Am I right?"

"You have learned your history well. But what of us now?"

"Your abhorrence of touch cannot be as great as most, Orram. You took my hand when we first met. I have assumed that you would let me know if I overstepped the bounds of your sensitivity."

"Then you lay the responsibility on me?"

"Yes, I believe I do. Forgive me, but I wanted to touch you. I *need* to touch you—to know you are real —and alien. Conn learned this about me when we first met."

"Ellls are very aware beings, Tandra, usually more intensely aware than you or I could possibly be. Awareness gives birth to caring; they go to extremes to avoid intruding on the varoks' tactile senses, even though their own similar senses contribute enormously to their awareness, which they value equally with life itself."

"I have always been something of a bulldozer, Orram. Most people would be more sensitive than I."

"But not so adaptable, so accepting, as you. I promise to be honest with you, Tandra. I am a difficult varok to bulldoze. And I find your combination of physical aggressiveness and mental passivity quite—appealing."

The varok stood up and pulled the length of his quiet form to its full height before the panorama of the moon. Then he turned to face Tandra again. "I would like to continue our tactile exploration immediately, while my sensory defenses are down. I will ask Killah if he can join us this morning for comparative studies."

He noticed that Tandra went cold with the suggestion, so he continued on a different tack. "Of course, we have charted all known anatomical and physiological differences between the human and varokian species. Our purpose would be to make subjective comparisons. If you are agreeable, we can do it anytime, when the mood strikes us. Now why don't we continue our tour of the base? Then we can pick up Shawne and go to breakfast."

They stepped down from the observation deck, passed through the recreation lounge, entered the hall leading to the quarantine facility, immediately turned into another short hallway on their left, glanced into what might be called Artellian's office (a small, comfortably pillowed, circular room lined with maps and diagrams and moss wet-sweaters) and the food center. (which was almost always occupied with nibbling ellls), and then walked through the bio-medical labs, the health examination area, and the isolation room, the latter three ingeniously grouped together on the other side of the hall. Soon they came to a wider, longer hallway. Like the others, it was draped with silver moss that glowed with a dim sheen.

"The peace of a mellow fall dominates this place," Tandra thought as she admired Orram's tall, brown presence in the soft red light of the artificial morning. Everything seemed full of life and its living. She recognized the large doors to the pool on her left, followed Orram to the right, and enjoyed watching him open the sealed panels of the geology and chemistry studies. There her impressions were not only confirmed but gratifyingly enhanced. The studies were rich, comfortable rooms dominated by plump couches and soft mushroom stools and thick growths of moss. But buried here and there in the cushiony elegance—in the elllonian way, so that it appealed to the senses—were contrasting crystal sculptures, transparent tangles of pipes and cups and electronic samplers: evidences of some elllonian Rube Goldberg's tinkering with moon dust.

Reluctantly, Tandra turned away and followed Orram down the hall. Beyond the studies, next to the hangar, was a small, relatively sterile observatory, and beside it perched the centrifuge room, a simple mossy cylinder fitted with nothing but body-molding couches spaced around its lower circumference.

"At Killah's insistence," Orram explained, "the ellls take turns sleeping and exercising here. It is not a pleasant experience to be whirled at speeds which simulate their natural g-forces, so this room is used strictly for reasons of health." He stepped back over the threshold and looked down the hallway. Shawne had emerged from the room nearest the entrance to the pool and was happily bouncing toward them. Orram caught her as she leaped carelessly at him.

Tandra gasped at the contact.

"It's funny to run here," Shawne told the varok.

"But you must learn not to get ahead of yourself, little one. Go more slowly." He turned to Tandra and set the child down. "You should see one of the apartments. They are all on the other side of this hall. The nursery is right here. The ellls would not be happy without raising a few children, so they have put six adults into one room and left part of the end apartment free for an incubator and elllonian-style cribs. You have seen the boy, Da-oon, run past the quarantine window now and then, haven't you? He is almost four Earth-years old now. He should be a good companion for Shawne. She will want to play here most of the time."

They turned toward the open room, but Conn suddenly appeared and stopped them at the door.

"No need to check here, Tandra. Everything is okay."

"I'm sure it is. But I'd still like to see it. Shawne will be in there most of the day."

"Look, Tan, Ellalon will be with them, and Aen takes over later. There are some good toys there—nothing that can hurt Shawne."

Tandra bristled. "Why don't you want me to see the nursery, Conn?"

"I'm sorry, but I've got reasons."

"Then I had better know them before I send Shawne there."

"You've got to find out some things for yourself first."

"Conn, I am stubborn about very few things, but one of them is Shawne. I want to know where she will be and what she will be doing when she's not with me."

Conn looked at Orram. "Hell," he grumbled, "come on then."

He ushered Tandra and Shawne into the room, glanced quickly at two large tanks built into one wall, and invited Shawne to sit with him on the warm mossy floor near a pile of three-dimensional puzzle pieces and a small smooth elll busily sorting them out.

"You know Da-oon, don't you Shawne?" Conn said.

The baby buried her face in Conn's side before she ventured to smirk at the small elll studiously ignoring her. Then a large moving model of a *kaehl* caught her eye. She ran to the toy and was carefully removing the eggs from its soft pouch when Da-oon, excited by the promise of fun on his own terms, began gathering up the generous supply of elllonian plumes which were scattered among the toys. Together then they began to build a nest for the great toy *kaehl* and her eggs.

Abruptly Tandra stood up and smiled at Conn. "I'm perfectly satisfied. It's quite safe here. I don't know what I wasn't supposed to see, but there is nothing that can hurt Shawne. Those tanks are too high for Shawne to fall into, and the toys look wonderful."

"You are finished, then, with the nursery?" Orram asked.

"This isn't the first time that I've trusted Conn." Tandra saw a prolonged, worried gaze travel between Conn and Orram. Her imagination flew wild again. Conn and the ellls were not being used by the varoks. Together they were *all* using *her*. The ellls couldn't work so closely with the varoks unless they were basically very much alike. What did they really want with her? What would happen to Shawne, to Earth? Conn had used her romantic tendencies to win her confidence and . . . The thought repulsed her, she erased it from her mind, and she relaxed again as she watched Shawne and Da-oon playing happily in the pleasant nursery. "Forgive me, dear Conn," she said to herself. But Orram's voice still made her shudder.

"Artellian should be awake. I will show you the room I share with him."

Conn followed Orram and Tandra back down the large hallway. They entered the last room on the right, next to the pool room. Like the rest of the base, it glowed warm and humid with a plush, lived-in elegance. Tandra wandered into the apartment's chaotic maze between two bed pads and two sleeping basins, invitingly rich with soft, blue moss. Behind Orram's meticulously ordered bed-pad was a great heap of Artellian's books, pink vials, pens, clean synthetic paper, and belabored manuscript set in and around the rough-hewn walls, which had been carved with great care and apparent delight into convenient drawers, long shelves, and broad working spaces.

From deep within a small niche above her head, Tandra saw a purple stone figure staring down at her with its one large black eye set menacingly into a fine, high brow, which grew like a cancer of smooth perfection and merged indiscriminately with a pitiful, bony abdomen and great bulbous legs, cruelly pitted and stained, that twisted into uselessness.

"What is that, Orram?" Tandra asked, running her fingers over the rough stone figure. "It is no varokian beast."

"Its name is *Gurahn*," Orram said. He stepped un-self-consciously over the literary heaps on the floor and took the purple monstrosity from its niche in the wall. "It is the personification of Varok, an interpretive sculpture made by the *ll-leyoolianl*, a species of great-fish who inhabit the deeps of Ellason. They convey their ideas through the use of three-dimensional images."

"Through three-dimensional images? How can you know that your interpretation is correct?"

"They have developed the art of their communication to a very high degree so that one cannot miss the meaning in one's own context."

Conn nodded.

"Does this ugly thing really tell you something significant, Orram?" Tandra's voice was no longer hesitant; it had an edge of disdain. Apparently the varoks were enough like men to be plagued by human-like pretensions. "I think you have fallen victim to a contemporary human fallacy. Ah! See the eight-by-ten-foot masterpiece: One giant splash of paint elegantly framed! The empty canvas conveys the hopeless void of existence that surrounds man. The rough edges of the paint trail here and there into the emptiness: the souls of men stretching out for truer knowledge, for fuller consciousness. But they end too soon, fallen in despair." Tandra laughed cynically. "A fine interpretation. But the true meaning lies closer to the fact that the artist threw his paintbrush across a piece of canvas and hornswoggled some little old lady into paying thousands of dollars for it. I think that this Elllonian great-fish has learned to dab mud into weird shapes that have tickled the ells' imagination and appealed to some varok's hungry search for meaning.

"What else have these fish done? Designed any tools, written any dictionaries? If they are so intelligent, why aren't they here at base? How do you know that they are intelligent at all, Orram?"

"So," Orram said, "you insist on equating verbal ability and technological prowess with intelligence?"

Tandra's eyes were caught by Conn's questioning look. Why had she challenged the varok? She didn't have the intellectual strength to match him.

"What else is there to equate it to?" she said. "On such evidence I would submit that you are the most intelligent species in this solar system; that the ellls rank second; and that we human beings run a poor third." She spoke, seeking to back off from the demand in Orram's gaze. "Yes, of course I equate verbal ability and technological prowess with intelligence. And you are the proof."

"And the great-fish are proof to the contrary. Their expression is entirely different from ours; they are brilliant and inventive in the ways they perceive and communicate. Yet you have rejected my evidence, the great-fish, with little thought and no real consideration." The varok spoke pensively, quietly, with nothing but kindness in his voice.

Tandra suddenly understood. She looked at Orram with new respect and less fear. "I am as blind to new concepts as most men. It disgusts me that we can't get past the assumption that human intelligence is some kind of unique phenomenon in this universe, much less admit to the existence of an entirely different form of intelligence. Only a few hundred years ago men were burned at the stake for denying that the Earth was the center of the universe! We haven't come much further! We still don't see ourselves in the total context. We are either blinded by our self-importance or overwhelmed by the realization of our insignificance. We can't even place ourselves in perspective within our own small planet. I think you are wise to avoid open contact with Earth. Men are not ready to relate rationally to a superior intelligence—especially not to a superior *alien* intelligence." The notion of men trying to relate to the great-fish of Ellason flashed through her mind as an impossibility.

"Are *you* ready to relate rationally to alien intelligence, Tandra?" Conn asked. "You are man."

As the elll spoke the sparse shadows grew deeper in Orram's face. Why was there such protest in the woman's mind, such denial?

"Come sit here, Tandra. Talk with me for a moment," he said. "You know that we have taken elaborate precautions to avoid accidental encounter with your species." He read her reaction to his words and knew that she emphatically, emotionally disassociated herself from man.

"I saw the disintegration and gas guns in Conn's isolation suit," Tandra said.

"We have a healthy respect for Earth's potential fear of aliens. Someday we hope to exert some influence in helping your planet find a workable stable condition, much as we advised the ellls, but we see no way to introduce ourselves effectively to Earth yet. The ellls were a docile, schooling people, capable of denying for themselves inventions of convenience if their manufacture proved costly or disruptive to their beloved oceans. I doubt that men are so capable, but we won't attempt to force solutions unless Earth enters a terminal crisis—a crisis endangering her potential to maintain life."

"What solutions would you force? What *could* you force? Almost anything, I suspect." She tensed and looked up.

Tallyn and Killah were standing in the doorway listening. Tallyn's rough, powerful torso was balanced skeptically, his eyes narrowed angrily behind agitated crown plumes. Finally, he spoke. "Earth once most beautiful diverse living planet by this sun."

"Tallyn, I know. It's my planet."

"Is it now?" he said.

"I care more for the life of Earth than for the lives of all mankind, that's why it is mine."

"Tandra, surely not," Conn said irritably.

"You came too late to know, Conn. How I wish you could have seen Earth twenty years ago. I remember when the sun made brilliant paintings on white and gray clouds as it set instead of slowly dimming to an orange ball behind the smog. The skies haven't always been uniform gray. And the trees were green and strong and grew without artificial stimulants and cleaning. You could still see deer in some of the open forests. I remember seeing one in the hills once. Have you ever seen a deer, Tallyn? Your water birds are exotic and lovely, but no alien creature I have yet seen can compare with the delicate beauty of a doe or the majesty of her buck. You will never make me assume the role of defender of man, Tallyn."

"You can't deny yourself, Tan," Conn said.

"Man is an integral part of the planet Earth," Orram

said. "Your concern for any part must of necessity concern the whole."

"When a pathogen infects a body," Tandra replied, "the whole is endangered until all the pathogens are destroyed. Earth doesn't need man. I wish I didn't need him. I don't *want* him! You are more than enough, Conn."

"More than enough!?" Conn laughed and then wondered why. "Your duty is with man; you are man whether you like it or not."

"About some of this you are right, Tandra," Killah said. "The state of your planet's life will continue to deteriorate until the human animal decides to contain himself. Earth is a closed test tube, eh? But perhaps man is an adaptable germ and will learn to survive on excrement, become *Homo effluetus.*" The elll ran his webbed hand slowly over his crown plumes. "More likely you will simply learn to ignore it all—become *Homo insipidus.* You are an adaptable species, too adaptable, capable of extraordinary repression. Well, we cannot know yet. I would like to see your best potential realized, myself. You are not a lovely animal but quite capable of creative thought and tolerant love— even acceptance. Tallyn might think otherwise. You human beings seem to be inordinately impressed by technological gadgets. This upsets him."

"Since some years," Tallyn said in a rising crescendo, "when *ecology* is common word everyone knows but use it too much as political handle, man's still-always misuse of Earth's life and resources is deliberate slaughter. You drive car, live in many-roomed house full with all-electric environment. What insanity is this?"

"Tallyn," Orram said quietly, "Tandra knows all this."

But the gruff elll raged on. "You do all *you* can, eh?"

"No, no, of course I don't," Tandra cried. "But would it help for me—one person in nearly seven billion—to forego electricity?"

"You are blind hypocrite!" Tallyn insisted in a deep

elllonian roll. "You do nothing! You see proud animal here, this varok? He is vastly more than wise you or I. Do know how he lives? Has he told you what is home?"

Further words failed him, and Killah picked up the point: "Master Oran Ramahlak lives in one room formed from whatever his land on Varok offers. He uses very little power, only some to communicate, some to see with light. Varoks use a collective transport system, but more often they stay home. He limits himself to two children, and he knows his race is secure. No life need fear him, except when he must eat."

Tallyn shouted, "Do you know that? Does no life fear you?"

"How can you accuse me, you ellls, living in this base the way you do?" Tandra asked tightly. "How much energy did it take to fill that pool full of water? Sleeping bowls everywhere to coddle the ellls! You are the hypocrite, Tallyn."

"Everything on this base calculated for maximum efficient. *Uuyvanoonl* increase surface area for moss to grow. Ellls need water and play. Pool was necessary— energy required is less than staffing with all varoks. All is known. All is accounted for. Do you know that?"

With that Tandra released the reins on her emotions. She got up abruptly to pace the room, tears crashing hot on her cheeks. "I account as best I can. No life need fear *me*," she cried, shaking with fear and rage. "I try to maintain *my* integrity. I am not *all* men. Don't you see? I agree with you. Human integrity exists mostly in the mind of man, rarely in fact. I do what *I* can, in spite of the rest, but I must find a way to survive first."

Orram read clearly the profound frustration she felt; more quickly than he thought possible his empathy reached the depths of his felt emotion. He rose from the bed pad and caught Tandra in a sympathetic embrace.

The vision of the varok's close contact with the woman jolted Tallyn into silence, and his anger metamorphosed to a more pleasant dismay.

"You know that Tandra is right in questioning this base, Tallyn," Orram said. "It was an enormous expenditure and required a moral compromise to build. The study of Earth was considered to be worth the price. Even though we are essentially self-sustaining here, our maintenance requires continual justification."

Tandra found no comfort in Orram's embrace or his words. Questions boiled through her mind, and she felt utterly alone: the ellls and Conn couldn't or wouldn't understand, and the varoks were in absolute control.

Conn, no less than Orram, had sensed her distress, and he was unexplainably relieved when Orram released her. Immediately Conn took the varok's place. He turned Tandra away from the others and tried to give her the verbal assurance she needed.

Tallyn's surprise at Orram's embrace remained, and his eyes widened with sympathy when he saw Tandra's warm response to Conn's attention. "Forgive me, Tandra, little *kaehloid*," he said softly, "M. Ramahlak, I not seen you touch anyone so before. And Conn—now I see how much is this schooling with Tandra. I would not if you. Human love is difficult—too much one elll to carry alone."

"Tallyn," Orram said, not wanting to let the conversation go without drawing a meaning from it, "human beings are highly competitive, egocentric beings like varoks. They are not like ellls. They have no innate sense of cooperative self-denial for their common cause such as you have. They must learn—their genetic makeup does not tell them—what is necessary to live at a maximal level within a balanced life-system."

At first Tandra was afraid that he was talking about her; then she knew he was. She denied it and tried to justify her denial with all the passion of self-assurance. Man was an entity apart from herself! But the impact of the varok's words left their mark; she felt degraded and shamed.

Her feelings of humiliation were not lost to Orram; the varok was profoundly moved. And her intense aloneness was also clear, as was her apprehension and distrust. But where was the focus of her mind? Was she trying to invent her own comfortable reality? If so, she was having some success; he must break the invention or she would be of no use to them later.

7
Identity and Comparison

In the weeks that followed, most of Tandra's time was occupied with microbiological studies. Cultures were made of throat swabbings and fecal and blood samples from all the crew, as she and Killah watched for an exchange of normal flora between the species. Their relationship was business-like and comfortable; she enjoyed Killah's habit of making biological observations with a philosophical bent. It kept him at an entertaining distance where her illusions about ellls were not challenged.

Conn, however, pressed closer, demanding more, and gradually Tandra's work came to provide her with a handy escape from Conn's hovering. At first he had not intruded on her while she was in the labs. But because her work left him too little time with her, he occasionally would interrupt her there.

One day, after Tandra had worked several hours at her desk, she suddenly realized that Conn was standing behind her. "Yes," she said, looking up from a microscope.

The cold in her eyes was obvious. "What did I do?" Conn asked.

Tandra smiled nervously. "I'm sorry, Conn. I'm just irritable from working. I'm glad you came. I'd really rather talk than work."

"All right." Conn sat down in a moss chair by her lab desk.

"All right what?"

"Go ahead, talk."

"I can't just go ahead and talk."

"So ask me a question," Conn ventured. "Sometimes

I wish you wouldn't accept so much so blandly—ask more questions or something."

"All right. Try this one again. And really tell me this time. Don't play it off," Tandra pleaded. "What does it feel like to be an elll?"

"It feels good, sometimes real good," Conn chuckled.

"Stop it, Conn," Tandra cried. "I asked you a serious question."

"Why the hell do you think I'm *not* serious?" Conn said. "I gave you a good answer. It feels good to be elll. I feel good. We feel good. What more can I say? I don't know how *you* feel to me yet."

"You see why I don't ask questions?" Tandra laughed.

They talked amiably then for a short while before he left—but he didn't try to intrude on her work again.

Through all this time, Tandra could not shake herself free of her apprehension over the varoks. They moved through their daily routine, it seemed to her, like zombies, always courteous, never offering more than they were asked. But the fantasies of fear burned in her mind only when she was alone. The warm rasp of Orram's voice snuffed them out, leaving her feeling paranoid and foolish.

Spontaneously, after just such an incident, she mentioned the problem to Killah. "Intellectually, I know its foolish," she said, "because the varoks are absolutely straightforward in their manner, but I can't rid myself of the idea that they are sinister, devious monsters: super-men in the worst sense."

His response was a hearty laugh. "There is nothing so dull as a varok, Tandra. You have read something of them, not enough. Put aside some time each day now and study them thoroughly. You will soon see why I laugh at your fears."

When Orram passed by their lab and disappeared into Artellian's office, she said: "Killah, he should have purple horns and slimy scales—at least a tail!"

Killah tossed his floppy plumes out of his eyes and

erupted again with hoots of laughter, but when Tandra grabbed his arm he stopped abruptly. "Please," she pleaded, "I need to know that he is really not human. The patch organ is the only significant difference that I can see."

Killah shook his head. "You had better do that subjective comparison Orram wanted. I see it is troublesome to be so much like the varoks. Crisis of identity, Tandra? What is man, eh? Well you know, we are all merely collections of molecules—hormones and what-have-you—sharing the gift of consciousness—complex blobs of obvious relevancy in an incomprehensible universe. So what do they matter, our intellectualizations and grand philosophies? We share cognizance and are grateful. That should be enough."

Tandra acted on Killah's advice then and became entirely engrossed with Orram and his species. It was like entering a strange, guarded room of hidden switches. She devoured all the information the varoks provided, but still did not dare to ask the difficult questions: Why were they really here on Earth's moon? And why had they chosen her? For what, beyond the obvious biological studies?

The answers lay within Orram, just beyond reach. When the varok sensed Tandra's uncertainty, he decided he had been too cautious, too passive. So he attempted to draw closer to the woman, and soon they had established a comfortable pattern of encounters: After the long, congenial dinner-hour when the lights had dimmed to a soft ruddy hue, they would meet at the pool to swim lazy circles or to play floating slow-motion games invented to test each other's physical stamina and reflexes. Then they would retire to the observation deck for long conversations.

Orram's patches were rarely idle at those times; he knew that Tandra's fear was balanced by a strong desire to trust him, by an odd reliance on him that he couldn't rationalize, and by a certain sympathy that superseded her defensive ego.

One evening while the ellls were gathered in the food center to choose their meals and to tease and push and chat companionably before they drifted off to the pool, Tandra noticed that Orram was alone, eating more hurriedly than usual. She made her way through the green mob to stand near him. Though she could find no clue in his expressionless face, an ill-defined uneasiness was apparent. When he had finished eating, she decisively followed her intuition and linked her arm in his. He looked down at her, his face still blank, then led her gaze with his own toward Junah, who was watching them from across the room. Junah disappeared into the hallway when she met Orram's glance, and Orram moved with Tandra toward the observation deck.

"I was going to spend my time alone with my thoughts this evening," he said. "Now I would rather not. You noticed Junah leave the room when you came over to me in the food center?"

"Yes," Tandra answered. "I noticed and felt sorry. She doesn't like me to touch you, does she?"

"No, she does not."

The woman and the varok climbed the stairs to the observation deck and sat facing each other before the great curving window.

"Tell me about Varok, Orram," Tandra said.

"What can I tell you that you do not already know? Our security restrictions are a nuisance. I would like to tell you more than I may."

"Tell me what it is like to be a varok on Varok. What the Mutilation means to you. I would like to know."

He stretched his long legs full over the couch and gradually submitted the control of his elegant form to its comforting hold. Then he began to talk in mild, rough-hewn tones.

"When our first space ships left Varok for extended exploration, an aging astronomer, Llorian Analahk, wrote poetry and songs that expressed what you want to know. I should memember something of his." The varok's warm, thought-filled voice slowed and paused and then moved on into a gentle crescendo:

Arise great orb, and moons sink low.
These lands float free in mist
Where color spins on ethereal webs.
Come home to this great swirling mass,
Come home where lands float free beneath the moons,
Where color spins.

Beneath the danger-veil, behind the storm,
Below the freezing crystal tones,
Come home to hues forever changing, color spinning,
Come home to mist, to warmth beneath the moons.
Come home where color spins,
Where lands float free.

Great orb arise and hide the moons.
Find shadows nowhere when you move.
Obscure the mist and pale the hues,
Become the sky itself.
Come home to mists retreating wildly,
Come home to colors maddened by the shade.
Come home to this great orb
Where color spins and lands float free in mist.

"You must have been magnificent creatures before the Mutilation," Tandra said quietly.

"Perhaps," he said, smiling with the word *before*. "We were tall, humanoid mammals with a wingspread of three or four metres. The historical reference *Mutilation* refers not to the mutants who died in infancy or left infertile offspring, but to the gradual altering of the entire population: the degeneration of the wings and the loss of flight, the increasing inability to function rationally under emotional stress, and the sexual aberrations which developed when our abhorrence of touch was maximal. Nature had to force us to mate again more frequently after the major die-offs; so it was that we came to resemble human beings, and we began to wear clothes.

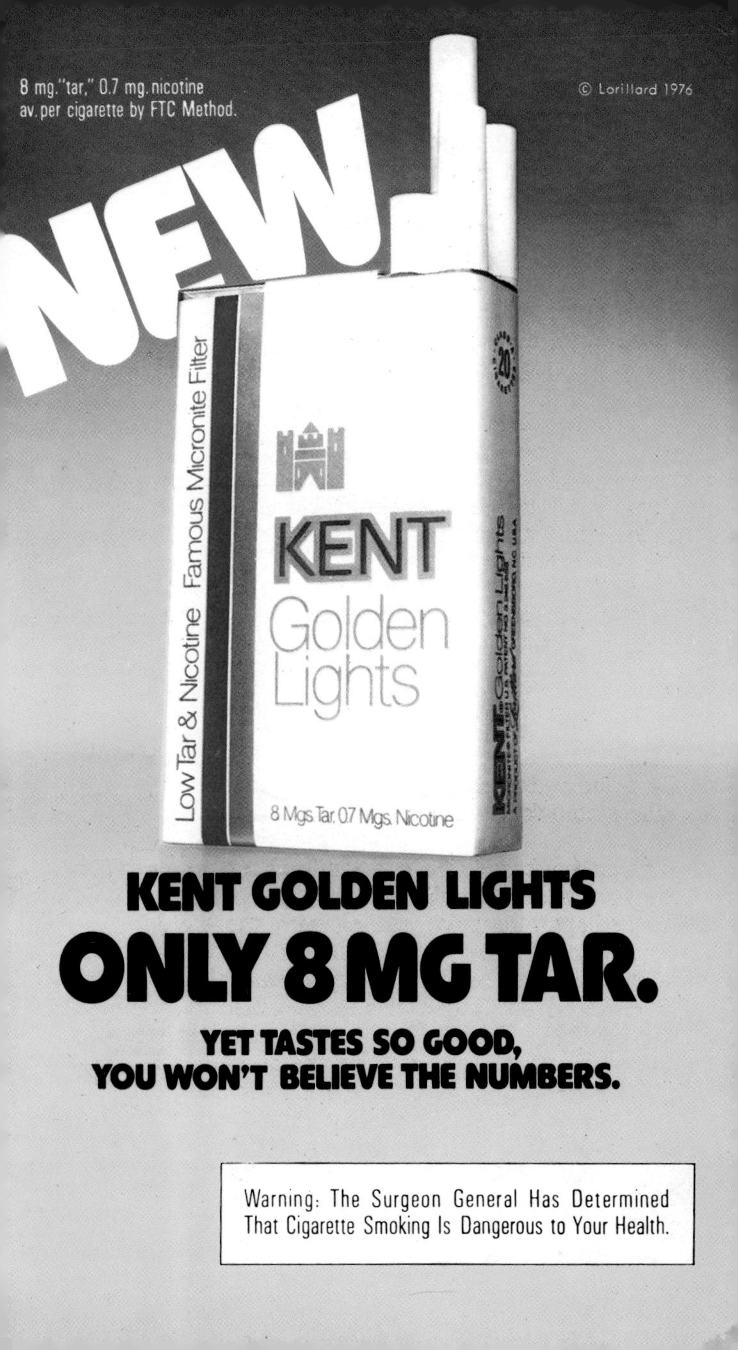
8 mg."tar," 0.7 mg. nicotine
av. per cigarette by FTC Method.
© Lorillard 1976
NEW
Low Tar & Nicotine Famous Micronite Filter
KENT
Golden
Lights
8 Mgs. Tar. 0.7 Mgs. Nicotine
20
KENT Golden Lights
KENT GOLDEN LIGHTS
ONLY 8 MG TAR.
YET TASTES SO GOOD,
YOU WON'T BELIEVE THE NUMBERS.
Warning: The Surgeon General Has Determined
That Cigarette Smoking Is Dangerous to Your Health.

NEW!
KENT GOLDEN LIGHTS
LOWER IN TAR
THAN ALL THESE BRANDS.

Non-menthol Filter Brands	Tar	Nicotine	Non-menthol Filter Brands	Tar	Nicotine
KENT GOLDEN LIGHTS	**8 mg.**	**0.7 mg.***	RALEIGH 100's	17 mg.	1.2 mg.
MERIT	9 mg.	0.7 mg.*	MARLBORO 100's	17 mg.	1.1 mg.
VANTAGE	11 mg.	0.7 mg.	BENSON & HEDGES 100's	18 mg.	1.1 mg.
MULTIFILTER	13 mg.	0.8 mg.	VICEROY 100's	18 mg.	1.2 mg.
WINSTON LIGHTS	13 mg.	0.9 mg.	MARLBORO KING SIZE	18 mg.	1.1 mg.
MARLBORO LIGHTS	13 mg.	0.8 mg.	LARK	18 mg.	1.2 mg.
RALEIGH EXTRA MILD	14 mg.	0.9 mg.	CAMEL FILTERS	18 mg.	1.2 mg.
VICEROY EXTRA MILD	14 mg.	0.9 mg.	EVE	18 mg.	1.2 mg.
PARLIAMENT BOX	14 mg.	0.8 mg.	WINSTON 100's	18 mg.	1.2 mg.
DORAL	15 mg.	1.0 mg.	WINSTON BOX	18 mg.	1.2 mg.
PARLIAMENT KING SIZE	16 mg.	0.9 mg.	CHESTERFIELD	19 mg.	1.2 mg.
VICEROY	16 mg.	1.1 mg.	LARK 100's	19 mg.	1.2 mg.
RALEIGH	16 mg.	1.1 mg.	L&M KING SIZE	19 mg.	1.2 mg.
VIRGINIA SLIMS	16 mg.	1.0 mg.	TAREYTON 100's	19 mg.	1.4 mg.
PARLIAMENT 100's	17 mg.	1.0 mg.	WINSTON KING SIZE	19 mg.	1.3 mg.
L&M BOX	17 mg.	1.1 mg.	L&M 100's	19 mg.	1.3 mg.
SILVA THINS	17 mg.	1.3 mg.	PALL MALL 100's	19 mg.	1.4 mg.
MARLBORO BOX	17 mg.	1.0 mg.	TAREYTON	21 mg.	1.4 mg.

Source: FTC Report Apr. 1976
*By FTC Method

"Under the harsh requirements of a marginal survival, our first successful mutants had no time to indulge self-awareness or sensitivity to others. To be lax or kind or impractical was to insure one's elimination in favor of the strong and the smart and the hardened. As you have seen all too well, Tandra, the Mutilation left deep psychological and sociological scars upon us. Emotional involvements of any kind, and especially sexual involvements, still cost us a great price. Reason cannot co-exist with emotional motivation in the varokian mind. We must seem extremely stolid to you."

Tandra shifted uneasily on the couch. "Would you prefer that I not touch you?"

"No, Tandra, obviously not you," he said. "Don't let Conn worry you. The ellls respect too much this tendency of ours to avoid touch. The ellls see us varoks as hopelessly cold because their lives are ruled by their senses, especially their sense of touch. Ours are ruled by the deadening power of reason.

"Do you understand that we varoks are entirely incapable of willing the control back to reason, once intense emotion takes over? If we allow ourselves to feel joy or anger or even grief at the loss of a friend, the emotion will rapidly overcome our entire minds until we are thrown into an irrational fit. Sometimes it is days before we recover some conscious control of our minds. That is why we must never allow ourselves to be driven into emotionally untenable positions. I have a problem to deal with now . . .".

"Junah?"

"Yes. She is imagining a relationship with me that goes beyond our original agreement to mate casually. I may have to terminate that relationship. I could not consummate a marriage with her, but she continues to look for signs of marital contact from me. You undersand our customs in this regard, don't you, Tandra?"

"Incompletely. I know that you marry infrequently and that consummation of marriage is a merging of identities which involves the patch organ in a way that I cannot know. Some varoks in consummation can lean on each other psychologically and experience some emotion rationally. I believe this is called release."

In spite of, or because of, their free relationships, Tandra knew, the varoks often remained with one mate for life, only rarely accepting another for short periods. Occasionally they solemnized their mating with legal obligations and ceremonies. But once these formal marriages were successfully consummated—consummated not with sexual union but with the aid of the patch organs behind their ears—they were never dissolved.

Orram had never touched a varokian female with compelling emotion or sensual desire, though he had mated out of a need for close friendship as often as most varoks. Junah had been a recent casual choice for him, but he knew that her emotional potential toward him was greater than his response toward her. It would take long, careful months of clear indifference to undo her increasing desire for him as consummate mate.

"I think you would find Varok quietly beautiful, Tandra," Orram continued, frankly changing the conversation. "It is an unhurried place. True peace of mind can be found there, and creative wills such as yours are quite free. We are learning to value life— savoring the quality of moments above all else, as the ellls do. Some men would say Varok is stagnant, for there is little desire for change—only for equitable stability."

"What price in human lives have we paid for our fear of stagnation?" Tandra asked. "Statistics come too easily; we don't seem to care for the massive grief that they represent."

"Perhaps the hunter prefers death to life without the hunt. Perhaps life has no quality if it is predictable and safe."

Tandra suddenly flushed with shame. "You are a species with integrity and intelligence superior to man's, Orram; I know that, yet I continue to place you in the role that men might assume—a role of domination and subjugation and hidden purpose."

Abruptly Orram sat up and a dark crease formed

between his faint brows. "So that is why you have feared us," he said. "I should not have postponed our physical subjective study. You must be assured immediately that we are not human. Will you agree to a physical study now?"

Tandra paused.

"Yes, I need to know you are not like man, to see you as a varok."

"You are more sensitive than we have thought," Orram continued. "We do indeed have hidden purposes for you, but we are not sure you can or will fill them. You must qualify and volunteer yourself for the jobs that you see must be done. We will force nothing on you. Indeed we will attempt to contain your ambition concerning Earth if we believe you fail to qualify for the task you assume.

"You still hold a narrow view, Tandra. In spite of your passion for life, you still think in terms of man. You can't know how we have grieved to watch the demise on Earth of irreplaceable species we have never seen equaled in our worlds. I wish that you could see an elephant or a kangaroo with the eyes of an alien! Earth is a showcase of evolution's wildest experiments; the planet is a menagerie resplendent with lush diversity. We humanoid species are rather ordinary animals, species to be expected, designed to maximize adaptability."

"I know that intelligence is more common, even on Earth, than man dares suspect," Tandra said. "It seems to me that superior intelligence must have a selective advantage in any environment."

"But you should realize that one cannot talk about superior intelligence when comparing different species," Orram said. "We have never found a thoroughly suitable yardstick for measuring intellectual capacity in more than one species. We varoks have an extra sense or two and our technology may be a bit more advanced than yours, but we have serious flaws in our nature. The ellls don't normally indulge in technological games, but they have far superior biological equipment for absorbing and interpreting sensual stimuli than either you or I have. The *ll-leyoolianl*, the great fish whose skills you disdained, have neither language nor tools, but they undoubtedly do have an enormous talent for conceptualizing experience and communicating their ideas with great clarity."

"Even more than the ellls?"

Orram glanced queerly at her. "You should know how poor they are at forming abstract concepts. The cllls' minds work in the present. They are so enmeshed in immediate experience that they simply respond without mentally stepping back to evaluate themselves as a third person might."

"Explain," Tandra said. "I don't understand what you mean."

"Has Conn been able to define his relationship to you—to understand his problem with you?"

"What problem?" Tandra asked.

"Then you haven't focused on it yet? Is this another example of man's repression, or just yours? But soon you will focus on your problem and Conn will not. He will probably never be able to conceptualize your relationship—even non-verbally to himself. The elllonian mind is continuously subjected to an enormous sensory input. If their minds were computers you would say that their bit-rate has a broad band-width and a high frequency. Lots of data, bits of information, coming in all the time. Much more than ours. We have fewer senses, hence fewer signals to sort out and interpret. On the other hand, the great-fish probably don't perceive bits of information at all. They simply understand what they focus on."

"And how would they talk to Conn about our problems?"

"They would school with him."

"You're serious," Tandra said.

"I'm rarely capable of any other mood." Orram almost smiled. "The *ll-leyoolianl* are a greatly respected species. They are more often correct than not and are looked to for counsel by many species, not just ellls and varoks. But more important than the great-fish, do you understand what I have said about the ellls?"

"Many impressions all the time, little integration. It fits. Immediate experience is what they are made of. Killah and Conn have both said that awareness is life to them. And I do know, Orram, that there are many measures of life besides so-called intelligence."

"I am sure that you do, Tandra." The varok searched the woman's eyes carefully. "I think that you are almost ready to trust me. Tell me now what you need to know about varoks."

"I need to know what you intend with Earth. Why do you watch and wait and do nothing?"

"We *can* do nothing but watch and learn. The reminders we see of our past mistakes are invaluable, Tandra, but extremely painful. We are not masochistic. Indeed, the reminders are double painful because we are so helpless."

"That can't be true!" Tandra cried. "There must be something you can do."

"That's the irony in it all. We could probably help relieve some suffering by sharing what we know; but any help we give will result in even greater suffering later. If we provide a solar energy technology to feed the hungry now, there will soon be twice as many to feed. It is well known that partial solutions only postpone and magnify such crises. There is no way we can impose the total solution on man, but I believe there might still be time to avert total collapse."

"You must try, Orram. Try anything. There is no predicting the reaction to alien contact. You might have great influence."

"Or none at all. We can say nothing new, and we cannot open closed minds or change those who prefer profit and expediency to the difficult answers."

A profound sadness settled over Tandra and the varok. He took her in his arms to comfort her as he had before, and throughout the night they remained together sharing thoughts and resting and searching for answers.

* * *

When the next day's light cycle had been established, Orram searched Tandra's mood and found no apprehension left. "You are still too much in awe of me, Tandra," he said, "but at least your fears are eased. Come now. Explore me thoroughly." With a few quick motions he undressed and stood nude before her. "Satisfy yourself that I am alien."

Tandra backed away from him and studied his taut brown body. Except for the uniform thin sprinkling of soft, silver and red hair that covered it, it was not obviously alien. She stepped closer to him and moved her hands slowly along his arms, over his elbows to the thick natural calluses on the tips of his fingers, and down his regular, firm sides. "No hedonic glands here," she said in an effort at humor. He did not smile.

She moved her hands quickly over his hips. His testicles were smooth and oddly bare; and the lack of pubic hair made his penis seem raw and vulnerable. As she moved her hands on down his legs she missed the expected feel of coarse hair. She looked at his feet, counted his toes, then stood up; and her gaze was drawn into the deep blueness of his eyes. For a moment she savored the good feeling their openness now gave her. Then she explored with her fingers Orram's silver and red hair, his high cheek bones and deep brows, his straight long nose, and his chin, smooth from lack of beard and shaving.

Suddenly she stepped back and slipped out of the robe that she had worn to dinner the night before.

"Surely you are not done," he said before she could remove her bodysuit.

"Yes, I am done."

Orram's face was grave. "But you have avoided the two areas of my body that are most unlike your own."

"I did avoid the patch."

"I thought that you were anxious to establish my alienness."

"I was. There doesn't seem to be any alienness to establish."

"Sometimes our deepest fears find us when we least expect them. Examine my arms and the patch organs behind my ears, and you will know that I am not human."

Again Tandra ran her hands over Orram's long arms; she noticed nothing unusual. She started to reach toward his patches when he suddenly grabbed her hands.

"You refuse to see, Tandra! You must learn now! You must know without doubt that I am not human. I am alien to Earth! My home is a floating oasis entrapped by a hostile, gigantic mass millions and millions of miles from here." He turned his hands outward and spread his fingers. "Run your hand along the inside of my arm and between my fingers."

Tandra obeyed, and the faint line of heavy tissue that had seemed like a scar loomed in her mind as an obvious vestige of an ancient structure. She traced the line downward to the tip of Orram's fifth finger, which was slightly longer than the others. Then she followed it toward his body and could see that it flared into a tough thin web for a short distance under his arm.

"My legs now," he commanded.

Tandra knelt and encircled his knee with her hands. "I see on both sides of your legs similar vestiges of what must have been extensive tissue. Killah said that your ancestors had been magnificent aerial creatures. I thought that they might have had wings, but these vestiges could be the remains of something like the alar membranes of bats."

"Indeed they are," Orram said. "Before the Mutilation, our ancestors were built very much like your extinct flying reptiles, the pterydactyls. The large wing, or alar membrane, extended from an elongated little finger, down the arm, and along the outside of the legs. The remaining four fingers were used for manipulation, as they are now. An additional membrane extended between the legs and a short tail. Now examine my breast. Isn't it broader than a human male's?"

"Yes," Tandra said, probing firmly with her fingers,

"and there is a short ridge running down its center. I can barely feel it beneath your muscles."

"A keel, really," Orram said, "very much like the keel on the breastplate of birds. It served as an anchor for the large breast muscles that extended into the wings." He looked at her with anticipation. "And now what do you think of me?"

"You are varok. It is resolved. You are also . . ." She stopped speaking, afraid of her thoughts, *also male,* she said to herself. But the meaning did not escape the varok's patches.

"Now touch the patch organs, Tandra. They are not sensitive."

She placed her hands behind his ears and felt the smooth raised discs of tissue. Orram bent his head down so that she could examine them closely. They were textured very finely with tiny slits and membranes, but no other details were obvious.

Then she backed away, finished undressing with almost no hesitation, and stood before the large wall which framed the lunar sunset, her long, dark hair spilling over her smooth shoulders onto her breasts and touching the fine, straight arms that contrasted gracefully with the muscled tension in her modeled legs.

Orram touched her chin. "You are a very beautiful woman, Tandra; I, too, am disturbed. Only your behavior tells me that you are most decidedly not varokian." His fingers brushed her temples, stroked the smooth skin behind her ears where there were no patch organs, and moved systematically over her entire body.

When his touch left her, Tandra pulled her head back, searching his stony face with bewilderment. "You belie everything that I have read about varoks, Orram. Your touch is sensitive, but you savor it. I thought you would have had to fight a feeling of repulsion."

"You could be no more surprised than I am. In some way that I do not understand you have made me forget my varokian inhibitions. I will stop now, Tandra. I need some time to consider my observations. Shall we relax now and swim?"

* * *

They descended the stairs into the recreation lounge, passed Conn, who was absorbed in tinkering with a solar concentrator, and entered the pool room. Killah was there with the elllonian girl Tllan.

"Well, well, *kaehloids* in the flesh," Killah said. "Going to enjoy your swim for a change, Ramahlak?"

"I just might surprise you, Killah."

"I hope so," the elll grinned.

"What did you call us, Killah? *Kaehloids?*"

"In effect this rude elll is calling us furry little beasts," Orram said.

"Ha!" Tandra came at Killah with curved fingers and a glare in her eyes.

"*Aeo-o!* Tandra Jekyll becomes Miss Hyde," Killah screamed. He backed away from her, leading her toward the pool. Orram circled behind her. Suddenly Killah lunged at Tandra. She pulled out of his grasp into Orram's, and in the next minute managed to pull all three of them into the water.

Tllan jumped in after them with an unearthly whoop, and the noise of their rough play brought Conn into the pool room. With wide, unbelieving eyes, he watched the game grow from hesitant chasing to unrestrained wrestling. They were handling Orram as one of them.

With sudden anger Conn dove into the fracas, found Tandra, and towed her to the center of the pool.

Her eyes glistened expectantly.

"You've read about varoks," Conn said. "You know that they hate being touched."

"Sometimes they don't," she answered firmly.

"Hardly ever. You and I can wallow in physical contact and enjoy it, take it, or leave it. But a touch is like an electric shock to a varok. Unless there is some very basic meaning behind a touch, they avoid it. I know Orram well. You don't. And you can't tell when he's had enough."

Tandra smiled. "All right my big lizard. But I think you exaggerate."

To her surprise he was stern, almost angry. "I don't exaggerate, damn it. Orram is a brother to me; I know him. You could break him. Leave him alone." His deep emerald eyes narrowed slightly, emphasizing his annoyance. "And *frog*, Tandra, 'big *frog*' is more accurate."

8
The Green Veil

There was probably nothing Conn loved better than to float suspended deep within the pool with Ellalon, indulging his elllonian nature while he waited for Tandra or Orram—with whom he indulged his loner's needs. Sometimes Tandra appeared first, and initially they would create good moments taping their beloved soundpictures. But now as the weeks passed, neither would admit that their music was becoming a crutch between them. Conn retreated more often to the sensuous comfort of Ellalon's soft body and to the more remote emotions he shared as part of his school: purely abstract sensual pleasure, little personal pride or desire, and an overriding collective joy in living that all but negated individual consciousness.

He also sought retreat in Orram's friendship. More often now, when the day's work was done, the varok's distinctive stroke called him to the surface of the pool and they cautiously experimented with the breaking of old taboos, searching more actively for the bond that had grown between them. The elll wondered if he shouldn't try schooling with the varok; and the varok pried more words from Conn, relying less on his patches to know the elll.

Orram discovered that Conn had been as drawn to Tandra as she to him on their first meeting. It was not surprising. They both valued the experience of life above all else. Apparently they had reveled in a simpleminded awareness together, enjoying stars and pianos and dancing with no murky thought between them. But it was clear that that period had passed.

Orram probed into the deductive channels and vacil-

lating emotions of the elll and finally unearthed in Conn
a surprisingly deep disturbance that centered on his
complaints against Tandra: Since she had left quarantine, their conversations had become two-sided, one
side at a time. Conn had found little to say in answer
to Tandra's probing for truths she could generalize;
and she had grown tired of his obsession with sensuous
experience, refusing to understand what it meant to be
part of a non-verbal, schooling species. In spite of
himself, Conn had continued to try to satisfy Tandra's
insistence on an intense level of verbal exchange, but it
seemed that the harder he tried to project himself verbally, the more foolish he sounded. It was certain that
Tandra didn't respond to his efforts. Nor did she appreciate them. He knew his anger toward her was not
fair. But neither was it fair for her to expect him to be
so human. If only he could get her to study elllonian
biology. She knew nothing of ellls yet.

Why did she seem more distant since she got out of
quarantine, he asked Orram. They were supposed to
really know each other now—use their favorite sense,
touch, to aid in the verbalization process. "It's got to
be a two-way exchange," Conn said. "You know I'm
finding this problem hard to verbalize. The point is, I
can't hack the words without some more meaningful input from her."

"I would try a combination of sensual and verbal
contacts," Orram suggested. "Isn't that how you first
met? And be patient, Conn. Killah and she invent more
projects for themselves than they can complete, and
Tandra is still trying to sort out varoks and men. She is
very tired. The number of new impressions she has to
absorb must seem overwhelming at times."

So Conn stubbornly worked with his pigeon-holed
mind, making it place tags of meaning on the words
he forced from his throat. But Tandra only became
more remote. "Give it up, Conn," she said one day.
"There's just not much we need to talk about. I can
accept that now; I don't love you any less for that fact."

It didn't fit. There was *too* much to talk about. Or

ought to be. Where was her curiosity? "I wish she'd vomited when she first saw me," Conn grumbled to Orram. "It would make more sense. I can't stand this indifference." But *indifference* didn't fit either.

As the Earth rolled toward a bleak, dry April, Tandra continued to study the varoks; and she grew to idealize Orram. She spent less and less time with Conn, until he found it difficult to see her at all unless he enticed her into the recreation lounge with a new sound. Finally one day she refused all his suggestions and retired to her room, and his exasperation drove him into a fury which spilled over his usual restraint. He had to have it out with her. He followed her to her room. She was alone, sprawled comfortably on her bedpad with pen and paper in hand. Conn stretched out close to her and wrapped a long leg around hers.

"Go away, Conn," Tandra snapped. "Can't you ever stop playing? I'd like to do some writing—"

"Let's do something that's worth writing down," Conn said, pulling her closer.

His eyes succeeded in capturing hers, and she was drawn into the crystal depths of brilliant emerald, down toward the unknown mind of the elll. But something there was more than frightening—it was almost horrible. Tandra jerked her gaze away, and shuddered.

Conn sat up, feeling unexplainably lost.

Tandra busied herself picking up papers. Then with growing irritation she stopped and stared at him. "Why did you come here—like that? What do you think I am?"

"You're probably soft and warm. I wouldn't know," Conn mumbled.

"Is that all I am to you? Something soft to feel?"

"You should be something old and homey and familiar to feel by now. It's been a long time since you got out of quarantine. I want to know you now the only real way I can, Tandra. We've talked ourselves out, or at least *I* have. Now I need to touch you, to feel your heat when you think of all that philosophy you love to toss around in your mind."

Tandra recoiled and got off the bedpad. "My philosophy doesn't put out heat waves."

"I'll bet it does—the way *you* care. It must. Let's try." He grabbed her leg and pulled her to the bed.

"Let me go!" Tandra screamed.

Conn flinched, but he let her go and tried words: "Damn it, Tandra, we ellls can't talk the way you do. We don't even experience emotions in a human way, individual to individual—or shouldn't, goddammit. Our whole culture—everything we are—is geared for collective emotion. Yet I feel longing, and it must be like yours. We both still look to our first hours together. Please understand that I need to learn, to explore. I'm a loner, Tan. Even I can't know what to expect of myself, but you might be able to learn for me. At least, you could do some reading about ellls."

"I don't—need to read about you."

"Why not, dammit!? You don't know a thing about us, and you're wasting your time studying a species you'll never have a tinker's damn of a chance to relate to."

"You talk to me about relating?! You've only memorized the word from some psychology text. *You* don't relate to *me*. None of you do. All Tallyn does is gripe at me, and Llorkin scribbles down everything I say. Killah does his work and then looks for something to joke about, just as you look for something to try your slang on. You don't seem to care about what I really feel—what I think. You won't talk about our lives—why we're here—the miracle of our existing together—what your idea of God is—anything at all that matters."

"God!? Oh, Tandra. What does it matter? Whatever made us also made beauty and love. That's good enough for me."

"That's just what I mean. All you care about is—how to enjoy life!"

"Isn't that important?" demanded a voice. Orram stood by them, his uncompromising gaze again making Tandra flush with shame.

"I don't know. I don't know! Between the two of you, I'm not sure of anything."

Conn stared at her, then left without another word.

As Tandra became more and more distant from elllonian reality, Conn became ever more tied to the human female: her musical, accepting, life-loving personality enkindled in him a deeply satisfying but, for an elll, strange love, directed as it was toward an individual; her rejection of him initiated a longing for personal acceptance and a rudimentary anger based on racial pride; and her arrogant capacity for bitterness and repression fostered a hate directed both at her and at himself—the latter because he feared the judicial self-righteousness he saw in himself. All of these feelings were new to him, new to ellls.

It was with great difficulty that Conn finished his work that month monitoring events on Earth. He floundered more and more until even Orram became entangled in the subjective chaos of Conn's emotions: Tandra's simple, friendly touching of the varok nurtured a feeling of inferiority in Conn; her growing mental contact with Orram initiated Conn's frustration at his own species' limitations; and the time she spent with Orram enkindled Conn's latent jealousy.

As Conn watched Tandra and Orram's friendship deepen and his once-fulfilling open contact with the woman become shallow and misplaced, his elllonian store of explosive emotions began to overheat. In desperation, he even decided to talk to Llorkin. But all Llorkin could tell him was that Tandra had a "belligerent" temperament. "She is bound to show us that she, not we, can touch varoks—and that she needn't touch *us*." It was no help.

In his increasing dismay, Conn found it difficult to work and impossible to study. He took to walking the halls, muttering to himself angrily. He was doing this one day when he felt a small, smooth, chubby hand work its way into his fin. "Where goin', Conn?" Shawne asked, rolling her enormous blue eyes up at him.

"Hey there, fat stuff, you're supposed to be in the nursery, aren't you?"

"I don't like that Lorka. He's got big, mushy green eyes."

Conn knelt down and set the baby on his knee. "He wears the same kind of contacts I do, Shawne," he said, rounding his lids affectionately.

The baby laughed and poked a finger at his face. "No, no, no. You got marbles. Like glass." She snuggled into his arms and rubbed her fingers over the soft hexagonal tiles of his skin. "Can I have a 'flume? Just one, okay, Conn?"

"What color do you want? Remember, I can't see much difference. You pick one out."

"M-m-m. Blue. Where are your blue?"

"I don't have any. Only the girls. Try again."

"Then I have—green!"

"Ouch! Hey, you've got to remember to ask before you yank. That one wasn't quite ripe."

Shawne hugged him generously and said, "I sorry, Conn. Good-bye." Then she raced back to the nursery shouting, "Take me swimming after dinner, Conn."

The elll stood watching her, longing for the same kind of acceptance from her mother.

Early one evening after he and Tandra had finished selecting the bass tones of a richly rhythmic varokian study for translation into the ellls' ultrasonic range, Conn became totally absorbed with his sound engineering. Tandra settled down with a book of Analahk's poetry and some varokian tapes which she had not yet heard. Soon she was completely immersed in a world of new word images and wrapped in the misty veil of the music. The words and the sound became one— sometimes strange, sometimes beautiful, often incomprehensible—and she imagined that she was on Varok, sharing the essence of what it meant to be varokian. She floated, ecstatic, searching—when suddenly Conn's insistent tugging brought her back to the moment.

"Tan, I've got it! This is the best we've done yet."

"Wait a minute, Conn. Don't disturb me now."

"Come on, let's try it out in the water."

"Later." She started to read again. The music continued arhythmic, haunting. Conn shut it off.

"Conn!"

"Tandra, you owe me some time. You've been putting me off too much. You'd spend all your time here, all six months, on the varoks if I let you."

"I'll hear the tape later—"

"If Orram walked in here and wanted to swim, you'd be in the pool before I could get the switch flicked."

"The switch flicked!? Conn . . ." Tandra laughed.

"Tan, I'm trying to tell you something."

"Well, tell me then."

"Goddam. You wouldn't hear me if I said anything. You're tuned in on the varoks and you won't even touch me. You know that touch means damn near everything to me—to us ellls. Yet you don't touch *me*, for chrissake, you touch Orram. You know varoks are supposed to hate it, yet you keep communicating with him the way you ought to be talking to me."

"I'm relaxed enough with Orram to be myself with him—like I am with you—or used to be before you started complaining so much about elll this, elll that. Be patient. I love you like—like my own brother."

"That's part of the problem. I'm not your brother."

"Oh, Conn," she sighed, exasperated. "A figure of speech, that's all."

"No. No. It's a hell of a lot more than that. I won't roll over and sit up for biscuits, Tan. We loners need something beyond the school, but not at that price."

"What are you talking about? If I'm as mixed up as you seem to think I am, you'd better have Llorkin shrink me."

"That might not be a bad idea."

"Well, go ahead then. I'll lay on his miserable couch, and you won't find anything."

"You're right," Conn howled. "Nothing but a few dried up stringy neurons!" He left the room, sure that he would be a target for her shoe, then disappointed that he wasn't and finally bitterly depressed.

He dove carelessly into the pool and let the full force of his pressure signals convey distress through the water.

From deep within the pool, Ellalon and Artellian responded by converging on the source of distress as if drawn together by a powerful magnet.

"Let's try schooling with Tandra," Conn pleaded. "I'm losing her; she won't confront me on any level now."

"I will get her," Ellalon said. "I have wanted to know her as you do Conn, but it is not possible. I don't understand why." She glided to the edge of the pool, disappeared into the recreation lounge, and soon emerged with Tandra, who was annoyed and more than reluctant.

"I don't want to swim now, Ellalon. I'm having a wonderful experience with Analahk's poetry and some varokian music."

"We need you, Tandra. You are fading away from us, and we want to stop it. Try knowing us in the school. Conn is in pain. Please help us. Come into the water."

"No, I really don't care to, Ellalon. Can't we talk here on the deck?"

Ellalon looked at Conn with a darkened, bewildered knit in her blue-trimmed brow.

"Tan," Conn sighed, extending his hand to her, "come in just for a moment."

"I told you I don't want to swim. I can talk more easily from here." She sat down on the deck and waited, immovable.

"All right, Tandra," Artellian said as he climbed onto the deck, "we can try to talk her, dry—in your manner."

"Damn it," Conn railed, "we can get along fine on your terms, but if I ask some respect for elllonian custom, you back off. You can't force me to it, Tan. I won't take the leash."

"Is that your fear, Conn?" Artellian asked. "I don't think it could happen. The varokian theorists say that the loner neeeds special personal contacts beyond the school, not masters. You have few canine tendencies."

"I just want Tandra to love me as she did at first. I

am not some kind of fearsome fairy-frog turned prince."

Tandra didn't laugh.

"I am elll. And you don't know what that means."

"I think Conn needs the assurance that you love him as elllonian, not as pseudo-human," Artellian suggested.

Tandra looked blankly into the broad open face of the older elll. "Of course," she said.

Artellian extended his golden-tinged hand, rolled in submission, hoping that the matter was settled; but Tandra shifted into a kneeling position on the deck and ignored his gesture.

Ellalon's eyes widened in horror at Tandra's cool, blatant rejection. "I think Artellian is right," she gasped. "You have never accepted us, and you can't face up to your own intolerance. You have always regarded Conn as human. No wonder Llorkin was surprised that you adjusted to our differences so easily." With a sudden agitated thrust of her soft blue-green frame, she stood up, but there was no anger in her eyes. "We took you in that first night after quarantine as one of us. But now you have lost us. Now we know that you never loved us at all; you loved only your own image of us. You are much more alien to us than we realized."

Artellian finally dropped his fin, reluctant for so long to accept her rejection, and the three ellls swam slowly away.

The water lay unnaturally empty. While talk at the food center rose to a gay crescendo and then gradually fell to an occasional murmur, Tandra sat by the pool. She clutched her knees and pressed her face into them, numbed by the tangle of confusion and self-doubt that spun unanswerable questions in her mind. Certainly she understood the ellls: mild, capable, colorful people, enjoying life like uninhibited children, intending harm to no one and no thing. She loved them. What was missing? How had she lost Conn? Was Ellalon right? Had she been avoiding Conn's touch? Artellian's? Yes, Artellian's. Why? What was it that she wasn't letting herself see? How does one become unblind? She lost track of time while her mind timidly approached and retreated from a set of new visions and untested concepts.

Suddenly she realized that the lights had once been dimmed and then had grown brighter again; another artificial day was beginning. There were no sounds coming from the food center now. The morning meal was done; yet no one had come near her. She understood then that her presence might have kept the ellls away from their beloved pool and the thought sickened her. A deep quivering frown imbedded itself on her face.

Coon had been watching her for some time, determined not to approach her, hoping she would seek him out, but when he saw her pained expression he hurried to her without further thought, against all the resolve he had built up in the past few hours. He pressed his arms firmly about her, ignoring the tremor that shook her body.

"Look at me, Tan. It's only me, Conn."

"I'm afraid, Conn. What am I afraid of?"

He pulled her hands away and gently lifted her face. She looked into the dark green lenses that covered his eyes and found only their crystal beauty. "You are still there, aren't you, Conn? Was Ellalon right? No one came to the pool, Conn. I want you all back. I'll read the books. I must apologize to Artellian. I—"

"Books and apologies, Tan?"

"I didn't think you would ever see me—come to me again."

"God knows, I shouldn't have," Conn sighed. "It's your turn, many times over. Take a cue from Shawne. You trusted her natural judgment when you came to the *Lurlial*. Watch her now, Tan. Forget the books and apologies."

"Ellalon said I had lost you."

"Lost today, found tomorrow," Aen grumbled. He came across the deck to stand close beside Tandra and Conn. "Right today, wrong tomorrow. We don't hold grudges, Tandra. We react when we react because that's how we must react when we're reacting."

The crushed-velvet figure of the aging elll stood over her, refusing to be ignored.

"So we are in trouble," he said, as she glanced up at him. "It will soon pass. Come talk with us. I have spent all my time these past weeks with Shawne and have neglected you."

Ellalon and Tllan joined them then and the four ellls made a tight circle on the deck around Tandra.

Conn said little. He was not sure he approved of this attempt to reassure Tandra. For the reassurance was being done solely in Tandra's terms, through words. He didn't like to see his fellows condescend to her in this way.

He tolerated the discussion until he realized that it was actually making Tandra feel comfortable. The words alone—tailored to comfort not to question her—were satisfying her. She was beginning to respond with animation to their comments and to analyze herself verbally with remarkable dexterity. But this would change nothing. The growing warmth and congeniality was superficial; they were all on a fake high. He left in disgust. Walking into the food center, he vented his anger on an innocent raw egg that had the misfortune of being left out on a counter.

Soon after, Ellalon and Tllan grew tired of the talk and left Aen and Tandra alone by the pool. The ellls had a feeling of depletion. But Tandra's sense of self-equanimity had been restored.

"Your mind enjoys exercise, I think, Tandra, like old Llowellian," Aen said. "I would like to take you to Ellason to meet her."

"Tell me about her, Aen," Tandra said.

"You would love her, Tandra," he said. "She has a universal outlook, a tolerant acceptance of and faith in life like yours, as well as a wisdom acquired the hard way. But she is very old now—over two hundred Earth-years I would say. She was born with no sonic capability, no sonar organ at all. And her chemical sensitivity was somehow impaired, too. In our environment on Ellason without her sonar she was as good as deaf, dumb, and blind. As a tad, a young elll, she worked hard to overcome her handicap with what senses she had, and eventually, she was even able to mate—quite successfully, I might add. Several times I was able to find her and to love her in the deeps." He smiled as fond memories flooded his aging brain. "Hm-m, makes me—how do you say? Horny? Delightful word. From the deer, eh? Yes, just thinking of that warm, dear one makes me very horny. I must go find Ellalon. She did not have Conn and Killah yesterday and, of course, last night none of us— But, do not worry, Tandra. We will survive one evening without the pool. Should I apologize for talking like this? We have tried to respect human custom. Now, of course, Conn realizes it's not been wise. Not quite honest from your point of view, eh? Well, off I go. Very horny. Yes. Delightful word. *Uleoon.*" He grinned with an enormous flash of white teeth and hurried off.

Tandra stared after Aen's bustling, round rear, decorated generously with brilliant, gold-fringed plumes. There was nothing so serious for an elll that joy would not soon take over. A smile found its way onto her face, and almost simultaneously her mouth went dry and a gripping pain tore through her stomach. Vivid images rose in her mind of ellls leering at each other, of ellls rolling together in the slimy mud of a lake bottom, of ellls laughing vulgarly at her naïveté. She slammed her hand down hard on the mossy deck. Then she looked down and saw the imprint she had left; she had crushed the life from the moss; its plump, tough leaves lay ragged and empty. For a panicky moment, she worked furiously to pull the life back into the tiny, intricate structures, but there was no restoring them nor what they represented. Her vision of the ellls was gone. Only a faint green blur remained.

"I need to talk," Conn said as he entered Orram's room. He carefully placed a fin on the varok's shoulder, and Orram laid his hand over it.

"Tandra?"

"I had a glimpse of something—" He couldn't continue. The silence tore between them for a moment, then

Conn dropped all regard for their specific differences. "Damn it, I can't talk, Orram, I need you in the pool."

He threw himself past the varok too steeped in himself to hear Orram's quiet response: "I'll try."

They slipped into the ruby water, and Orram watched Conn glide around him, trembling and beating out pressure signals with the outpouring of his frustration. His grief covered the varok like a pulsing blanket of agony in the warm water. Almost instantly, Orram felt as if his every nerve was stripped raw by the insistent drumming. The intensity of the pressure signals rose, throbbing and tearing. Too much, Conn! Piercing pain!! He couldn't stand it. Too much!!!

Suddenly it subsided. Orram looked for Conn and found him contentedly throwing himself high out of the water and falling haphazardly back in. Before long he swam to the shaken varok.

"Schooling with a disturbed elll is certainly an experience no varok should miss. I am honored—intellectually and spiritually honored. Emotionally and physically, however—"

"Should I get Killah?" Conn asked.

"No. Just float still for a moment. Don't make any waves. I must be bleeding from every pore."

"What the hell made me bring you here?!"

"I have a mind of my own, usually."

"You also usually don't give a damn for yourself. Why the hell did you get in my water, Orram?"

"You needed me here, Conn."

"I wanted Tandra, so I took it out on you. That's a hell of a price—you won't have to pay it again! I've tried all the talk I can. It's her turn to learn some elll-talk."

"As I just experienced?"

Impulsively—perhaps to avoid Orram's mind-search —Conn dove to the bottom of the pool, where the weighty blanket of water did much to keep him calm.

Through the following days, since nothing else seemed to work between Conn and Tandra, Orram insisted that they keep strictly to their music. Reluctantly, Tandra joined Conn each day, and gradually they became engrossed in comparing the styles of Earth's classical and modern composers and in reshaping them with Ellasonian and Varokian music. More often than not, elllonian rhythm was high above Tandra's audible range, since it was written to stimulate the ellls' sonar receptors. So Conn reversed the operation that he had performed on Tandra's records and devised a system that generated low driving tones from the ultrasonic beats. The resulting sound was wild and rich in harmonies scattered between tones western civilization calls notes. Tandra loved it.

Conn silently rejoiced as the music began to pull him closer to her again. Finally he relaxed enough to beg her to teach him classical western harmony; but all her efforts failed.

"I just don't see what's so special about combining sounds with frequencies of 261.63, 329.63, and 391.995," Conn said.

"I'm sure I don't know," Tandra admitted. "Just call it a C major chord and let it go at that. Doesn't it sound—well—happy—or solid or finished to you?" she said. "If I had a piano I could show you what I mean. Remember the arpeggios I played for you at my house?"

"No, and I didn't hear anything solid in those frequencies, either."

"Conn, you have no real sound appreciation. Only half of it goes in your ears . . ."

The elll interrupted her, suddenly very serious. "You have done a subjective physical comparison with Orram, and you know he is truly alien. Right?"

"Yes."

"Do one with me. Now."

"It's not necessary. You're obviously alien."

"Am I?"

"Not too many Earthlings run around in green feathers and velvet hexagons, Conn."

"Nevertheless and notwithstanding, I want to do a formal study."

Tandra hesitated. "If you insist." She undressed,

and closed her eyes while Conn moved his fins slowly over her body and through her hair. His touch stopped on her cheeks, and she felt the soft, dry tip of his tongue on her eyelids.

"Look at me, Tan. Please know me now," he said.

"I do know you, Conn. I don't like set-ups like this."

"Feel me all over with your eyes open, the way I felt you." Conn's breathing became shallow, and his eyes started to narrow.

"Don't order me around that way, Conn. I won't."

"You will! By God, Tandra, you will know me as elllonian!"

Then the emerald lights of his eyes dimmed and went out, and his mood seemed to reverse itself. "At least you'll swim in the same pool with me. Right? Into the water, landlubber." He suddenly lifted her, ran to the pool, and flung her in. Then he somersaulted after her and disappeared beneath the surface of the wine-red water.

Tandra clung to the side of the pool and waited for him to resurface. She waited a long time, knowing that ellls could remain underwater for at least several minutes. She waited minutes more before she became anxious. She searched her mind. How long had she seen them stay under? Could Conn have hit his head when he dived in? Probably not. The pool was over twenty feet deep. She swam quickly to the spot where Conn had disappeared and dove toward the bottom. She saw nothing but the deep red of the pool's mossy lining. She surfaced and her stomach tightened in alarm. More than twenty minutes must have passed since Conn dove in. His lung capacity couldn't be that great.

She climbed out of the pool and searched the clear water for Conn's dark form. There. But he wasn't moving. He seemed to be floating upside down. Fear gripped her as she entered the pool again. She swam over Conn's long body, filled her lungs, and dove, determined to ignore her fear of the dense liquid ruby water, rich with reflected light. She found Conn's shoulders and managed to cross her left arm over his neck and under his right arm. Then she kicked furiously, her free arm pulling hard toward the surface. Slowly she rose, and finally, with a gasp, she surfaced with her burden and began to move toward the pool's edge. She was making good progress when suddenly she realized that Conn was kicking, and smiling into her strained face. He clasped her in his arms and rolled underneath her, supporting her in the water.

"Conn, you devil!" she gasped, struggling to free her arms for an angry strike at him. But in the warmth of the water, he was too quick for her. Pinning her arms behind her back and winding his legs around hers, his central back fin erect and undulating rapidly, he supported Tandra's body above water and floated her slowly across the pool. The elll's fragile, velvet belly, rippling with the concealed effort of firm muscles, felt delicately soft beneath Tandra, and his feathered loin pressed provocatively against her. She began to relax into his tender strength.

"You are ready to talk my language, Tan. Now you will know ellls as no varok can."

The probe of his sexual organ grew more obvious, then insistent and undeniable.

"Conn, stop. I can't—we can't do this."

"We can," Conn murmured, pressing her closer. "I've checked the geometry. It should be a good fit."

"No!" she cried, struggling against his embrace. "Don't, Conn. This is ridiculous."

"Ridiculous, hell! You've wanted us to communicate better. Now we'll play it my way for a change." He placed his long, velvety arms along her sides as they sank deeper into the crystal red warmth of the pool.

"Conn!" The voice reverberated above the water. "You are needed in the hangar."

It was Orram. Tandra tore out of Conn's arms, and the elll glided toward the edge of the pool where Orram was standing. "I'm not on duty now, Orram," he said. He climbed out of the pool and stood before his varokian friend, a half-smile on his lips, a furious expression in his eyes, and his male organ thrust out from among his groin feathers.

Orram studied Conn's eyes for a moment before he

slowly and deliberately moved his glance over Conn's flushed body and erect organ. "What is the meaning of this challenge, Conn? Ellls don't display themselves."

"What is the meaning of your challenge?"

"Why were you here alone with Tandra?"

"Why not?" The quizzical ridge deepened on Conn's brow. He waited, belligerent, his eyes narrowing.

Fear grew within the poised frame of the bewildered varok. Why couldn't he reach Conn? Why now a price on honesty? And what feeling was this? Fear? Yes. And anger, too. Both emotions were alive within him, and he was not able to rationalize them into either understanding or repression. Ellls care nothing for the social implications of sex, he thought systematically. Conn's belligerent display makes no sense. Yet he has come to the pool alone with Tandra. This is no simple teasing. This is— What? What is this? Conn cannot prove anything this way. He will push Tandra completely out of reach. She is not ready for this. It will not work. I care. Why? Pushing Tandra too hard . . . I care too much! Suddenly the varok's emotions crashed over him and possessed his mind.

"You will get nowhere this way. It's mindless bestiality!" he raged, his clenched fist slashing toward Conn's disappearing organ.

The elll jumped to one side into a crouch as he blocked the attack with a powerful sideways thrust of his joined arms.

"Orram, what's happening?" Conn cried. "You are losing control to emotion. Listen: I must make her know me again. I am too alone!!"

Conn spoke in a wail of passion, and the desperation in his voice sent the varok back to reason. Orram trembled inwardly, badly shaken by the sudden thrust into emotion and then out of it again. "I thought I was strong enough for you. Perhaps I am not. But leave Tandra to me. You are not helping her. You are only deepening the dream."

"No, Orram, you are wrong," Tandra said. "I am not in a dream. I can see clearly." She stood beside them. "I love you both as the dearest friends, Orram, and I suppose I would have submitted to Conn if you had not come in when you did. He is not a beast to me, and neither are you."

With a cry of protest Conn took Tandra by the shoulders. "No, Tan, no. You miss the whole point. I *am* beast. I am elll!"

9
The Sounds of Grief

"Orram, I would like to go with you on this next expedition," Junah said.

"That is a strange request," he said. "There is no
need for you to go."

"There is need in it for us perhaps." She was probing
deeply, trying to contact him beyond mood. But he resisted her probe, denied her entrance to his mind, and
warned her that logic must deny her desire.

"We have no need for time together," he said quietly, turning away.

The invisible pull of yearning, buried and denied,
distorted the pale light in Junah's eyes, though her face
displayed no expression.

Tandra, working in Killah's lab, saw the exchange,
and briefly wondered why the varokian woman seemed
so upset. Then she resumed her work. She took culture
tubes inoculated forty-eight hours previously out of the
incubator and set them on the work bench. She selected
a turbid reddish growth marked with Roen's name,
and her little finger and side of her hand automatically
uncapped the tube under the sterilizing cone as her
thumb and forefinger manipulated a long narrow probe
with a small loop on the end. The culture was viscous
and ropy with a common elllonian organism usually
found at the back of the ellls' long tongues. The tangled
masses in the culture would have to be avoided if Tandra were to isolate the other bacteria. Her probe became entangled in a sticky string of the teeming life.
She pulled it from the tube and let the heat and radia-
tion of the sterilizing cone destroy it. Then she rein-
serted the probe into the tube and trapped a drop of

turbidity. Quickly she recapped the tube, carefully opened a large, flat octagonal disk of gelatinous nutrient, and made several streaks on the surface with the bacteria-laden probe. She sterilized the probe and crossed the end of her first streaks three times, dragging fewer of the millions of bacteria out across the nutrient. She sterilized the probe and crossed the last three streaks again—and repeated the process five more times —then carefully closed the flat dish. The process diluted the bacteria by spreading and separated them by friction. With luck a few individuals had landed on spots isolated enough so that with proper incubation they would multiply undisturbed until a distinctive colony of genetically identical individuals would grow to visible dimensions and identifiable characteristcs.

Tandra repeated the process four times for each culture tube; there were two culture tubes for each member of the crew. Hours later she finished the two hundred and forty streak plates, labeled them, organized them into their trays, set them with some difficulty into the varokian autoclave, waited while the pressure mounted, set the timer—and then remembered that they should have gone into the incubator, not the sterilizer. She stood staring at the autoclave in dismay. Most of the organisms so meticulously separated for cultivation and identification would already be dead.

There was no point in trying to work. Her mind was preoccupied, struggling to free itself from an entangled green veil. She must try to find the ellls again.

She wandered about Killah's labs searching absently for something to write on. She picked up a sheet of synthetic and stared at it. It was very empty. She tried to concentrate on Conn. Nothing. His features: straight nose (yes, she was sure of that); short, tousled plumes (they looked so much like hair); brow line cocked at a permanently amused tilt (eyebrows? No. Must be tiny plumes there); long legs (taut with wiry muscles, powerful yet soft, firm yet gently grasping, sensual); wide, smooth, muscular chest. Quickly then she wrote a detailed description of Conn and hurried to find Orram.

Artellian stopped her in the hallway. "Are you all right, Tandra?" he asked.

"Yes. No," she stammered. "I must find Orram."

"He's in the hangar. Go slowly, Tandra. There is time for everything."

She smiled gratefully at the Master elll, but his green alien countenance no longer seemed fatherly, just strange and bestial. She shuddered and hurried down the hall.

When she reached the hangar she strode directly to Orram, who was standing beside the plump gray-brown vehicle, *Arlaht,* with Junah and two ellls.

Slowly Orram's face turned away from the land craft toward her and, before she spoke, Tandra watched it return to its usual placid veneer as he locked away a look of frustration.

"Orram, please read this."

He took the synthetic sheet, read it, and handed it back with a grim, plain face. "This is no elll you have described, Tandra. It could be a human or a varok. Where are the pressure plates and sonar lines, the back fin, the lack of ears, the webbed extremities, the large eyes covered with contact lenses?" He led her away from the others and chose his words carefully. "Have you confronted the fact that you may find the ellls unacceptable, even abhorrent, now?"

"After loving Conn so well . . ." Tandra began. "I'm obsessed with a vision of Conn as a green blur, wallowing in the mud with whomever comes along."

"What is it that you love about Conn? Try to define that," Orram said.

"I love his easiness and wit, his directness, his competence, his modesty, his—his beauty."

"And what has destroyed all of that for you?" He paused. "Why do you fear knowing more about the ellls?"

Suddenly Tandra was shaken with an insight that seemed to come from outside herself. "Can you read my mind?" she asked. "Is that what the patch does?"

For a moment Orram stared searchingly at her, his

brow heightened in surprise. Then he gently touched her chin. "Not quite," he said. The dim caution in his face lifted, and he spoke lightly, with a touch of excitement in his voice. "Tandra, come with us on the expedition to the lunar poles. There are things we must discuss. I will assist you in your adjustment to the ellls. You will have a fresh perspective after two weeks away from Conn. Come, look here."

She followed him to the map built into the *Nalkah's* control panel. "We will go to the lunar north pole, swing back toward base on the side facing Earth, and stop briefly before we make the southern loop. This is an old, well-worn route for us. It was scouted in orbit from the *Lurlial* before we tried it on land, so we know the rough area northwest of here quite well. We regulate our speed so as to take advantage of the more moderate temperatures and better light within the terminator. It should be an interesting trip for you, Tandra. We shall be gathering data, taking samples, and doing maintenance on the experimental probes and communication web along the route. And we shall have long periods of time to talk."

Tandra listened with rising excitement. "When can we leave?"

"I agree," he said in answer to her unspoken thought, "the sooner the better."

Within forty hours, Tandra and Orram, accompanied by Aen and Ellalon, boarded the comfortable monstrosity, *Nalkah,* and before long the pressure lock of EV base swung open and deposited the vehicle and its passengers onto the moon's surface. The *Nalkah* was a versatile craft, designed to travel—or, as Conn once said, hover, galumph, or tip-toe if necessary—over any terrain. It contained all the equipment one might expect. There was a complete life support system for four oxygen breathers, including storage tanks for water, oxygen, and dried food. Most of the rear compartments of the vehicle were crammed with sampling equipment, repair tools, and life support suits for lunar exposure. These Ellalon and Aen made frequent use of in order to collect data, to catalogue samples, and to repair faulty equipment at the EV experimental lunar substations.

But the vehicle also was designed to maximize the pleasure of its passengers. The interior was draped with the tastiest of Ellasonian mosses, and the couches were spacious and carefully contoured. Tandra and Orram spent most of the time relaxed into the four large couches of the resting cabin in the rear of the vehicle. There they talked of Varok and of Earth and of themselves while they watched the lunar terrain slowly move by. When it was Orram's turn to take the controls, Tandra moved up to the control deck with him, and the ellls always gave her their seat without question.

Tandra was as fascinated with Orram, and the strange depths within him, as she was captivated by the harsh panorama of the moon's tortured surface. For many days neither mentioned Conn. Nor did Orram say that it was clear to him that she was avoiding Aen and Ellalon.

On the tenth day of their journey, after Tandra had been watching Orram maneuver the *Nalkah* for almost an hour, he suddenly stopped the vehicle and stood up, motioning for her to take his place. "It is quite simple, simpler than driving an automobile in traffic, I would guess," he said. "You want to give it a try, don't you?"

"I've been longing to. You're not about to take any chances, I see," Tandra laughed, for he had stopped more than a mile into the flat wastes of the Sea of Cold, where she could hardly do any damage to the vehicle if she tried. She slid into the driver's couch and reviewed the controls. Then carefully she eased her knee against the velocity bar, testing the *Nalkah's* response.

"Aen, we have a fourth driver," Orram called over his shoulder.

"Could not resist any longer, eh?" Aen said. He moved up to the control deck and patted Tandra on the shoulder. She recoiled, and he shook his head slightly. "I wonder how Shawne is doing alone at base with all the aliens?" he asked, watching Tandra's expression.

"I have no worries about Shawne," Tandra said carelessly. "Conn promised to watch over her carefully. She didn't even want to come with us."

Aen shrugged and turned away.

"Tandra, you are a master of selective repression," Orram said abruptly, "You are seeing Aen as smoked, green glass, and you will not rediscover Conn when we return to base unless you face your intolerance squarely."

"I am not intolerant!"

"You do not accept the ellls as they are. Nonacceptance is the child of intolerance."

"Orram—"

"Tandra, what would it mean . . ." He stopped talking, then his words emerged gradually, as if he were experimenting with them. "What would it mean if our two species were interfertile?"

"Not much," Tandra laughed, relieved by the diversion. "We are too calloused to new realities, even to the bizarre, these days."

" 'We' you say. The loss of man's uniqueness would have no significance? No influence?"

"Only insofar as man's pride might be damaged."

"Man's pride would be threatened by our interfertility? His uniqueness? Anything else? Tandra, what would it mean to you?"

"It would also upset a few atheists," she said. "Such complete biological convergence might imply direction in universal evolutionary processes."

"I'm not sure," Orram said, "but I am sure that you are evading my last question."

"I'm— Yes, I was, wasn't I?" she said, feeling foolish. Why was she trying to protect herself from Orram? Because she was trying to be more than she was? "Certainly love is more important than biochemical accidents. Should it matter that you—or Conn for that matter—touch me for a moment? If love motivated the act, isn't it justified?"

"Are you trying to argue with me?" Orram asked.

"I assumed that you would not approve of inter-specific sex."

"I have no opinion, really. I do not care to make such generalizations."

"Am I making tribal judgments without realizing it?" Tandra asked.

"Decidedly," he said. "But your eyes are opening, Tandra. My question was foolish; we have better things to worry about. And wouldn't *all* agree that love is more important than its particular expression?"

"Most men would not," Tandra said. "We attach some kind of cosmic significance to all our acts, even our sex play. Ridiculous, but it's true. And yet what are we? What is man? Our existence must mean something. We may be tiny blobs of pompous protoplasm in terms of geologic time and space, but at least we are capable of love. Isn't love the integral, shared force that holds the cosmos together?"

"You and I and Conn are reaching toward some such common denominator across differences we have only begun to understand," Orram said.

"Surely our similarities, our understandings, our shared experiences are more important than our prideful differences."

"Yes, Tandra. That is exactly the point. Hear me. Focus. You are above differences. You are capable of awareness that transcends your experience. You can know Conn again. Ask the right questions. Ask the questions that we all share, the questions whose answers shape the patterns of our existence: Why have formless gases and minute particles come together in the enormities of space to form complex organisms capable of cognizance? Why have molecules molded themselves into forms of beauty? Why have they become self-conscious? Why have they learned to love?

"You almost took Conn's sexual touch as a natural extension of his friendship, for you know that he needs sensual expression. I think you have enough sense to love him for what he is—to accept, to appreciate, and finally to cherish those unique elements that make him different from you."

"You must be wrong, Orram. I can't face the ellls now that the dream has been denied. I am too human. I am man—and man is so insecure that he hasn't yet defined *himself* comfortably. He looks to differences too easily for an excuse to hate and to reinforce his self-love."

"If that is true," Orram said, "then you will have to go beyond your idea of man if you are ever to know Conn as he really is."

As the *Nalkah* picked its way south across the Sea of Cold, skirted the rim of the crater Plato, and dove between the Straight Range and the Teneriffe Mountains into the Sea of Rains, Ellalon watched with interest the growing bond between Orram and the human female. She was keenly disappointed when Tandra consistently avoided her, which was no easy feat in the close quarters of the lurching, crawling vehicle they shared. Eventually, Ellalon learned that Aen, too, was searching for ways to awaken Tandra's awareness of himself. The ellls' instinctive pull toward shared experience made them ignore Tandra's coolness and continually probe her defenses to find chinks into which they could stuff bits of humor and easy comment and some honest affection.

One twilight day after they had swung toward base in their looping course around the moon, Tandra was threading the *Nalkah* through the lowlands around the Lansberg craters toward the gray-brown wastes of the Ocean of Storms while Aen and Orram checked maintenance data taken from the experimental station near Copernicus. Ellalon awoke from a restless sleep, and seeing that Tandra was alone and trapped by her duty at the controls, the delicate blue-green elll slipped quietly into the other couch before the control panel and stared for a moment through the window to the endless craters that surrounded them. Then, without warning, she spoke: "Tandra, if you can't let yourself know us, then at least open yourself to us. We want to know you the way Conn has."

The blood drained from Tandra's face. "I'm sorry," she said, meaning it. "I can't face you, Ellalon. When I look at you, at any elll, I feel as if—as if I'm drowning in . . . I can't say. I feel this even while I admire your beauty. And—and it sounds ridiculous, but I—perhaps with you I'm jealous. I didn't know until recently that you were Conn's mate."

"Jealous?" Ellalon asked with a shake of her long, blue plumes. "I'm not sure what it means. Something to do with possessing a person—or wanting to? But Conn is not here now, and I am not his only mate. He mates with many ellls at base, though not as often as we would like."

"I suppose he does," Tandra said. "Jealousy may be the wrong word, Ellalon. I didn't expect to monopolize Conn. No, I think my problem with you is—more like a moral confusion."

"Moral confusion? Oh, Tandra, I don't understand you at all." She laughed. "I thought we were talking about mating with Conn. How could our morals confuse you? They are quite simple. We insist on honesty and hate physical violence; we abhor anything that dulls consciousness. That's all. Morals have nothing much to do with mating."

"Nothing much?"

"We have no words in our languages that will translate *bigamy, extramarital relations, premarital sex, adultery, jealousy* . . ."

Tandra laughed as a wave of affection for the elll washed through her. "You mean so much to me," she said. She reached for Ellalon's arm, but before her hand touched the green, mossy skin, the elllonian girl grabbed for the controls and threw the *Nalkah* out of the path of a large boulder that was bounding lazily down on them from its precarious position high on the wall of crater Grimaldi. The boulder skidded past them but brought behind it a slow-motion cascade of smaller rocks. Rapidly they engulfed the *Nalkah*, bringing it to a halt.

"Well," Ellalon grinned. "Let's go throw rocks at each other."

Tandra laughed with her. The warm regard was there again. Now if only she could clear the blurred vision.

Orram was at the back of the craft with a lunar exposure suit already pulled over his long legs.

"It will save time if we all help repair the road," Ellalon said. "Tandra and I need some exercise and a good stretch. Aen, are you coming?"

"Wouldn't miss the chance. I'll do some exploring while you three do all the work."

They helped each other into the exposure suits as quickly as their good humor would allow. At last they were all dressed, and the *Nalkah* was depressurized. They disembarked to scramble about the boulders that blocked their path. Aen tossed a few small rocks away from the *Nalkah* and clambered up the hill leading to the bowl of the crater Grimaldi.

"I don't see any loose rocks," he said into his communicator.

"Look around some more," Orram answered.

Aen climbed higher while Orram and Ellalon and Tandra quickly cleared the path. They were moving the last of the boulders when Aen carefully turned on the steep slope above them and started back. Suddenly he stumbled into a depression that had escaped his carefully ranging eyes, blinded by the brightness of the sun's reflection on its rim. He grasped at a large boulder as he fell, but it tore out of his hands, then rolled slowly down the hillside, ricocheted suddenly off another precipitous outcropping, and before it hit the path, mindlessly crushed the life from Ellalon.

No sound told the tale. Tandra thought she heard Aen grunt and mumble into his communicator as he made his way down the rock slide, but she didn't realize that anything else had happened until she turned away from the *Nalkah* and saw Aen roughly drag Ellalon's limp body to the side of the path and strip off its space suit. Tandra screamed and ran to him, tugging desperately at his hands doing their gruesome work. "What happened? What are you doing?" she cried.

He looked at her blankly. No sign of grief, no indication of care or regret showed behind his helmet. "Go to the *Nalkah* and get an injector of the disintegrating compound," he said calmly. "I fell, and this was in the path of the boulder I knocked loose."

Horror grew within Tandra. "This? *This? Aen!*"

"Do not excite yourself. There is nothing more to care about. There is no more to Ellalon."

Orram came from the *Nalkah* carrying an injector. He picked up Ellalon's delicate green arm, probed its vein, and waited quietly while the powerful chemical found the elll's blood pools and quickly converted her back to the elementary particles from which she was created.

"Pea soup," Aen said, and he smiled with warmth at Tandra.

Incredulous, she broke into wild, angry sobs. Orram pulled Tandra to her feet and urged her toward the *Nalkah.* "We must continue our trip," he said.

"Even you," she sobbed, "even you will just leave her here without—with nothing."

"I have no choice." His voice was very tight. "I must get us back into the *Nalkah* safely. Then I can allow the grief to break me apart. Remember, Tandra, I am varok. I cannot function rationally and feel an emotion like grief at the same time."

"But kind Aen—how can he do this!?" Tandra shook uncontrollably, her mind a fierce tangle of confused concepts and emotions.

Orram held her firmly. "Please try to calm yourself, Tandra. Ellls have no grief. Ellalon no longer exists in Aen's mind, as she does not exist in fact. The school has changed its composition; that is all. There is no human counterpart to what Aen feels now. This is a real difference Ellalon would want you to understand. Accept it. The ellls will miss her in their own way, for they will have to adjust to her absence from the school; but they will not grieve. They will not curse fate and storm against what is unchangeable. But I shall. When it is safe and when I am somewhere where my shame will not be too great, I shall release the grief that is within me. It will be much like yours. I shall grieve for the loss of a gentle friend—a selfish emotion really. I want what I clearly cannot have. I want Ellalon to be alive. Is there more to grief? Ellalon does not need our tears. She needs nothing. The ellls know this better than we. I shall grieve as you do, Tandra, but when I do, that will be *all* I shall be able to do. Therefore, it would be unwise for me to succumb to emotion now. We must continue into the highlands immediately."

They followed Aen into the *Nalkah,* sealed it against the moon's vacuum, took off their exposure suits, and watched Aen start the drives and guide the vehicle down the rough path, leaving Ellalon's tragedy to itself. Somehow Tandra managed to do what had to be done. Then she found a couch and sat frozen, unmoving, her eyes fixed in a glassy stare. She was only dimly aware when Aen took the controls from Orram with a kindly insistence.

"You had a friend named Ellalon who was like a daughter to you, Orram. Do you have grief that you wish to release?"

The varok nodded; already the smoldering pain of his grief threatened to burn the tethers of his reason.

"There is no need to wait," Aen said. "I will take the *Nalkah* to base. We are only twenty hours away."

Orram moved slowly toward Tandra and sat heavily beside her. "Forgive me, Tandra," he said. "Aen is right. I wanted to spare you from watching my grief, but I should not wait the length of time that it will take us to reach base. Twenty hours is too long to contain this pain." Suddenly his powerful mind was shattered by the impact of his grief, and his straight, invincible body was bowed and crumpled with great heaves that left him helpless, lost to reason, his consciousness nothing but incoherent fragments.

Tandra took his head in her lap, smoothing his silver-brown hair. The books had not exaggerated. The threshold was crossed; Orram would not be rational for hours, perhaps days. She longed to give him what human strength she could. "You can live and know and feel such pain too, Orram," she whispered.

Aen stopped the *Nalkah,* moved quickly to the resting cabin, and tried to pull Orram away from Tandra. Angrily, she resisted his pull and would have clasped Orran even closer if the elll had not prevented her.

"Tandra, he must do this alone," Aen said. "He must maintain his own way back, or he will go too far, and you may not be strong enough to hold him."

Aen had worked with varoks during most of his long life, and even Orram, who was no ordinary varok, rarely surprised him. Now, however, he drew back amazed, for Orram straightened and took Aen's arm, supporting himself back onto the couch next to Tandra. "She is strong enough," he said, and he put her hands on his forehead. Tandra looked at Aen questioningly, but he could only shrug in bewilderment.

"Orram, are you out of your grief?" he asked.

They waited for his answer, submerged in silence. Finally, Orram spoke slowly, with considerable effort. "No," he said. "I am neither out nor in. I am held somewhere between reason and emotion by what I receive from Tandra. I am aware—and controlled—and still full of pain. How odd to know both at once. I will be out before we reach base, Aen. Continue, please."

"So you were right, Tandra," Aen said with a smile. "But you must be very strong now. You are taking Orram along an unknown path." He returned to the controls, and the small, gray craft bumped and turned and groveled its way through the highlands at a painfully slow pace.

Orram did not move for several hours nor did he say anything until they were well into the d'Alembert Mountains. Then he rose silently, found three packets of food and drink, and took one to Aen. When the elll had eaten, Orram returned to Tandra and offered her one. Then he sat again on the couch and ate.

"We are only three hours from base. I have reported the accident," Aen called over his shoulder.

"Then I will put away this grief. Aen, come and rest. I will return the *Nalkah* to base."

The elll stopped the craft, walked back, and knelt beside Orram. "Are you really able, Orram? So soon? Yes, I see you are quite out of your grief. Perhaps the human element has introduced another factor into varokian existence, eh?"

"Decidedly, Aen," Orram said. "Stay with Tandra now. She is in a limbo even stranger than mine."

During the remaining hours of their trip Aen spoke continuously to Tandra with all the understanding and gentleness that his kind soul possessed. But the state of death meant nothing to him, so he could offer little relief for her shock. The mindless glint that formed in her eyes when she looked at him told him that she could not focus on him, that she barely heard him. But still he talked. He talked of Shawne and the tad Daoon; love of children they could share.

Finally, Orram drove the *Nalkah* over the rim of the small crater which lay in partial blackness near the crater Schlüter and guided the land craft across its floor to the sealed entrance of the base.

Conn waited in the hangar for the *Nalkah*'s arrival. He started to insert his light-limiting contact lenses so that he could turn the lights back up to the brightness required for the varoks—then hesitated. Until Tandra had left on this trip, the lights had not been dimmed, as a courtesy to her. Now, Conn suddenly decided, the lights would remain at elllonian levels. He put his contacts back into their case on his wrist and reset the elllonian-light-only warning system.

Finally the *Nalkah* entered the dark hangar and settled to a halt, and its passengers climbed out of the hatch. A dim red light reflected like fire in Conn's enormous black pupils as he searched Aen's face. In response, the elder elll glanced at Tandra and shook his head slowly, but then he suddenly brightened: "Look here, Conn, Orram is already out," he said.

Conn clapped the varok heartily on the shoulder. "In

and out? That must be some kind of varokian speed record."

Rare, bitter tears rose in Tandra's eyes. "How can you joke? Ellalon is dead. Her blue plumes are all that are left, smeared with her mashed green. Your mate, Conn, she's dead. Crushed! Care, Conn. You must care!"

For a moment Conn's eyes narrowed with anger. "Yes, I care—because the school will have to go through adjustment when it is already small. I have lost no mating. There are plenty of others."

A wave of nausea swept over Tandra. Conn's voice was hard, and his appearance was blurred, unfamiliar in the dark red Elllonian light. "Conn!"

He relaxed and grew easy again. "I respect your grief, Tandra," he said gently. "And I thank God that Orram is out of his so easily. Respect me now. Anger is not what I need from you." He placed his hand-like fins under her chin and waited.

Tandra stood with her eyes averted, understanding what he wanted—and fearing it. Finally, her determination crystallized, and she raised her eyes to his. "You are elll," she murmured. She searched, but she saw nothing—nothing but the great black circles of his unmasked eyes. She turned away from the vision and ran blindly toward the door to the labs, but Orram caught her.

"Tandra, the *Nalkah* is proceeding to the south pole, with Conn in charge. Will you go? You are well qualified now to navigate."

"Aren't you going?"

"No. I will stay here and consolidate our data for transmission to Varok."

"I don't want to go with Conn now," she said. "I need time to find my way out of this wilderness." Her consciousness was centered in Orram. He was the key to reality, a stable reference to play her fears against. "I cannot go," she said.

The elll had joined them. He nodded curtly and walked back toward the *Nalkah*.

Orram called after him, "I shall send Erah and Tllan to fill out your crew."

"Erah can't go," Conn said. "She is still in grief from the news of Ellalon's death. Junah never went into grief. Send her. Tell her we'll eat before we leave."

Orram took Tandra's arm and turned her firmly toward him. "Go help feed Conn and the others," he commanded.

"Orram, please, I want to see Shawne."

"The vision must be cleared, Tandra," he said. "Do it now. With delay it will become only more difficult."

They left the hangar, and while Orram continued down the hall to Junah's room, Tandra turned into the food center. Moving mechanically and with difficulty in the dim red light, she selected some leathery Elllonian fruits, cut them into squares, and was adding black Varokian *hoats* when Conn entered the room.

"We'll just eat a few raw eggs," he said crisply and set four large blue eggs on the central table.

Tandra spoke without much awareness of what she said.

"The eggs are very large. Where did they come from?"

Conn looked at her with disbelief. "They're ours, Tandra," he said.

"Yours?"

"Certainly you know—No, you don't, do you?" He grabbed her shoulders and shook her, his desperation rising. "Tan," he said slowly, "our girls produce several eggs every six weeks or so."

"They do? These? These are your eggs? You are eating your own eggs? You are eating your own . . ."

Suddenly then she saw him, stark and real—alien—denuded of fantasy: *high, green cheekbones on a hollow, straight face, and a mouth so broad!* She could not tolerate the new strangeness of his face, once so familiar and loved. "It's like eating your own children!"

"They're eggs, Tandra, not ellls," he cried.

She answered as if in a daze. "All potential life should have a chance for continued existence." *An angry alien image wavering over her, a dim black-green shadow, mocking her.*

"That's semantic nonsense. I'm not talking about a carefully nurtured, incubated egg or a quickened fetus that awakes love in its mother with a stir; I'm talking about the first bit of tissue that has no awareness, no knowledge of pain or joy—not even in its mother's mind —except perhaps as a suspicion or a fear."

"There is meaning in potential life," Tandra said. *Where were his eyes?! Black, hollow, gaping holes, looming huge and empty!*

"Potential meaning, Tandra, for the developing individual—and potential horror for the real individuals who must make room when there is no more room!"

"But where is your respect for life?" Tandra pleaded. *Strange, branched hairs waving stiffly, grotesquely, planted at odd angles all over his head.* "The right to life is more fundamental than the right to happiness."

" 'Happiness? Happiness!?' Freedom from starvation is *ecstasy* if it can be found on your miserable planet. You can't mean to place the rights of an insensate, organic growth above the rights of a conscious, feeling being!"

"What is there to value, if we don't value all of life, Conn? I thought that's what ellls value most." *Vile, inhuman, long tongue. Ears gone. Slimy, black-green mouth, so broad! How could she stop him, make him go away?*

"Yes, we value life above all else—life that feels soft touches and knows love, life that sees the stars and knows the wonder of eternity, life that tastes the bitter, poisoned gruel called pain and knows the terrorizing degradation of eating garbage in order to survive. Tandra! Tandra! You human beings can't continue to make actual life so meaningless just to satisfy the potential in fertile eggs."

"It doesn't have to be that way, Conn," Tandra whispered. *Great cloacal lips, emerging eggs, closed probe, wet and smeared with feces. Vomit rose in her throat.*

"It-*is*-that-way!" Conn screamed. "It-is-already-that-way, Tandra. It-has-been-that-way-for-decades! Learn to drink your waste, Tandra! Go mad for lack of living space! Watch the boils of hunger rise in Shawne's mouth! All for the sake of eggs!" Violently he smashed an *el* egg and in a furious rage born of true ellonian grief threw Tandra into its slippery remains and left her sobbing hysterically on the floor.

10
Beyond Self

"Master Ramahlak! Oran Ramahlak!" Junah called. An unusual tightness in her voice betrayed some urgency as she hurried down the hall. She found Orram in the nursery with Shawne. "Come to the food center," she said in Varokian. "Dr. Grey is very ill."

With his usual sandpaper monotone, Orram told Shawne that he would soon return, but when he reached the hallway, he broke into a full run. He composed himself before entering the food center. Tandra was sitting on the floor with her head bowed between heaving shoulders.

"What is it, Tandra?" he said, kneeling beside her.

She shook her head slowly, fighting for composure. "Conn," she said, "Conn." Words tumbled from her dry throat. "Conn! Killah! Hollow eyes. Swamp things. Eggs and waste and sperm—all from one—all from the cloaca. And they mate all the time, underwater, with anything!"

Orram's face darkened. "Yes," he said.

She grasped him with cold hands. "Conn said hedonic glands and a spermatophore. They're alien, Orram, really alien. They're like amphibians. They're not even remotely human! They have no mothers!"

If he could only reach her now, perhaps he could project to her his own conception of the ellls. Slowly, with gentle assurance, he joined her grasp while his mind reached toward her, concentrating on ellls, their love of life, his love for them.

Gradually, in his secure hands, Tandra began to relax. The revulsion subsided, and the shock dissipated. She knew, somehow, that Orram was showing her a view of the ellls that she had not seen before. Her mind began to focus clearly on them again: Killah—handsomest of the green, aquatic frog-men. Yes, frog-men. No, ellls. Handsomest of the ellls, fond of phrases and ideas; slave to his work. Aen—aging; an aging frogman. Isn't there a better word? His golden plumes framing his dark face only barely frog-like. More like a collie or an Egyptian drawing. *Green* and *water* mean frog; that is all. Kind, simple Aen. Artellian—strong and competent, golden statue elll, dressed in patterned velvet, firm and wise, like a father. Ellalon—so beautiful; light green framed in blue: now pea soup beside some rocks, and she needs nothing. But the life that she lived had been full and good. That's all, and that's enough. And Conn—tall gangly big thing, with an untamed brow; a face lit by fun or wild anger that flashes and goes out as the lightning of a summer storm; and a capable mind, more really, a brilliant mind that loves sound, words, and music and ultrasonic beats, loves to make it and shape it until it becomes his own; predictable and warm, like part of myself, like home and family and pine boughs crackling in the fireplace.

"Orram, tell me more," she murmured, aware only of his help, not his silence.

For long, vibrant minutes he held her face against his and transmitted as simply as his patches would allow a set of concepts that defined elllonian existence. Finally, she began to stir and to resist his thought patterns.

"I must learn for myself. Let me go, Orram. I am ready to face them alone now. It is cleared. Let me go!" She struggled to free herself with a violence that surprised them both.

"Yes," Orram laughed. "You are quite ready now. I, too, am alien at last."

"You have strength and depth no man could match." She kissed his fingers as they knelt together on the floor, and without conscious design their forearms met in an intimate varokian embrace.

"You have learned, Tandra, that we are hard and brittle we varoks—and too soon you will learn that we are also fragile and difficult. You have many strengths that we lost long ago. I love your flexibility, your reasoned passion."

Tandra smiled wanly.

"Tandra, tell me what happened here."

"Nothing, really, and very much. Conn was enraged at my—attitude toward eggs. I was less than honest. He had become so horrifying to me, I couldn't accept anything from him. I didn't want him to exist."

"He no longer spared you?"

"That's right."

"I wish I could promise that it won't happen to you again, but I'm sure it will," Orram said. "Come. Shawne wants you. She is in the nursery. It's time that you saw all that the nursery contains. If you have accepted Conn's alienness, then you are prepared. Do you feel capable of it?"

"Yes, I want very much to see it now."

Junah was waiting outside when they emerged from the food center. "Can I help?" she asked.

Tandra saw her as if for the first time. It was obvious that she adored Orram. The unvarokian quality of her emotion was abruptly clear.

"Dr. Grey is recovered now, Junah. You had better get something to eat and board the *Nalkah*."

Junah watched Tandra and Orram as they turned the corner into the large hallway. Then she moved swiftly to the hangar to join Conn.

The nursery door was open. Tandra could hear Llorkin's voice within: "Shawne, *va. Sense*."

The baby saw Tandra and ignored the command, running to her instead, shouting, *"Da, lelea."*

"Well, finally, you speak, Shawne," Llorkin said. Then he turned to Orram. "Why is Dr. Grey in here?" he demanded.

"She's here at my direction, G. Llorkin. She will begin her elllonian studies now."

"Are you aware that our life cycle approximates that of Earth's amphibians, Dr. Grey?" Llorkin said, peering expectantly into her face and fumbling in the clutter on his desk for a pen.

Tandra took Shawne's hand. "If you don't mind, I

would prefer that Shawne introduce me to her friends
first, Llorkin. I recognize your amphibious nature now,
and I'm sure that nothing will shock me sufficiently to
justify your jotting it down."

Ignoring him, she quickly surveyed the room. An
incubator contained one large blue egg, and within a
wall-sized aquarium swam two foot-long humanoid tad-
poles. A confusion of toys on the floor surrounded a
small, featherless, green elllonian figure, still sporting
a sizable tail.

"Dat's Da-oon," Shawne said. "He goes potty in da
udan. I do too. This is Malkan. And Ellan is a girl.
They can swim real good." Shawne ran over to the
tank and thrust her hand in. The two elllonian tads
swam toward her and playfully nibbled at her hand.
Then, as Shawne swished her fingers through the water, they tried to grab them with their rudimentary
prehensile fins.

Orram followed Tandra to the tank. "Their legs are
still buds, developing rapidly now. In another two years
the tail will become a vestige, and its adult extension,
the retractable back fin, will develop until maturity. The
hexagonal pressure-sensitive plates mature while the
tads are still in the tank. The light green outlines of
the plates are sensitive to heat and ultra-sonic vibrations. Ellan has a large ultra-sonic vocabulary already,
and they will both learn to communicate with changes
in water pressure before they leave the tank. We are
lucky to find them here. They spend most of their time
in the centrifuge room." Orram turned from the tank
and knelt beside the small elll busily working over one
of Shawne's puzzles. "Da-oon is almost four Earth-years
from hatching now. Mental development is a bit slower
than man's. Llorkin," he said, "Da-oon and Shawne
are approximately the same mental age now, don't you
think?"

"Yes, in terms of abstraction and mathematical con-
ceptualization. But the human infant's social age is
much lower."

"What do you mean?" Tandra asked.

"She is very egocentric and possessive. She expresses

the individualistic survival demands of a year-old hatchling."

"We don't expect human children to learn to share until they are four or five years old, Llorkin," Tandra said. "We encourage generosity, and babies can demonstrate an amazing amount of it at times, but we also encourage individuality and self-reliance. We are not group-oriented creatures, like yourselves."

"Neither are varoks," Orram assured her. "The ellls school in both a psychological and a physical sense. In fact, they find being cut off from their own kind very difficult. The crew of this base is rather unusual. All had to pass rigorous psychological tests for adaptability to isolation. But you and I, Tandra, are naturally independent souls. We stubbornly refuse to equate ourselves with any other creature alive or continuously to rub elbows with our fellows, as, quite to the contrary, the ellls must. Since they need to school and we require individual territory, the optimal density for our species is comparable to yours while the elllonian density is maintained at three times that."

"Whose eggs are these? Are their parents known?"

"No. *El* eggs are selected at random and checked for fertility and apparent good health. At the present time, application can be made by a group of four to six ellls to raise five eggs. Tllan, Killah, Ohln, and Tallyn are sponsoring these three infants, and a new sponsor must be found to replace Ellalon. They are responsible for the incubation of the eggs, their nursing in the tank until their lungs develop, and their education, which begins immediately upon emergence from the tank and continues for four Varokian years, fifteen Earth-years. The five sponsors establish a special relationship with their young; they are a family unit of sorts."

"And the unselected eggs are eaten?"

"You have enjoyed many *el* eggs yourself without knowing that they were elllonian," Orram replied. "No doubt the difference in pronunciation between *el* and *elll* misled you." He paused and observed her with an unseen sense. "So that is what happened at the food center. Conn told you, I suppose, in rather crude terms."

"No, that wasn't it. I accused him, in effect, of can-
nibalism—" She stared at the varok. "Orram! You're
reading my mind!"

She expected a denial. But the varok touched her
chin, and his eyes filled with warmth. "What made you
think I was reading your mind?"

Llorkin watched with wide eyes as the varok accepted
the woman's hand on his own and they moved closer
together.

"Tandra, I need to know. Can you tell me what made
you think I was reading your mind?"

"I felt watched."

"But not with eyes."

Llorkin busily noted their conversation; his broad
mouth was unusually dry.

"Not with eyes," Tandra agreed.

"Where's Conn?" Shawne interrupted. "I can swim
with Conn. I do. He says I'm *Shawnoon* now."

"Conn is going to the moon's south pole, little water-
Shawne," the varok said with the hint of a smile.
"Come, let us brighten the lights so you can show us
what Conn taught you while we were gone, *Shawnoon*."

Later beside the pool, while Shawne slept, the varok
and the woman talked: they reviewed Tandra's changing relationship with Conn; they worried about Conn
and his anger; they grieved for Ellalon; and, Orram
realized, they also exchanged thoughts with more than
words.

When Tandra took Shawne to the food center after
the child awoke, Orram stayed by the pool stretched
full length on its soft deck, thinking of the diffuse mood-
reading that Tandra had been doing. He wondered if it
had any relation to her ability to hold him suspended
between crippling grief and rational self-control. He
was suddenly jolted from his thoughts by Artellian's
voice.

"Are you quite sure you are out of danger now,
Orram?" the Master elll said. "Aen said that you never
went completely into your grief for Ellalon." He folded

his golden green form onto the deck beside Orram.

"Yes. I am out. An interesting phenomenon really. With Tandra's help I was able to experience the anger and regret of grief and to maintain some conscious control simultaneously. We have just communicated again on a similar level."

"Orram, are you able to read her?"

"I can read her mood quite easily. And sometimes specifics. Also, she reads me, Artell, though she doesn't seem to know it yet."

"How can she not know it? You always know it, don't you?"

"Yes, it's a conscious act on our part, the use of the patches. But she has no patches. What she does must be an unconscious learned response." He stopped talking and sat up. "I think we should run fertility studies between our species. I'm sure Tandra would be willing to contribute a few eggs."

Artellian jumped to his feet. "Are you mad, varok? We have joked about such tests, but we have never considered them seriously. Tandra has had a difficult time with us. We can't ask her—I think you are in need of more time with Junah. Perhaps Erah?"

"Neither. Sit down, Artell. Tandra is now one of us. She will understand that fertility tests are a logical addition to our comparative studies."

"But why speak of fertility as you mumble about patch capability?"

"Both functions are extremely personal ones, closely related in varokian life, are they not?" Orram said.

"True, true, my dear friend. But spoken of in one breath only in reference to consummation."

"Yes?"

Artellian stood over the almost-grinning varok with a golden head cocked at full tilt. "I think you're asking a bit much of yourself, Oran Ramahlak. Or are you released, already?"

"Already?! Do you expect that my emotional release is inevitable—with this human being? Release is a life-long goal of consummated varoks. It means nothing more than that with mutual help some varoks can learn to express emotion occasionally without sacrificing rational consciousness."

"Isn't that precisely what happened to you after Ellalon's death? Tandra kept you in touch with reason during your grief, did she not?"

"That may have been a phenomenon related to release. But connected to fertility studies? I do not think so." Orram stood up and clasped Artellian's shoulders. "Don't worry, M. Artell. I am well under control."

Taking Orram's hands from his shoulders, the golden elll sighed, then looked at the varok's hands, pondering his unusual gesture. "Take care, Orram. Take care with all this mood-reading."

While the *Nalkah* crawled around the southern pole of Earth's moon, the elllonian crew at base began their adjustment to Ellalon's death. For more than a week they put aside their Earth-studies, brought their experiments to a pause wherever possible, and reduced their Earth-monitoring activities to a minimum while they schooled, huddling together in the warm water of the pool around a throbbing nucleus of distress signals.

Tandra watched them from the pool's deck as she studied elllonian books. At first the ells treated her cautiously, afraid of imposing on her, but soon they found in her a new acceptance and a hesitant yearning, so Killah was dispatched to invite her to join in the adjustment.

"Our grief is different from yours, Tandra," Killah said. "Come join the school—without Ellalon. Know us again before Conn returns."

Without hesitation, Tandra followed her colleague into the pool, where the ells gradually embraced her with the gentle tapping of their pressure signals. As the tapping grew more intense, she relaxed and floated at ease in the gentle massage until, finally, acceptance was won. In an unconscious, symbolic act, she entrusted her life to the school and slept.

Killah was the first to notice that she had slipped beneath the surface. Swiftly he dove under her and lifted her face out of the water. In her sleep she took a deep breath and fit her body onto his. And there they stayed for more than an hour, his velvet green form making a bed for her in the warm, throbbing water, while his back fin undulated tirelessly to support her.

Nothing was said when she finally awoke. She clung to Ohln and to Killah for a long time before she climbed out of the pool to return to her books.

In that way the week continued. Tandra learned to know the ellls—not as near-humanoids nor as unfathomably alien amphibious beasts—but as mild, handsome, unique creatures of rare intelligence and appreciative nature, who, by good fortune or divine plan, had escaped the worst of nature's demands and had learned to live happily with existence as they found it, reshaping and exploiting it only slightly for their real needs, rarely for their convenience, and never for their aggrandizement.

One evening soon after the adjustment had been made, and a relaxed schedule of analytical work had been reestablished, the elder varokian astronomer, Ahl, came to Tandra as she lay on the floor of the room she shared with Orram and Artellian reading *The Cultural and Political History of the Ellls of Ellason*.

"Dull, eh?" Ahl said, as he sat on Tandra's bed pad and looked over her shoulder.

"Beautifully dull. Yet exciting. Reading elllonian history is like reading about a very large, complex child searching for awareness and meaning in life and finding it, and finding that that is only the beginning."

"So now you love the ellls, Tandra?"

"Even more than I thought I did at first. And I have no more fear of varoks. But, then, I have had fewer delusions about your species, Ahl."

"Orram did not allow them to grow, did he? Do you know that varoks have dreams that lead them astray, too?"

"I'm aware of at least one such problem," Tandra said. She sat up and gazed expectantly at the dark, silver varok.

"Yes, Junah; and she is in some danger, for none of us can reach her, nor reason with her. But not all of our dreams lead us to disaster."

"Do you want to talk about Orram?" Tandra asked, surprised by her own question.

"You read me well, Tandra. I am curious to know how you have unlocked the secret of the Master varok's smile."

"A varokian smile is a rare and beautiful thing," Tandra said. She glanced up as Orram entered the room with Artellian. There was something formal in their appearance. Her voice faltered as the deep blue entrance to Orram's mind seemed to open to her. Abruptly, unthinking and afraid, she denied the possibility.

Artellian sat down close to Tandra on the soft moss floor. "You know, Conn predicted that you would accomplish integration with us, Dr. Grey. I was wrong in assuming that acceptance on human terms would be easy but integration impossible."

"Perhaps only for a dreamer like myself," Tandra laughed. "I think your assumption is valid for most human beings."

"I wonder," the great elll mused. "Be that as it may, you are ready to begin the more difficult work we had in mind for you. You must help us decide whether to contact Earth or not—and how it should be done. In just a few days three astronauts will be sent to explore the Straight Wall. We did not expect that extensive exploration would be attempted again, especially now that our projections are being realized: time grows short for many lives on Earth. Somehow, perhaps, we should try to influence the fate of your planet. For the moment, we are decided that there should be no contact. If these lunar studies continue, however, our presence will be discovered eventually."

"Does anyone besides Jesse Mendleton and myself know of your existence?"

"No one. We have not yet seen any possibility for making official contact with your world, Tandra," Artellian explained, "because there is no central government or agency which all peoples trust. The World Federation is representative only of those who possess military and economic power. If we contact any partially representative government, we immediately prejudice our position with everyone else. All we have to offer is the shock of our alien opinions drawn from experience, so we must not jeopardize our credibility in the least."

"The task looks impossible," Orram said. "We must not only counter many of man's cultural imprints, but his ancient survival instincts and his remarkable talent for repression as well. In spite of increasingly sophisticated computer analyses and the steady and predictable increase of major disasters, many human beings refuse to believe that there is a problem."

"Apparently that is correct," Ahl said. "But we are ultimately more concerned with meaningful contact with Earth as a single entity than we are with the fate of the human species."

"I'm not sure I understand. Do you mean you will stand by and watch millions of men die?" Tandra asked.

"We already have," Ahl said. "If Earth requires a repeat of Varokian history, then we can only grieve, nothing more. I doubt that the human species is capable of the give and take required by a stable economic state. Therefore, something will give, and I doubt that it will be the human appetite. On the other hand, you are rapidly outbreeding your industrial excrement—if you see what I mean. Of course, there is always the possibility of nuclear war when competition for food and water and energy becomes intolerable. I am no prophet, and the solutions are not simple nor easily understood. However—whatever happens—while man ignores the necessity of restraint, he will have destroyed many of Earth's other species. That is the real tragedy, Tandra, for they are innocent.

"This is sad talk, my friends. This old varok needs some sleep. We will not resolve Earth's problem in one evening's discussion." The silver-haired astronomer turned away from Orram and Tandra and, with a twist of his hand to Artellian, left the room.

Tandra watched him go. "It's hard for me to grasp the possibility that man, too, could become extinct," she said. "We have always assumed that we were a super-species, somehow not subject to natural law. Yet we are. We evolved into dominance with superior adaptability and a larger brain; and as a result of natural law, we have inherited the Earth. Many species have suffered, been lost, because of our dominance."

Artellian stared at Tandra. "Repeat what you have just said."

"What? That men won't believe that they themselves are subject to nature's laws, that they too could become extinct?"

"You don't realize what you have said," Artellian groaned. "We know your cultures' assumptions all too well. That is not the point. Orram!" He looked to the varok for help. "Think what you have said, Tandra."

Orram spoke slowly at first. "You said that the extinction of Earth's species in the wake of man's dominance is to be expected as a function of natural law."

"Did I really say that?"

"It was assumed in your statement."

"Yes, I suppose it was. But isn't that true? Survival of the fittest is an old biological dogma."

"Tandra, not with reference to a total world system," Artellian said. "Survival of the fittest is a truism concerning differential reproduction—the strongest normally produce young within a single species." Artellian was growing more agitated. "Ahl, come back here," he shouted into the intercom. "Orram, you must make her understand. If she is so oblivious to her own mind, of what use is our effort for Earth?"

"We see in your statement, Tandra, a very serious flaw in human thinking," Orram said. "Surely you would agree that it is *not* a law of nature that species must become extinct by the hand of man—even if he were superior. Quite the contrary. Nature is most stable when she is most complex. Man has remodeled the systems of life on Earth at his own peril. It is a cliché. Biological systems evolved over millions of years, and man will pay a heavy price for his insistence on dominion—perhaps even the price of self-extinction."

"Tandra," Artellian said grimly, "your statement was possible because you are man, and man has assumed that other species must give way to make room for him. This assumption lies so deep in human nature that it overrides any intrinsic tendency you may have to revere life."

Ahl entered the room as Artellian spoke. "So you are demanding more from her. Good. I thought I heard a strange remark from you when I left, Tandra. Realize that your assumption of man's right to dominance is a direct threat to us as a species different from you. I'll be boiled in *lohn* juice before I will concede that ells or varoks or dolphins or ants *should* give way for man or his damning technology. *Our* laws of nature don't state that man should dominate and control all other life forms—that man can drive us to extinction with impunity."

"I made that assumption without realizing it," Tandra said.

"Consider the consequences to us if we had evolved on Earth," Aen said. "Our ability to speak with throat sounds was latent; we developed it with the help of the varoks. Had we evolved here, you would know us only as amphibious swamp beasts. Before you bothered to learn anything about us, you would shoot us for green suede and white meat. You would drain our homes and gardens for new housing developments and ignore the fact that we cared."

Orram continued: "Your statement contained an implied insult to the ellls and everything that they have *not* accomplished. What would have happened to them if men instead of varoks had found them on Ellason? There was no obvious technology to provide clues to their intelligence. How far would you go to establish communication? To the extremes that the varoks went? Would you spend one hundred centuries developing a common language?"

"I think that it would make no difference if they *did*

know we were intelligent," Artellian said. "Look what men do to dolphins. They hunt them for sport, dump garbage and oil into their ocean homes, rape their good will by enslaving them. Though men have known for decades that dolphins have a sophisticated system of communication and considerable intelligence, there have been only token attempts to contact them—and cynical ones. Men care nothing for their grief."

"No!" Tandra cried. "If men fully realized—"

"Listen to me, Tandra! We know them!" Artellian said with intensity. "We ellls can communicate with dolphins. They are playful, loyal beings, utterly without malice. Yet men have assumed that any species not physically or technologically superior must give way; therefore, the dolphins must give way, in spite of their innocence. And if this had been our home, *we* would have given way temporarily, because we would have lacked your terrible ambition, preferring to float around discussing experience in sonar rather than to mumble sounds in your audible range or to develop an inventory of destructive gadgets. We would wait—then survive while the masses of men died off. We would probably co-exist more equitably with the survivors: the self-sustaining men whose needs are simple."

Orram sensed Tandra's anguish and sought to ease it. "In many ways your culture implies that nature—or the nature of things—is a benevolent personality, a miracle-worker always looking out for man's existence. But you see, the ellls have never assumed a superior stance, and, even though we are the only highly complex form of life on Varok, we varoks have had faith in our specialness utterly denied by our history. Tell me, Tandra, what are you: humanist, spiritual ecologist, or theist?"

"I'm not sure I understand, Orram," Tandra said.

"Tandra!" Orram's eyes were demanding, penetrating. "You will see with the eyes of ellls and of varoks and add your own dimension. That is why we need you; we are not able to encompass so much in one glance—if you will only open your mind and damn your pride. You can understand what I ask. Are you humanist, spiritual ecologist or theist?"

Tandra forced her reluctant mind to work. "If the theist places ultimate responsibility for man's acts on God, especially a god defined in the image of man, then I am no theist. Nor does my God give special privileges to man, for He is not only Earth, but everything beyond Earth. And I am no longer humanist, for I believe that man's welfare, indeed his very survival, is dependent on the subjugation of his person to the total life system of Earth. This must be what you mean by spiritual ecology. Man is not the *raison d'être* of the universe. Am I talking sense, Orram, or merely reiterating varokian philosophy?"

"Your thoughts are close to Analahk's, but they are your own," Orram replied, feeling a surge of joy. "We believe in the unity of existence. Men might use the word God or Allah or Brahman, but we varoks have learned from the ellls that precise definitions and conditions tend only to restrict the concept. The point is that there is no reason to believe that our consciousness is distinct from the forces that shaped it."

Artellian plucked some moss from the wall and munched it quietly while he opened the water inlet of his sleeping bowl. "I can take only so much philosophy in one evening, my friends. No doubt we'll make you grow beyond man before we're done with you, Tandra. Perhaps we'll even force your mind beyond Earth." Without further comment, he climbed into the *uuyvanoon* and slipped beneath the warm water.

"I'm too wrought up to sleep," Tandra said. "Will you join me in the observation deck for a while?"

In answer, and as a gesture symbolic of their shared thoughts, the two varoks offered her their arms, and, lost in thought, they walked slowly toward the food center. There Tandra poured them cups of a tart Ellasonian red algae, which they carried to the observation deck and sipped absently as they stared out over the moon's landscape.

"You have climbed beyond disdain, Tandra," Ahl

said. "We will work well together now. You are not
alone in shame; we too have had severe growing pains."
Then he stretched out on a couch and quoted in low,
grating tones from the varokian *Songs To Life:*

Though our minds run narrowly in small, straight rivers
And never branch nor feed large pools
As do the flaming crystals of Varok's streams;
Though Life has now denied us freedom of the passions,
And we are chained to reason, sanity required,
Mindless joy denied, forgetful love impossible;
Though Life is drawn in squares and we dare not tread
    the lines
Lest we plunge to destruction on wild fires,
Encindered at the edge of reason and the fringe of love
Or the precipice of hate;
Though Life enchains us,
Denies us her most precious gifts,
We have remained her friend
And found our freedom from her dreaded sister, Time.
Enchained by Life, yet free now, free from Time,
Whose passing no longer fills our minds with terror.
Eternity is ours; and we may once again embrace our
    lives.

11
Contact and Detachment

Slowly the *Nalkah* retraced old paths through the maze of craters southwest of the base until, finally, it reached smoother terrain near the lunar south pole. After a routine stop at the experimental station between the craters Amundsen and Boltzmann, it hurried into the Southern Highlands facing Earth, clambered over the roughs east of Clavius and west of Maginus, and headed for the rim of crater Tycho, where the terrain became almost impassable.

Conn sank lazily into his couch as his long arms played the *Nalkah's* controls. They moved deftly and surely like extensions of the craft itself. As a rule, he loved this rugged part of the trail. Not only did he enjoy the sensuous pounding of the lumbering craft but he often relished the challenges of finding the easiest path and leaving the least trace through the extravagant debris, of rolling or climbing or hovering over the larger boulder piles with a minimum of shock, of dodging the sudden pits and small craters and swinging back before the craft threw everyone too violently. When he grew tired of the necessary concentration, he would shout a warning to Junah, Aen, and Tllan and let the vehicle careen wildly in and out and around and over the tortured landscape.

Now he drove the *Nalkah* as if by instinct. His mind was not on the rocks ahead of him. He felt dull and heavy, too dry—much too dry with all this gray dust surrounding him and the warm, wine-red water of the pool still days away.

Junah, too, was restless. While Aen and Tllan slept, she made the final entry in the South Highland Maintenance Log with some difficulty, put on an elllonian wet-sweater, and climbed into the couch next to Conn. "You look like you have eaten a *kaehl's* sour-gland," she said in clipped Varokian.

Conn tried to smile but failed. "Did you ever think you'd get tired of twilight and long shadows?" he said. "Oh, hell! Screw the whole works," he roared in English.

Junah started. Conn's unpredictable fierceness frightened her. "I've never seen you so ugly in mood, Conn," she said. "Is it the woman, Tandra? Is it her sickness?"

"What sickness?"

"I found her in the food center after you left her. She was holding her head in her hands, shaking all over," Junah said.

"Is that all?"

"Yes. I called Orram. She left the food center with him a short time later, apparently recovered."

"Human beings aren't like you varoks, Junah," Conn said. "They can wallow in emotion and enjoy it almost as much as we do. She wasn't physically ill or incapacitated, just crying. She was probably dancing around with Orram ten minutes later."

"Dancing? With Orram? M. Ramahlak wouldn't dance. He'll probably never dance."

Conn smiled weakly. "Junah, when are you going to learn not to take me seriously? But now that I think of it—don't be too certain that Orram isn't capable of the *Vrankah*. Tandra has him worrying about differences in your species for more than academic reasons."

"Conn, that can not be true. Do I read you correctly?"

"You read me," Conn laughed darkly. "I think Orram went away from that game of feelies with Tandra with a psychological, if not a physical, hard-on—but he won't admit it, even to himself."

"Conn, no, not Orram," Junah cried.

"I'm sorry, Junah, I'm not being kind to you."

"I lose my grasp on reason when I think of Orram. Conn, may I confide in you? I think it will help."

"Of course."

"I will, if you will tell me more about you and Dr. Grey first."

"All right, Junah," Conn sighed. "I'll try. What the hell. *A-la-oon!* Where can I begin? I'm so damn sorry I blew off at Tan. Her face, Junah! She looked at me and all the love was gone. There was nothing left but horror. Damn it, Junah. I wanted her to love me. Really me! So I raged at her about eggs, of all the damn things."

"Surely she will recover from the shock and remember your good times," Junah said.

"How I wish I could *forget* them. I see Shawne paddle to me and Tandra beam at us—so glad I could teach her Tad to swim. Every night when the water fills my lungs I remember—and then her face comes to me twisted and frozen with horror—her face—*aeyull!*"

"Damn her! Damn her goddam prejudices," he roared in English. "Junah, we spent hours with the tapes, and our sound was going to be good. Really good. We didn't need to talk. Who needs words when you have so much else?"

"But she was not being honest with herself. The lie would come clear sooner or later."

Suddenly, Conn's face relaxed. "Now spill your beans, Junah. I've done mine."

Junah hesitated, adjusting to his instantaneous change in mood. Then she put down her natural reserve and dove into unknown waters. "I treasure Orram's words, his appearance, his voice. I long to meet his arm with mine. I think that I could love him always."

"You too, eh?" Conn said. "I'll put in a good word for you." He tried to stop himself, but his confused bitterness drove him on. "Forget it, Junah. Orram is twice your age and three times your maturity. The best you can expect is an occasional pat on the head and a poke in the ass."

Conn's words lit the passion that Junah had dared to touch within herself. With an emotional violence that men rarely suffer, reason and control succumbed, and she jumped at Conn with a scream of rage, tearing at his crown feathers. Instinctively, he dropped the steering bar and struck out at her patch organs with a lurching attack that spun the *Nalkah* out of control and sent it spinning over the sharp rim of a treacherously deep crater.

Delight bubbled up from a hidden spring within Orram, and he laughed as he watched Killah's reaction to his boisterous approach.

"What sound is this?" Killah chided. "Let me give you a sedative."

"Your tail feathers are curling, Killah," Orram said, peering behind the elll, "but fortunately I am quite sane, just partially released, indulging in a bit of joy, if you will allow me. I am relieved that Tandra has integrated with us. We were cautious when there was no need for caution; from the time she met her first varok Tandra's assumption has been that fertility tests should be done."

"So—you finally dared a probing on the subject?"

"No no no." Orram's stolid face cracked with a hundred lines of amusement. "She suggested it herself, and I have already captured some human eggs."

"So you are released, Orram," the elll said, marveling at the varok's transformed countenance. "Do we have a whole new varok to know?"

"No, I am not released, at least not in the classical sense. Yet, you see now that I am capable of some emotion."

"And Tandra is the cause of this emotional indulgence? Can she control it?"

"She could, but she won't—consciously. What is incredible, Killah, is that I have some control myself. It seems to be related to my patch contact with Tandra. We will have to watch it closely."

"I don't like to see you experiment with yourself this way, Orram," Killah said.

The varok nodded gravely. "I am in no danger, and, of course, Tandra is very strong now. She has found reality and purpose with us. I guarantee that she will not suffer any harm. Shall we proceed?"

Not by the congestive flow of blood, but with voluntary muscles, acting in accordance with reluctant involuntary ones, the varok managed a penile erection. Killah extracted the required sample, and Orram retreated quickly to freeze part of it. Another part was immediately prepared for microscopic analysis and viability tests, and the rest was allowed to incubate with two meticulously nurtured human eggs, recently taken, with careful timing and considerable surgical skill, from Tandra.

During the following hours, Orram and Tandra tended the small incubator like anxious parents, as it lay poised beneath a recording microscope. Finally, a hint of sperm penetration could be seen in one of the human eggs. Then, as the hours passed unnoticed, the development of pronuclei became obvious. Tandra's glance met Orram's. Then they looked again through the lenses to the newly fertilized egg—and watched it die.

Tandra sighed and started to turn away, but Orram clung to her; his hand was shaking.

"Orram?" She turned to the varok and placed her fingers on his patches. "It's only an egg, you know." She looked into his eyes hoping to find the deep open blue again, but it was not there.

"Of course," he said with a face stolid again; already his hands had stopped shaking. "A momentary lapse, Tandra, nothing more."

In the recreation room, though disappointed by the egg's death and Orram's denial of emotion, Tandra felt contentment cover her like her soft varokian robe. Several ellls were scattered about the room studying Jesse Mendleton's latest transmission of scientific papers, where the most important news was the fact that the Earth had scheduled another lunar landing. A microtape of Conn's favorite melodies was softly driving lyric sound from the walls. Tandra's mind was open, free to explore and to find whatever was there to be found;

she would have her elllonian studies completed by the time Conn returned. How she loved him now: the free, intelligent loner among the schooling ellls, his easy slouch as he worked over their tapes, his quiet "plunch" as he slipped into the pool to leap and cut through the water. She saw him meet Ellalon briefly in the center of the pool, dive with her in casual acceptance and re-surface minutes later as if there had been no interruption in his swimming. What a stable, joyful, integrated existence his amphibious culture had made for his species and for him—even him, a misfit really, a loner, probably a mutant of evolutionary significance.

Tandra was shaken from her musings by Orram's hand.

"I thought that you might like to listen to the lunar landing."

He switched Conn's maze of electronics from stored tapes to the radio interceptor and homed in on the transmission from the lunar module.

"Where are they landing this time?" Tandra asked.

"They intend to land on the Straight Wall northeast of the South Horn Mountains and west of crater Thebit."

"It's rough in there, isn't it?"

"It's all right if they stay just south of the Taenarium Range and near the precipice."

As the varokian receiver picked the astronauts' voices out of the moon's airless space, Tandra smiled at the familiar banter. But soon the radio conversation crackled with tense excitement as the lunar craft turned to give the astronauts a view of the Straight Wall:

"There she is. We're right on it. Sixteen thousand at eighteen. Sailing over Birt now. Beautiful! Up a bit. Keep it up. Fifty-five hundred at eight. Eleven hundred at five. There's the Wall. *Who-ee*, look at that—a mountain climber's dream!"

"Or nightmare," a second voice interjected.

"Roger, Bob."

"One thousand at four point seven. Nearing the Wall, Midpacific. Looks rough over there. Nine-fifty at three point five. Approaching Wall. Twenty-five at two point two. Boulders, by God. Let's try—over this way. Fifteen at two point one. Poor visibility."

"Can't see a damn thing down there. We're kicking up dust."

"Take your time, Bob."

"Roger, Midpacif . . ."

Suddenly the voices were interrupted by a loud crunch—and silence.

"Orram!"

A controlled but frantic call came from the receiver: "Bob! Carliano, this is Midpacific. Can you read us? Jim, can you read us? Inclinometer critical. Confirm."

Tandra grasped Orram's hand, and they waited interminable seconds. Finally, a thick slow voice grumbled through space. "Roger, Midpacific. Carliano here. *Dove Two* has landed, so to speak. Too much dust kicked up. Couldn't see. Apparently flipped on a large boulder or something and fell flat on our face. Confirm eighty-eight point six."

"Report status, Bob."

"Roger, Midpaf. No obvious damage. What we need is a crane. We're completely over on our side. Jim Wright was thrown against the front panels. He's unconscious. Ted Bardeane seems to be in shock. Hold on while I check them out."

"Orram?"

He looked hard at Tandra. "Can you understand why we may not help them? We could put the *Lurlial* into low orbit and pick them up within a few hours. But you realize that our most recent decision was to avoid contact until we could devise an effective introduction of ourselves. There is much at stake, Tandra."

Tandra turned up the volume on the receiver. An hour passed, and it became clear that the lunar craft was lying helpless on a craggy ledge near the upper rim of the Straight Wall, with no hope of rescue.

"I'll ask Artellian to call the base Directorate together immediately," Orram said.

*   *   *

Hundreds of miles from the toppled *Dove* at the bottom of a smallish, deeep crater, the *Nalkah* also lay helpless, crippled beyond immediate repair. Three gray-green figures sprawled motionless on the craft's cushioned wall, which now lay against the moon's surface, and the fourth figure, Junah, sat in a half-crouch, quivering violently—a creature broken on the rapids where varokian reason and emotion meet but rarely blend.

More than an hour passed before Conn regained consciousness. Without moving, he tested the air and tried his body. Then, momentarily satisfied that the life-support seal of the *Nalkah* was still intact, he sat up and surveyed the interior of the overturned craft. Nothing alarming. Its large balloon tracks were still extended, apparently undamaged. Then he saw Junah huddled near him, and he knew that major damage had been done, not to the ship, but to her. He crawled to the pitiful brown figure and enfolded it in his long, velvet arms.

"Junah. Junah. *Ae-yul-ll!*" He searched for a sign of consciousness in her eyes. But there was none. Blank and gray, they stared dimly ahead through her convulsive sobbing.

With Conn's groans, Aen regained consciousness. His shoulder ached where he was thrown against the *Nalkah,* but he got up without difficulty and stepped around Tllan's prostrate body. She was either dead or resting well and needed no treatment, so he turned his attention to Conn and Junah. The blank look in the varokian girl's eyes jolted him into elllonian grief and he missed Conn's more subtle injury.

Conn tried to stand, but the *Nalkah* seemed to reel from under his feet. He grabbed Aen for support. Slowly, the vehicle resettled in his mind, and he tried again to stand. There was no steady reference. In the weak gravity of Earth's moon, his mechanism for balance, evolved in water under gravitational stress, was extremely vulnerable; it had ceased to function. "I can't orient," he said. "Call base, Aen, if you can set the probes. We won't get out of here without help."

* * *

After some time, Aen's belabored message sped north and west through the moon's crust to base—while Tandra listened to the sporadic, quietly anguished conversation between Midpacific Space Center and the stranded astronauts. She jumped from her chair eagerly when Orram reentered the recreation lounge.

"When will you radio the *Dove?*" she asked.

Orram's face was grave. "I'm not sure we will, Tandra. Come to Artellian's office with me. We need your viewpoint so that we might reach a consensus." He stood very still as he spoke, probing the strength of Tandra's mood.

"The *Nalkah* has also had an accident," he said. "It is trapped in a small crater near Maginus H. Conn has lost his sense of equilibrium and Junah—Junah has been injured, too."

"You are not telling me everything, Orram," Tandra said.

"How can you know, Tandra? You read me before I know myself. We will talk later. Artellian is waiting for us now."

They turned to enter the base's small, crowded office. Artellian, Ahl, Llorkin, Killah, and Tallyn were sprawled in awkward angles around a topographical lunar globe which was set into the living moss floor.

Artellian turned to Tandra anxiously. "You know how undecided we have been about contacting Earth's human society. Should we let circumstances force us to reverse our current decision?"

Llorkin's large green eyes focused sharply on Tandra and he stood up stiffly. "We are not prepared to encounter more men, Dr. Grey. We have only begun our talks with you in order to reexamine our options. We had decided some time previously that no contact should be made except with spokesmen truly representative of Earth's total life complex—which, it has been our observation, men are not."

"If men knew of your existence, that point could be

made and have some influence," Tandra interrupted. Her voice was firm.

"There is no hope for world-wide cooperation of significance, not even among human beings," Tallyn said. "I see nothing to do but to watch. After the die-off surviving mutants might be sane."

"I can't half blame either of you for your little regard for human life, but don't forget that we are sensitive, conscious beings. In spite of our obduracy and our adaptability, we suffer as much as any other species."

"I'm not sure such capacity for repression makes for strong animals, Tandra. Perhaps it is best man dies so Earth try again, eh?"

"No. You don't mean that, Tallyn. You value life—even human life—too much."

"Yes. Yes," Tallyn complained. "But we must try to save some sort of living-support capability for Earth."

"Yes, Tallyn," Tandra cried. "Yes. But when we go, we'll take everything else with us. So if you care at all for our rotting oasis, you'll be very careful not to prejudice any influence you might have. You can't let these astronauts die. Eventually it would be learned that you had been here—capable of rescue." She whirled to face Orram. His blank face nodded slightly toward Artellian.

"Though some might suspect we could do much more for man in the category of stop-gap rescues, this, at least, would be expected by all; and it would serve as a gesture symbolic of our good will," the Master elll said thoughtfully, looking to Orram for agreement. "I believe you are right." He rolled from the moss onto his feet and opened his hand, signifying the end of the meeting.

But Llorkin began to puff and stammer. "I must insist on submitting a contrary report if this outlook prevails," he said. "We cannot predict what effect a sudden revelation of our presence will have on the human population. We endanger this base and the entire life system of Earth in order to save three men."

"I think that you overestimate our ability to influence Earth under any conditions," Ahl said.

"I for one do not intend to stand by and watch the further degradation of life on this beautiful planet," Llorkin announced.

"Then you may return to Ellason on the next ship," Artellian snapped.

"I think it's rather a good play, myself," Killah chortled. "Hopeless astronauts are suddenly rescued by an unknown, benevolent intelligence from outer space. It's a good entrance, I think."

"I agree," Artellian said. "The entrance is as good as we could hope for. The stage would be set for maximal influence. Llorkin, I will take full responsibility for this decision. The cost of this base is not justified for our studies alone. We can't ignore this opportunity to minimize Earth's peak death-load. We will put the *Lurlial* into polar orbit, land near the *Nalkah,* and do what we can there, then make a ballistic shot to the Straight Wall and pick up the astronauts."

"Since one of them is injured, perhaps we should pick them up first," Orram said. "The *Lurlial* is equipped adequately for medical treatment. We don't yet know the nature of the *Nalkah*'s damage. We may have to spend some time there."

"Let us proceed at once," Artellian said. "Tandra, all security precautions will be enforced. No scientific information is to be revealed to the astronauts except as specified by this Directorate. What you may know or may have guessed about the varok's patch organs and the probable locations of Ellason and Varok will remain private speculation.

"The *Lurlial* will be decontaminated before embarkation. Since at least one of the astronauts is injured, we will reverse normal procedure and wear isolation suits ourselves while *en route*. They will disguise us if we deem it necessary not to reveal ourselves. We will effect repair if possible and bring the astronauts back to base only as the last resort. Tandra, you will accompany Tallyn and Orram in the *Lurlial*. Assume responsibility for proper isolation procedures and the maintenance of psychological balance in the astronauts. Come with me now while I make radio contact with them."

Tandra followed Artellian down the hall and into a corner of the hangar stuffed with a maze of transmitting and receiving equipment.

"Vohn, attempt to lock onto Midpacific Space Center and *Dove Two*," Artellian said to the young varok working there. "High frequency directional to Earth, and try the lunar e.m. web to eight degrees west, twenty-one degrees south, full power."

A few seconds later Vohn said, "Full power, locked in and receiving."

At first no sound came from the receiver. Then a slow, steady voice broke the silence. "No change in Wright. He's still unconscious—looks pale. Bardeane is sedated. I've done all I can for them. I'm going to sleep for a while. Give me a buzz in a couple hours and I'll continue EVA."

"Roger, Carliano. We're with you, exploring every possibility for getting you out of there. Hold on."

"I'm not going anywhere." A grim chuckle was barely audible.

"I'm impressed with that man's stability," Artellian said. "I see no reason to delay."

Tandra nodded and smiled as he absently pulled at his golden crest. He set his expression and flipped on the transmitter. "Calling *Dove Two*. Calling *Dove Two* at Straight Wall. Do you read me?" Artellian spoke into the transmitting web slowly and distinctly without dampening his elllonian accent.

"Midpacific? This is *Dove Two*. Reading you loud and clear."

"Bob Carliano, this is Midpacific. I didn't send that transmission. Picked it up here, too."

"Midpacific and *Dove Two*. This is Elll-Varok Earth-moon Base. We can effect rescue of *Dove Two* within twelve hours. Repeat. This is the Earth-moon Base of Elll-Varok Science. We can accomplish rescue of *Dove* or *Dove's* crew within twelve hours. Do you read me?"

"Where the hell's that coming from, Midpaf?" Carliano cried. "It's a damn poor joke."

Artellian continued. "Until we make contact with you again, we prefer, for security reasons, that the location of our base remain unknown. We will cease transmission until our space vehicle is in lunar orbit. Approach will be from the north in approximately three hours."

"Bob, did you receive that last transmission?"

"Loud and clear, Midpaf. What's going on?"

"The transmission didn't come from us. We can't get a directional fix unless they keep transmitting."

"That's your problem. Just get them off the frequency."

"Could you place the accent?"

"Negative. Forget it. I need some sleep. Keep those kooks off my back."

"Roger, Bob. Better watch the language. We're still open."

Tandra turned to Artellian. "It's not surprising, you know, their response."

"Yes, of course," he smiled in spite of his disappointment. He turned off the transmitter and spoke into the base's intercom. "Ready the *Lurlial* for immediate insertion into polar orbit. Decontaminate. Crew: Ramahlak, Grey, Killah and Tallyn. Isolation suits readied for Conn, Tllan, Aen and Junah."

Tandra ran quickly to her room. As she expected—without knowing why—Orram was there waiting for her.

"How did they receive you?"

"They didn't believe it. I don't think any amount of talking would convince them that it wasn't a hoax."

"Tandra?" Orram stared at his hands and waited for a question to surface in her mind. "Your touch has become an aid, a small part, or an introduction—I don't know which—to a much deeper communication between logic and passion within myself. I need that now, Tandra. I need your help. During the *Nalkah's* accident Junah went negative."

Tandra stared at the varok and dismay darkened her face. "What happened?"

"We don't know. Aen talked to me from the *Nalkah*, but he wouldn't elaborate. Like all ellls he is perhaps too afraid of triggering varokian emotional release. I might have saved her, Tandra. I should have ended our mating when I sensed that she was over-reading me."

"Over-reading?"

"Fantasizing identity with me. Looking for a marriage, for consummation. Eventually all varoks who forsake reality or reason succumb to their psychoses. But perhaps I could have reclaimed her by making my position clearer. She was reading me incorrectly."

"Reading you?"

"Yes. You read me now, Tandra."

She looked into his blank face and made a considered guess. "I sense regret. Surely you can't blame yourself for her demise. You never encouraged her."

"I tried to discourage her, but I was too kind. Read me again."

"Orram?"

"Read me, Tandra."

The woman searched the varok's eyes, but found no clue to his demand. "Do you need something, Orram? Reassurance?"

"There is nothing in my eyes, Tandra." He moved his arm over hers. "Try moving closer. Your sensitivity may be limited to a shorter range than ours."

Timidly placing her fingers behind his ears, she said, "You need support—support in bearing guilt. But you are not responsible for her going negative."

"Don't deny it. I cannot live with self-delusion. I am varok. I cannot survive if I deny reality. I am partly responsible for her illness. At least I could have postponed it. And again you read me correctly. I bear guilt, and I look to you to bear it with me."

"Orram?" Tandra began to sense the import of what Orram was attempting.

"Read me once more."

She closed her eyes and searched for intuition. Nothing spoke. She relaxed and tried to let her mind go blank. No clear suggestion came. She opened her eyes and looked at Orram and tried to find a spontaneous, obvious answer in his eyes. No. His touch. No. His presence. No. Nothing spoke. "I can't read you now, Orram. I think that the others were only logical guesses."

"Perhaps," he said, going entirely still. "We must board the *Lurlial* now."

The ship glided through the hangar locks and leaped toward the black lunar sky, then fell into a low elliptical orbit that passed over the poles and skimmed crater Maginus.

"We have you spotted, Conn boy," Tallyn twanged in English on the Midpacific-*Dove* frequency, hoping to reassure his bewildered human audience of their real presence and good will.

"Go to Hell in a fruit basket, Tallyn, you jerk," Conn snorted moodily. "And don't take all day playing hero. It's not getting any more pleasant down here, you know. Who's your crew, Orram?"

"Tallyn, Killah, Dr. Grey, and I."

"That all? How'd you get that thing off the ground?"

Tallyn laughed in rollicking tones that tumbled and played all the way to the Midpacific Space Center and across the stark wastes to Bob Carliano in the *Dove*.

"Who the Hell is this?" he called.

"We'll be with your shortly now, Carliano," Tallyn said.

Orram broke into the conversation with data indicating their approach to the wall.

From the window of the upset lunar ship Bob Carliano had a fair view of the dark horizon. Suddenly his excited voice sent a shock of hope and fear through his audience at the space center.

"Goddam if there isn't something up there. A faint glow. It's coming in fast. Looks like a huge kite. It's gone out of sight now."

"Easy down, Orram," Tallyn said. "Engines off. Good aim, varok. We can't be more than twenty metres from *Dove*."

"Dove Two, this is *Lurlial.* We are approximately twenty metres directly east. Can you prepare for lunar exposure?"

"Who are you?"

"We will discuss everything when you are safe. We assure you we intend only your well-being. I repeat: Can you prepare for lunar exposure?"

"Dove Two, this is Midpacific . . . *Dove Two?"*

"Midpacific, we are going out. Whoever you are out there, we are ready for lunar exposure. Depressurization commenced. I'll check our position. I think we're on a ledge down the Wall about twenty-five metres. In any case you'll need something to get us out of here. Two of us are injured."

"It will take us twenty minutes to dress for exposure and walk to the rim. We will attempt visual contact first." Orram turned away from the controls and strode to the rear of the *Lurlial.* He spoke into the intercom. "Tandra, I do not see any reason for you to come. Stay here and receive the men."

Orram, Killah, and Tallyn quickly donned lunar exposure suits over their isolation suits, sealed their helmets, and disappeared through the hatch onto the lunar surface. It was treacherously pocked, and strewn with enormous boulders. At intervals the cliff dropped away forty or even two hundred metres to ledges below or plummeted the full three hundred metres to Rima Birt overlooking Mare Nubium. The three aliens searched the face of Straight Wall for a sign of the human ship, but they failed to see it.

"Dove, this is M. Ramahlak. We are at the precipice above you, but we cannot locate you from here. Do you have any light source that will give us a vertical signal?"

"Dove Two, this is Midpacific. We have directionals on the interference. Moon is apparent source. We advise caution."

"Affirmative Midpaf. Going EVA again to signal whoever is out there."

"Repeat. We advise restraint in signaling."

"I'll have to respectfully ignore that advice, Midpacific. We're being upstaged beautifully, but at this point we are willing to believe in anyone's fairy tales."

"Do you like being called fairy, M. Ramahlak?" Tallyn said, straining his accent to its heaviest lilt.

"I can think of worse things to be called."

"Signal Ramahlak. This is Midpacific. Please identify yourself."

"Midpacific, this is Master Biophysicist Oran Ramahlak, Director of Scientific Operations at the Elll-Varok Earth-moon Base. We are visitors to Earth's moon from Ellason and Varok. Our purpose is scientific observation, and our policy has been one of strict non-interference with man's affairs. We will make no official contact beyond the effort necessary to effect this rescue until we can deal with a fairly representative body from all the peoples of your planet. When such a body is firmly constituted, we look forward to an exchange of information that will benefit us both."

"Please identify Ellason and Varok."

"That information is not available for human awareness. I have defined the conditions necessary for any exchange of scientific or technical data. *Dove,* do you have a signal for us?"

"Depressurization is complete. Hatch open. I'm coming out onto the struts. The ship is in shadow. Light signal deployed now."

"There it is, Killah, behind that pinnacle," Orram said, pointing to his left. Below them a light flickered in the deep shadow and reflected off the gold cloak of the lunar ship, which was wedged almost horizontally between the face of the sheer cliff and a huge angular boulder perched on the narrow ledge.

"We have nothing on the *Lurlial* that will get that ship out up there," Tallyn said.

Almost an hour passed before Orram and Killah climbed into the *Lurlial* behind Tallyn and Bob Carliano. It had not been easy hauling the injured astronauts out of the *Dove's* trap. Orram had also decided to take all the camera equipment he could find.

Midpacific was frantic for news. Carliano had said

nothing for the last half-hour except to grunt acknowl-
edgments. He was physically exhausted and at the same
time in a state of acute tension: The tall, anonymous,
square-helmeted figures could not be human. One was
stiff and calculated and his movement had a strange,
defined pattern to it; the other was unjointed and powerful, his torso and limbs stacked all out of proportion.
Their space suits were definitely not Russian, Chinese,
German, English, or Japanese. Their voices were harsh
and alien. No human throat could make such sounds.

He stood in the passageway of the strange ship, still
dripping from the entry shower, with two aliens beside
him and his disabled companions at his feet. He watched
a figure come toward him looking humanly feminine in
spite of her isolation suit. He tried unsuccessfully to
think. Was this someone he could trust?

"Welcome aboard. My name is Tandra Grey. We're
almost neighbors. I work at the medical labs near the
mid-southwestern megalopolis. I just recently took a
leave to do comparative microbiology for the ellls and
varoks. We are in isolation garments for the trip, and
you will be quarantined at base as a precaution. There
is no need for fear—and very little risk of exposure."

Carliano decided he had no choice but to trust her.
Impulsively he took his helmet off. "You at least *look*
human to me."

"I am," she said, turning to help Killah and Orram
remove their lunar exposure suits.

Carliano watched anxiously while his rescuers unsuited. He was visibly disappointed that they remained
hidden in their isolation garments.

Killah bent over one of the astronauts. "This one was
conscious for a while."

Carliano tried to protest as they unsuited Ted Bardeane, but he was easily overruled, and they carried
Bardeane down the hall to a cabin and bedded him
down in an *uuyvanoon*. At the instant that he touched
the soft moss he regained consciousness, took one look
at Killah's strange, suited silhouette bending over him,
and bolted out of the basin. They were able to subdue

him only after a struggle, and to still his panic, Carliano helped them administer a sedative.

Killah left the room in a temper to check on the more severely injured man, Jim Wright, still lying in the passageway. Orram and Tandra followed.

"This man has had a concussion. There may be a clot," Killah said. "We should get him to base as soon as we can."

"Can we take time for the *Nalkah?*" Orram asked.

Tandra gasped.

"We'll go get your Conn," Killah laughed. "We'll have you two healed together before these men are out of quarantine."

As the elll grasped Tandra's shoulders affectionately, Bob Carliano appeared in the passageway and watched closely, his mind whirling with curiosity. He followed Orram and Tallyn to the control panel and had to be reminded to secure himself while they arced through lunar space and braked over the lunar highlands.

"Tycho, Street, Maginus," Tallyn murmured into the communicator. "We have Maginus H. Conn, give us locater signal. We have to be choosy just where to set down in that mess. How are you, old frog? Still dizzy?"

Conn's voice mumbled an affirmative, and Aen talked the *Lurlial* down onto a relatively uncluttered space in their entrapping crater.

"Bull's-eye," Aen said for Midpacific's benefit.

"Aen, I think we can jack you up and get you on your tracks," Orram said in an unperturbed monotone.

"Roger, varok. We're ready for you."

"*Dove Two,* this is Midpacific. Can you give us a status check?"

"One minute, Midpacific," Orram said. He turned to Carliano. "Commander, the communicator is here on the control panel. Midpacific wants a status report. Aen, Ramahlak here. Can you continue the expedition with Tllan?"

"Yes. Mare Humorum station needs some maintenance, and we should erase the trail through the Cordilleras. We'll bring Junah and Conn over to the *Lurlial* now. They both need immediate care."

Tandra moved back to the entrance hatch. When she heard the decontaminating shower turn on, she opened the inner hatch and found Conn under the cascade clutching Junah's frozen, blind figure, trying vainly to expose it entirely to the spray. Tandra reached in, manipulated Junah, and led her out of the chamber. Conn tried to follow, but he fell into the passageway, knocking Tandra down.

"Conn, let me help you."

The elll remained silent and motionless while she dismantled his lunar exposure suit.

Suddenly, Junah jerked spasmodically and dug her hard fingertips into Tandra's arm. Her eyes grew less than dull and her fingers clutched with their full strength. Tandra set her teeth against the pain and tried to wrench the fingers from her arm, but they tore ferociously into her flesh.

Conn focused on their struggle and threw himself at Junah. She tried to steady herself against his attack and momentarily her fingers left Tandra's arm before they grasped out again toward the source of her pain. Conn grabbed her throat in his wide prehensile fins, pinning her down with his legs.

"Conn, stop it!" Tandra screamed, pulling violently at his shoulders. "You're cutting off her air. Stop it. Stop it, Conn."

"I'm just putting her out so you can strap her down. There. Now take her quickly to the nearest *uuyvanoon*. Leave it dry, for God's sake. Then come back and get me."

While Tandra obeyed, he made his way down the passageway with maddening difficulty and climbed into an *uuyvanoon*.

Tandra returned and stood over him uncertainly. "Can I get anything for you, Conn," she said, hating the self-conscious timidity that plagued her. "Perhaps Killah has some medication."

"No, no," Conn said, closing his eyes.

"Conn, I've learned to love you—so much more than I could have before. The books . . . You are a magnificent, beautiful people. I——"

"You've done your homework at last," he said, not unkindly. "But it's too late for us now, Tandra. I need Orram—lots of time with Orram. Even the pool seems too empty. I destroyed Junah with cruel, bitter words because of us—because I was angry and frustrated with you. So *us* is gone. I can't be your pet lizard anymore. I never should have been. I can't sit up and bark; it just won't work. You know what I mean? You are man, and man has always seen himself as master. We both made the same kind of mistake, Tandra. You are too human for me. And now Junah . . ." He tore off his helmet, turned his face away from her, and sank into the warm water, letting it flool his lungs and ease the torment that shook his body.

Tandra closed the sleeping basin and stood looking down on Conn, her beloved elll, cradled in moss and sealed in water like a giant, tortured fetus. She would win his love again somehow. But now, she thought, the loner needed to school in the manner of fish, needed to mate in the manner of amphibians, needed to rollick in the manner of porpoises—and she would never again know his friendship on her own terms.

12
Encounter

Killah had no talent for what human psychologists might call healthy repression. Within the fluid, formless culture of his elllonian fathers, where passions rose and fell with their own impetus and washed over the life-essence of that mild green species to enrich its collective awareness, there was little need for self-delusion. And no need for tact. Hence Killah was unpracticed in the numb-minded arts required of human bureaucrats. As a result, when he talked to Midpacific Space Center about Jim Wright's condition he saved no adjectives in outlining the necessary surgical procedure, he drew precise though indelicate analogies to the tools he would use, and he presented the odds against error in judgment, technique, and the physical idiosyncrasies in Jim Wright's injured cranium to six places. His human audience was impressed, even awed, and ready to give him unanimous approval to do the operation—but then the television cameras were set up.

When the first transmission in living color reached Earth showing the competent elllonian doctor, his be-plumed assistants, and his array of unfamilar tools and support equipment, it was immediately cut off from public broadcasting "for reasons of national security"—and Killah was besieged with questions about elllonian life and technology. Jim Wright was completely forgotten.

Desperate over the loss of time, Killah called in Orram. His humanoid but strange appearance precipitated a new round of curiosity and fear in the human audience. On the Earth, contingency plans were immediately revised to include attack as well as defense.

It was only because Orram's rasping monotone was so unwavering and insistent that he was able eventually to pull the conversation back to the wounded astronaut.

Then the human beings began to question Killah's instruments and to debate his proposed technique; there was skepticism about Killah's skill. Finally they decided that Orram would be better suited to do the job, in spite of his explanation that he was a biophysicist not a practiced surgeon as Killah was. His objections did no good. Killah was gradually ignored as the questions were directed more often to the varok. Orram patiently redirected each question to the elll, but Killah's answers were largely unheard.

Carliano understood what was happening, was chagrined at the odd display of racism, and tried to be helpful. The astronaut Ted Bardeane was openly hostile. There was little doubt in Orram's mind now: he should have left the cameras on the *Dove*.

Hours passed and still the *Dove's* command at the Midpacific Space Center could not decide who would decide to allow the repair of the crushed skull that was endangering the brain of astronaut Jim Wright. They could not agree to let the aliens do what they could not in fact stop them from doing.

Killah could no longer contain his impatience. With heroic restraint he excused himself from the cameras; then he grabbed Tandra from watching his would-be patient, tore down the hall screaming "Do they really believe they have a choice?", pulled Tandra into the pool past an amazed Conn standing beside it, embraced her firmly, took her deep into the clear red water, remembered in time to tow her to the surface, and then unburdened his overloaded psyche on his human colleague with a torrent of ellonian anger.

"Never! Never never never have I ever—ever wasted so much valuable time," he screamed as he sliced furiously through the water around her. "Never—never in all my life have I ever sat on my ass with my feet in my mouth for so long. Sat on my ass and played word games while a normally conscious being lay blind to his own life, losing not just minutes, but hours, Tandra, hours and hours of consciousness. He's losing all that life while they sit around inventing circumlocutions to avoid making the decision to operate. Of all the unfathomable, cruel— You human beings have no sense of priority!" He slammed his hand down on the water where Tandra had been a second before. *"We'll* make the decision!!"

Tandra found Conn's eyes fixed steadily on her, probing as deep as he could. Did he think she would be offended by Killah's rage? She smiled wryly at him as Killah continued to tear up the pool, but he made no overt response. Behind him, she saw Ted Bardeane enter the room and watch Killah's tantrum with increasing horror.

"We ellls do not repress our emotions," Conn tried to explain. "We get them out and over with in—"

Bardeane turned away and ran from the room.

Suddenly Killah surfaced again and stopped ranting; he rolled onto his back to let the ruby warmth of the pool damp the quiver of his velvet hexagons. Then he leaped through the water to Tandra and placed a dry, lippy kiss on her nose. "Well, that's enough of that," he said with a broad smile, his mood already completely placid. "Let's return to the great debate. A good tantrum like that gets the venom out of the blood pools in a hurry, right?"

He boosted Tandra out of the pool and leaped onto the deck beside her, draping a stocky arm on her shoulders. "Swim, Conn?" he said to their sullen observer. "You missed the adjustment, and you're still unstable. You'd better take some vibes before you go back to the centrifuge."

"With Tandra? I had better not. I can't fake it." Then he hobbled drunkenly away.

"Conn," Tandra cried, but he walked on and disappeared into the hall.

"This will pass," Killah said softly. "Conn needs your love more than he realizes. Don't abandon him yet, eh Tandra?"

"Me? Abandon him?"

"You're not going to let pride have its way. We ellls

are a schooling organism, Tandra. It is difficult for
Conn to understand your feeling of alienation from your
own species. I think that is why he is still upset with
you. Now wipe the eyes. We have surgery to do, Midpacific or no Midpacific."

Conn made his way to Junah's room and sat beside
her. A wave of grief washed over him as he stared into
her great brown eyes. They were dull and empty.

"Junah? It's Conn. Junah?"

He sat near her for more than an hour, calling her
name and reaching toward her patch with his mind. It
was useless. There was no channel for his thoughts to
follow, and he was sickened by the continual spinning
of objects around him.

He went to the food center, trying to ignore his
injury, and prepared a softly textured meal. He would
feed her, exercise her, devote all his time to her cure.
He returned to her side and cautiously placed a small
amount of food in her mouth. If she refused it, the job
would be nearly hopeless; her survival instinct would be
too weak. The food lay suspended for a moment, but
then she began to chew mechanically. Finally she swallowed.

Conn made his way back to the food center with a
surge of hope. Tandra and Killah were there, eating
hurriedly.

"We're in for it now, Conn," Killah remarked acidly.
"They've made it clear that we are solely responsible for
Jim Wright's fate."

"That's the most accurate statement they've made
since we contacted them," Tandra said. She watched
Conn fumbling toward the fruit cupboard and a sharp
yearning welled up in her. "Conn, Artellian needs help.
His throat won't stand much more talk. Midpacific
insists on information from a reliable source, an 'elll of
authority.' Bardeane's got them all upset again."

Conn's body wavered as he tried to answer. "I'll be
with Junah," he said.

"You'll do Junah no good unless you do some time in the centrifuge first," Killah snorted.

"You don't look well, Conn," Tandra said.

"Don't tell me what to do," he snapped.

"*I'll* tell you what to do," Killah commanded. "Three hours a day in the centrifuge—minimum!"

"I'll help you with Junah as soon as we have operated on Jim Wright," Tandra said.

"Stay away from Junah," Conn warned and lurched through the door.

"Wright is losing more life-joy than Conn at the moment," Killah said. "Call Orram and meet me in the lab, Tandra. We'll set up our isolation booth within the quarantine room. Lock that madman Bardeane in the shower if you have to."

In the wake of Killah's decision to operate, Earth needed to be mollified. Midpacific raised such a series of threats and charges that Killah was forced to set up the television cameras in the isolation booth so that the human audience could monitor the surgery. Killah agreed to the compromise only when Artellian reminded him that their future influence with Earth was at stake. "We can't jeopardize all our chances for effective contact," Artellian had argued. "The more exposure we have the better."

In spite of the cameras, the operation was soon done. And when it was over Killah indulged in another elllonian temper tantrum to clear his head, for the tension generated by the skeptical astronauts and their bosses at Midpacific was more than he could absorb.

"Never—never again will I appear before those damn cameras of theirs. Orram and Conn can do the honors. No-thank-you! Forget old Kill the Doctor! They would have listened to a three-hour demonstration lecture on alien life while that man lay losing the precious minutes. Even after we promised them regular broadcasts, they continued to harass me with nonsensical questions. Proof indeed! Well, here I am, not proof enough: laying their astronaut's brain bare in alien quarantine on the moon with instrumentation they haven't dreamed up yet, and they don't want to believe it!"

Killah knew that Jim Wright would recover with no brain damage, for the repair had been successfully accomplished. But it was impossible to convince the human beings of the fact. They were determined to sit grim-faced for all the hours that it would take the astronaut to regain consciousness. Well, let them. Paranoids. Vulturous paranoids! Insisting that their *kaehldin* TV cameras focus on the grisly procedure. Miserable, frustrating beings.

But Jim Wright did not emerge into consciousness when Killah expected. Tandra became moderator between skeptical men and disdainful aliens. How easy and comfortable it was to assume that role—conversant to all and loyal to none but herself and her child—so different from the activist role she had discarded long ago, cynically and in defeat. This role would cost her nothing; her real tension was well hidden in the compromising, calm exterior.

Conn didn't like the role and he told Tandra so. To his surprise she agreed: "I would much rather take a position and watch Orram and Artellian demolish it than grease along like this," she said. "But it is not possible with men. Pride and money are always at stake; honest opinion hasn't a chance. Besides, Orram wants to go easy until Wright regains consciousness."

"Why isn't he conscious yet?"

"We don't know, but there should be no real danger; the EEG and mind probe are good."

"Somehow you seem more conscious now, Tandra."

"So you really *have* noticed. It is because the varoks prod me whenever I doze mentally. Ahl pursues every questionable inflection in my voice. I will never think like a varok, but I'm learning to question my first impressions." She cupped Conn's face tenderly in her hands. "We are in contact again, dear Conn. Can't we extend it?"

For a moment they tasted their old joy. Then Junah's specter rose to destroy it. "No," Conn said. "I don't know where to begin, Tandra. We'd just better leave each other alone. We would do more damage to someone." Reluctantly he turned away. "I must go to Junah."

* * *

In spite of the continuing medical debate concerning Jim Wright, Orram's regular telecasts were well received. By the time that the astronauts' required quarantine was completed, their immunizations pronounced successful, and their exposure to normal alien flora accomplished (after considerable human objection to the inclusion of the unconscious Jim Wright in such treatment), the world was well acquainted with Tandra's moderation, Artellian's rambling erudition, and Orram's bland, masterful composure. Human curiosity was surfacing from within the initial morass of fearful hate: once the appearance and intelligence of the ellls were accepted elllonian culture had a charming appeal. And after all, they had been on the moon over a century; they wouldn't be about to come down *en masse* now. That tall man (what's his name? Orlan?) is quite definite about that.

Orram underplayed his varokian heritage. The harder issues could be introduced once confidence was established.

"You mean once Wright comes to," Killah pointed out. "His lack of response would shake anyone's confidence. Still, our tests say he's okay." The ell admitted to no one but Tandra and Orram that he was worried. Wright should have showed signs of consciousness before now.

Carefully they considered more corrective surgery and rejected it until Wright's danger was clearly defined.

"We can't operate on him again just because political pressure dictates it," Killah said. "We rescued these astronauts for the sake of politics and look where we are—we now run the risk of being more demons than heroes in most eyes."

"I am very discouraged," Artellian agreed. "I have seen faith and an inclination toward trust in too few men. It may be that our efforts on behalf of man are quite useless."

* * *

Conn played little part in the televised conversations and cultural presentations. In fact, he played little part in anything but the attempt to revive Junah's sanity. As the weeks passed hope wore thin; Conn regained his health, but his spirit grew raw with fatigue and grief and estrangement from the school. Only his growing friendship with Carliano and his deepening dependence on Orram created enough joy in his life to maintain his elllonian wholeness. Then, like the precious gift of rain on a drought-stricken seedling, the news of Junah's first spoken words reached Conn.

He made his way quickly to her room, waved Erah away, and lay down beside Junah on her bed pad. Should he touch her? Would it help her or drive her deeper? Reality. Life seeks its own, doesn't it? He moved very close to her so that his entire body was in contact with hers. Then he murmured the words that she had said to Erah: "Orram's *alyakah* is Tandra. Junah is here. Junah minds Junah. Say it again. Orram's *alyakah* is Tandra. Junah is here. Once again, Junah. Say it again. It is true. Junah directs Junah." He stopped, nauseated with self-reproach. "I was wrong, Junah!" he cried. "Hear me! Orram will always love you as friend, a first friend, his best mate before his *alyakah*. *Alyakah* loves you too, Junah. I love you. I was wrong. I was bitter. I made you suffer for my pain. Conn was wrong. Conn says so. Conn knows it. Know it, too, Junah. *Ae-yul-l!* Junah come to me. Conn suffers."

He tightened his arms around her, and gradually, in warm, mysterious ways he could not know, his suffering penetrated Junah's wall against consciousness. She stirred in his arms and knew nothing but that she must comfort him.

"Conn. *Uuyvanoon,*" she said.

Conn leaped for the water inlet to an *uuyvanoon* and set it to half-fill. Then he supported Junah as she groped her way across the room and braced her as she stepped into the sleeping bowl. He followed her into the warm comfort and lay beside her, holding her head against his chest.

"Tell me your pain," Junah said with incredible effort, as she stroked the elll stiffly.

"O, *aeo-o!* Junah. Words are difficult for me. Read me, Junah."

"No, no. I cannot. Words, Conn," Junah said more easily, as her full consciousness and some control began to reemerge.

"I have too much to sort out," Conn said. "I loved Tandra. She was special to me. But she would not know me as I am. She refused to know me. I begged her to know that we were elll, but she saw me as a humanoid pet. The shock in her face when she understood about the eggs, Junah! *Aeyull!* I knew then that she would hate me for being such a creature. God, I'm a creature that eats its own eggs, a creature that mates only for pleasure. They care so much for mating, these human beings. They care more for how things are done than why they are done. I hate her, Junah; at times I hate her for her humanness. And I hate her all the more because I love her and want her—for what I don't know—and I am jealous of every moment Orram spends with her, every moment that he can accept her for what she is—whatever that is—and I can't."

"Jealous, Conn? That is not an elllonian emotion." The comment was perfectly normal, but Conn did not notice.

"Yes, jealous. A goddam, sonofabitch, human emotion that no sane elll has any business feeling. What an irony, eh? I'm a mutant, Junah, a loner. And I'm forced to watch myself indulge in a *human* emotion! I blame Tandra for making me feel jealousy and personal desire. Yet I know it's not her fault. I hate her prejudices and love her closeness and ease, and I am bitter that she refused to know me. How can I sort this out? I might as well be varok. I'm just a mass of emotion—not rational at all."

The word *rational* jolted him, and he sat up to look at Junah. The amused glint in her eyes told him that she had returned to a natural, controlled sanity. Great crystal green tears boiled up in his eyes as she smiled at him and accepted his prolonged, intense embrace.

"No one could stay repressed under the onslaught of language like that," she said. "I don't know what sonof-asomething means or many of the others, but the flavor is unmistakable. I must find Orram, now. Where is my robe?"

Conn didn't wait to help her. He ran from the room and with an ear-shattering whoop that soared into the humans' ultrasonic range burst into the pool room— where the crew and the astronauts now spent much of their time—and threw himself against Orram, Tandra, and Artellian, tumbling them all into the water. Then, wild with joy, he leapt out of the pool and shouted down at them, "Junah's back. She made it. I got her back." With that he dove on top of Orram in an embrace that took them both to the bottom of the pool.

In stark contrast to his entrance, Junah walked quiet-ly into the large room, a beautiful silver and brown goddess, commanding and statuesque. She accepted the welcome of the jubilant ellls with controlled pleasure as her mild dark eyes searched, then found Orram climbing out of the pool. He approached her, question-ing, measuring with silent probes, until their forearms met and their fingers slowly interlaced, growing strained in each other's firm grasp. Then—surrounded by silence and a roomful of tense, watchful ellls, two bewildered humans, and one silent man awaiting consciousness in his chair—they sought a solution to their relationship. The pool room breathed with them and waited, while they spoke without words:

"Dreams repressed. Now forgotten," Orram's patches read from Junah.

"Admiration. Friend," Junah read from him.

"Yes. And no longer mate."

"Erah?"

"Not necessary."

"But your need?"

"Partial consummate release with Tandra. Unex-plained."

"And your physical desire?"

"Denied. Complications for Tandra."

"Tandra loves you."

"Yes, but far too well. Exaggerated admiration."

"Which you deserve. Her view of you: very little distortion."

"Consummation implies imposed alienation from Earth."

"Her choice. Make it possible," Junah insisted.

"No. Other cultural factors operable. Pressure too great to impose."

"You are too protective. She is strong now. She gives you partial release? How can that be?"

"Unexplained. Still uncontrolled. And she is unaware of her ability. It occurs with close contact."

"Then consummation is possible?"

"Perhaps."

"You savor her touch."

"You have known that."

"Settled! I desire your happiness. You will never consummate with anyone else now."

"Junah! Do not force her! Do not tell her. It is too much to ask."

Junah smiled, dropped Orram's hands, and approached Tandra. Taking Tandra's arm in her hands, she pressed it against Orram's. A hushed murmur traveled through the ellls. They pressed around Tandra and Orram now, and a chant began. Slowly at first, it gradually gained momentum, then broke into a varokian melody. Artellian tried to stop it, and Orram shook his head, denying the demand, but with hesitation. That hesitation was enough to drive the ellls on. The tempo of their song suddenly increased, and they began to stamp insistently.

Tandra was completely bewildered. Surely not the *Vrankah*. The ellls wouldn't demand that of Orram.

Suddenly, Orram's hesitation was gone. His feet joined in the syncopated beat of the ellls' stamping and his hands began to tell a story with the flowing varokian melody. Or was it an invitation? The meaning became more clear as Tandra watched his hands talking to her, inviting her to come to Varok or to him or to both. Without volition her feet began to move with Orram's and her hands retold his message. They danced in unison then, the flowing movements of their arms contrasting with the changing hard beat pronounced by their steps.

When the story was told, the invitation complete, the carved mahogany varok and the shadowed, soft woman stood locked in mutual awareness.

"And Junah?" Tandra asked.

"She has reemerged into a state of mature reason," Orram said.

The music continued then with a slower beat as the two astronauts watched the ellls dance. Some moved with familiar human steps, distorted and extended by the moon's light gravity; others cavorted in the angular style of their own species, which took them into the water more often than not. Tllan passed trays filled with fermented elllonian fruit and rich, dark nuts. A celebration was in full swing, but no one was sure why.

Bardeane watched with growing disgust. It seemed to him unpardonable that the ellls should exhibit such joy while Jim Wright sat like a vegetable, destroyed by them.

"I'm getting Wright out of here," he snapped. "They're sick. They don't give a damn for him. He needs rest."

He started to wheel Wright from the silenced room when a distinct groan of protest emerged from the medical chair.

Killah leaped toward his patient and shoved Bardeane aside. "Make another sound if you are conscious, and we'll really celebrate!" he shouted.

Obediently Wright mumbled "Sound" and managed a weak smile at the sight of this weird green character who seemed so interested in his recovery.

The celebration broke into full bloom then and the television cameras were brought in to record and announce the event. Indeed, as Wright emerged into full consciousness, he responded to his alien benefactors with such an infectious, intellectual joy that he inadvertently boosted Artellian and Orram's TV ratings. Confidence on Earth grew, and it was decided that the astronauts should stay at base several more weeks.

Now that Junah was fully recovered, Tandra hoped to reestablish some contact with Conn. She tried bringing tapes to him, she invited him to school, she even approached his *uuyvanoon*—but he refused her with strange, mixed messages: "I don't have to stay here for anyone," or "All I give you is pain," or "I can't mean what we ought to mean, like Orram."

Killah insisted that Conn join the school so they wouldn't have to readjust to his absence. He tried, finally, but had little success; essentially he remained estranged from it. He voluntarily approached no one but Orram and Carliano. The astronaut became a substitute for Tandra—another accepting, open mind who loved life and relished experimental sound as she had.

Orram, meanwhile, had as little success bringing Conn closer to Tandra as he had had earlier trying the reverse. But his psychic link with Tandra seemed to grow stronger and stronger.

"Tandra, during the celebration last week we danced a kind of *Vrankah,* during which you were tracking me, and I, you." He offered her a wet-sweater from off the wall of the pool room as the base crew sat down to eat. "It is a much more specific function than mood-reading. The fact that you accomplished it so readily indicates that your potential may be considerably more extensive than the varokian. Do you understand what I am telling you? This is extremely important, this tracking that you have done. If the men should question you, please tell them it's a dance, a game we invented."

"Some game," Conn said drunkenly from behind Orram, his mouth crammed with rich, potent fruit. "You're treading on thin ice in more ways than one, M. Ramahlak. You seem to assume that Dr. Grey here is one of us. She is not approved for security information, you know. You were talking about tracking—direct spinal communication—right?"

"I have told her no specifics, Conn. You should know that I have good reason to trust her entirely. You would do well to rediscover that yourself."

Conn's brow deepened and he dropped his head. "You'd better shit or get off the pot, man."

"Don't be ugly, Conn," Orram said.

"What do you mean, Conn?" Tandra asked. "Take those berries out of your mouth. You're drunk."

"Leave-me-entirely-alone!" Conn hissed, grabbing Tandra's wrists fiercely. "Everything you vomit is a command. You have learned nothing."

"Release her!" Orram shouted. "You are irrational."

Conn backed away at the sound of Orram's command. "They didn't put all the details into those books you read. Varoks can't forever walk a tightrope between rationality and subjective horsecrap. And they can't afford to play around with emotion, especially sensual emotion, as much as he has lately. I'm not talking about the kind of crack-up Junah had. I'm talking about sex and—"

"There is nothing more that Tandra needs to know about it, Conn."

"First myself, then Junah, and now Orram. How many of us are you going to destroy before you leave here, Tandra?" Conn strode unsteadily away from them toward the pool.

Tandra did not need to look at Orram to know that he shared her bewilderment. "Surely I haven't been the cause of destroying you," she said.

"Remember that he is elll, Tandra. His emotions vacillate wildly and quickly. Conn is suffering from some very mixed feelings toward you, and he is dramatizing my danger."

They joined hands and followed Conn, passing the astronauts, who stood watching them with a variety of expressions on their faces. Ted Bardeane rose to stop them. "What is this?" he demanded.

"What is what?"

"This!" he shouted, knocking Tandra's hand from Orram's grasp. "I've seen enough. First that dance and now this. You represent man here by whoring with aliens. You degrade us all."

"I have done nothing to shame anyone. Man degrades himself; he doesn't need any help from me."

"God, I should have known. You're a stabilist!"

"A what?"

"You know damn well! Are you a stabilist or not? What side do you take?" Bardeane shouted.

"What is a stabilist?"

"Hold it, Ted," Jim Wright said. "How long have you been at this moon base, Dr. Grey?"

"Almost five months."

"And have you had any news from Earth lately?"

"Very little. My life has been—focused in other directions."

"Yes. I understand. Our focus has also changed since we have been here."

"Don't tell me you don't know about the stabilists!" Bardeane said. "They have gone *wild*. They don't care how they get their way now."

"Let me explain," Wright interrupted. "The stabilists are, in effect, a revolutionary party, demanding that all economic and population growth must stop immediately. They are desperate in this belief; they are completely out of patience with any attempt at rationalization. There have been increasing numbers of industrial bombings and two assassinations. That's the lengths to which they are willing to go. The situation is extremely dangerous now, for the people of many countries are divided nearly equally on the stop-growth issue."

Another rare silence settled over the pool room as the ells surfaced to listen. Killah exchanged a knowing look with Orram. The conversation was leading toward a confirmation of the impressions they had gained from their first experiences with the society of human beings. The astronauts' first fearful reactions, the interference with the operation, the moon-base broadcasts so easily misinterpreted—all led to the same conclusion: man was not ready to listen to a strange voice.

"The position you take in this controversy, Dr. Grey,

could have significant influence," Carliano said thoughtfully.

"Isn't it clear what her position is already!?" Bardeane exploded.

"I am interested in *no* one's position but my own and Shawne's," Tandra said.

"You write off man very easily!" Conn said.

"Man has written *me* off!" The conversation had not mattered much before Conn entered it. Now Tandra's voice and body shook with an undefined emotion. "The solutions are clear, Conn, the limits are defined; but men still fight and claw for profit—and they leave nothing. Your pool may be the last clear water Shawne will ever see, the stars from here, the last stars. And there is nothing I can do to stop them."

"So they're stupid or greedy. I can't follow their thinking. But it's no reason for hate."

"They are tearing apart Shawne's life, Conn. How can you blame me? I don't want to teach her survival tactics. I want her to live with beauty. Because of them, I'll have to teach her to accept horror. God, I don't know, maybe to eat corpses!"

Suddenly Orram's cool, steady hands covered Tandra's tight grip on Conn's arm. "You care too much," he said to them both. "It is misplaced. Anger does not dissolve hate, nor should hate replace anger."

"So that's your game," Bardeane said to Tandra. "You'll choose no side because you don't have to. You'll sit around up here in pink bathtubs with your damned survival instincts while the rest of us fight it out!"

"Yes, we probably will," Orram said. "It has become clear since we contacted you: in the end we will have no other choice. There is nothing we can do if man chooses an irrational course."

"But where is the *rational* course?" Wright asked, with an admonishment in his voice more analytical than Bardeane's. "The stakes are very large. No man can escape. His choices affect every aspect of his life, sometimes in opposing ways."

"Yet you see it in terms of battle!" Tandra said with an old familiar grief tightening her voice. "You have no capacity for political accommodation, much less economic compromise. You can't imagine gearing production to the return of materials or restricting yourselves to local resources. You don't think man could survive without all his powered contraptions. He couldn't possibly walk to work or have fewer children or live in simpler homes! You refuse to see that man must do with less of everything or he will soon have nothing—certainly not a life worth living!"

13
Beyond Love

While scientists on the blue planet Earth grew more frantic for details of the aliens, for explanations of their origin, for assurances that a full exchange of technical information was forthcoming, for detailed plans to return the astronauts to Earth; and while Tallyn and Bardeane confronted each other over priorities in human values and the God-given rights of all living things ("Obviously I, too, am animal only, Bardeane," Tallyn said)—Bob Carliano and Conn spent their time together with Conn's sound equipment in the recreation lounge.

"How does that translate?" Conn asked, as he fed his ultrasonic tape into the low frequency generator.

Carliano listened to the rich music for a moment and shook his head slowly. "It's wild—but beautiful. You've combined some of the best styles from all three planets."

"I'll leave this one alone then. Do you want to take a duplicate tape back with you? No regulations against cultural exchange. I'll copy this onto one of Tandra's old tapes. They'd probably confiscate our tape for chemical analysis and ruin my music."

"They'd confiscate a lot more than that, if they could."

"You sound like Tandra," Conn complained, suddenly angry.

"What's the problem between you and her? You pick at everything you can find. She's no different than the rest of us."

"That's half the problem."

"She loves you like a brother."

"That's the other half of the problem. I'm not human."

"She's beyond that now," Carliano said. "I know what she went through. She's spent a lot of time with me trying to explain what happened. She knows you're elll. Good grief, how could she miss? I still lay awake nights trying to believe you're real! And what a shock you give me every morning! Real honest-to-God alien intelligence! Every nerve in my brain wants to pull back and deny it. 'No,' they said, 'I am Man, the image of God. This elll is only imitation.'

"Once in a while we get a glimpse of the stars and we know that the probability of life on some planet out there has got to be high—and still we come home believing we're God's great gift to the universe. Think what we're exposed to all our lives: The moon! Hooray! We've done it again! 'Man, the king of Earth, now prince of the heavens,' a pope once called us. Can you blame us for being a bit nearsighted? We'll no doubt go over the cliff with head held high, breeding like mad, proud of our humanity to the end. We're *all* products of this incredible no-think. It takes time to adjust. Tandra fled into romantic identity with you. Don't blame her. She's grown out of it now, and I'm getting there slowly." He paused and looked squarely into Conn's wide eyes. "Bardeane will never make it though. He still sleeps with a knife under his pillow."

"And Jim?"

"That guy is like a machine. He's had his nose in all the books Artellian could dig up. It's just an intellectual exercise for him. No sweat."

"Have you told Llorkin all this?"

"We couldn't get rid of him for the first few weeks. Yes, he's got it all down in red and white. He seems more convinced than ever that rescuing us was a mistake."

"We'll probably never know," Conn said, "but we're in it now—with a sizable audience guaranteed when we deliver you to Midpacific."

Carliano was silent for a moment. "You're not planning to land the *Lurlial* in public?"

"I assumed we would. So far we've been received rather well."

"But why sacrifice yourselves?" Carliano asked. "You wouldn't enjoy living in the Bronx Zoo."

"You mean that, don't you?" Conn laughed. "You'll never catch an elll indulging in martyrdom."

"Then don't take any chances when you take us back. Don't announce our return. Set us down on an island somewhere. We can salvage signal devices and survival gear from the *Dove*. There are influential characters who would go to any extreme to get some alien material to study—or to sell. And there are nuts at all levels determined to blow the alien menace out of the sky before it attacks. Then there's always those bureaucrats determined to enhance their national prestige by getting a piece of you before the other guys do. Need I go on? I'm serious."

Conn's eyes narrowed. "Perhaps we've been a bit naïve and sloppy in our thinking lately. Let's go talk to Artellian."

Because the base Directorate decided that there could indeed be substantial risk in landing on Earth in public, Carliano's suggestion was adopted. The *Lurlial* made a side trip to the downed lunar craft at Straight Wall, retrieved its survival gear, traveled in minimal time to Earth, and simply deposited the astronauts on a remote corner of an island not too far from Midpacific Space Center.

Conn listened as the astronauts made radio contact with their colleagues at Midpacific:

"What in hell do those coordinates mean, Carliano?"

"They mean we're sitting in the middle of someone's pineapple plantation waiting for a pick-up."

"What do you mean 'pick-up'? Aren't the aliens bringing you in?"

"No. They had a previous engagement, Midpacific."

"You can't let them go. You've got to bring them in."

"They're awfully shy," Carliano said.

"Where are they now? Where are they?"

"About one hundred metres straight up, I'd guess, Midpaf, but——"

"What are they doing? Why aren't they bringing you in?"

"They've got strong survival instincts, Midpaf. Radio contact established, Conn. You'd better bug off."

A new voice broke in like the crack of a whip. "Hold them there, Carliano. That's an order. Midpacific security, scramble jets. We can't let them get away."

"Hey, wait a minute. When do we get a pick-up?" Carliano yelled.

The *Lurlial* disappeared into the sky above the ocean, leaping in a great arc toward the North American continent.

"Where the hell are you taking us, Orram?" Conn hollered. "We're not making orbit."

"I don't intend to go into orbit. Artellian picked us as crew for this trip so we would have some time to relax together. He hoped we could resolve our relationships before we returned to base."

"More likely we'll *dis*solve them."

"Just that, Conn. Your humor turns the air sour around you. Where is the source of life-joy that usually emanates from your feathered brain, *aloon?* You're still not adjusted to the school without Ellalon. I suggest that we land in the Rockies, somewhere in the high country. It is June. Most of the snow should be gone now. Junah, what do you think? Tllan? You're least involved. Tandra? Llorkin? Shawne?"

"Let us risk it," Junah said.

Llorkin and Tllan and the child nodded in agreement.

"It should be beautiful there now," Tandra murmured.

"A bit cool for lizards, but I'm game," Conn said.

Orram intercepted from Tandra the crest of a painful wave. "Then it's agreed."

He and Conn headed the *Lurlial* toward a small, isolated basin somewhere southwest of Denver and expended a good deal of energy maneuvering their ship between its steep rocky slides.

The basin cradled a fragile pool of icy water which was collared with the delicate greens and yellows of alpine flowers and marsh grasses. The morning sun skipped lightly over the deep blue of the lake and glanced sharply off the *Lurlial* as it touched the soft brown earth carpeted with needles of fir and pine and spruce. Soon several green and brown figures emerged from the belly of the pregnant bat and began dressing her in a comouflage of snow and pine boughs. Then, drinking in the hot sun and the crisp thin air of the high Rockies, Conn and Tandra, Tllan, Llorkin and Junah lay on the snow-dappled edge of the sky blue lake and watched the changeless rim of rock that surrounded them capture and release white puffs of clouds. While Shawne chattered on with endless questions about the scattered snow banks and pine cones and tiny flowers, Orram improvised a sled from the *Lurlial's* galley equipment and spent more than an hour tumbling up and down a small snow bank with the baby.

"It is so beautiful here," Junah murmured when Orram finally sat beside her to recover his breath. "Reminds me of home. How long can we stay?"

"We have provisions for ten days. We can stay here for eight if we're not discovered."

Conn stretched his long legs and absent-mindedly traced the hexagonal patterns on his skin with his forefinger as he watched Tllan toss bits of snow into the freezing water.

"*Aeo-o!* Look!" she said. A small rabbit-like animal suddenly appeared from behind a pile of rocks at the far end of the lake and darted across the meadow. "Is that a rabbit?"

"I think it's a cony," Tandra whispered.

"Looks delicious," Conn growled, throwing out his tongue full length.

"Conn, you scared it away," Tllan protested.

He ignored her exasperation. "Come on. Let's go for a swim."

"No, you beast," she said. "Do you know how cold that water is?"

"No water could be that cold. In we go, *leel. La*

oon!" All at once, clasping her with his legs, he took her deep into the lake.

A moment later the surface of the water boiled and trembled, then explored with the thrashing of struggling ellls. Orram jumped up and watched with alarm as Tllan attacked Conn, thrusting the hard tips of her stiffened fingers into his groin. He sank, and the girl glided to the edge of the lake, accepting Orram's hand and stammering furiously, "I—I'm not going to be used as a—a depository for his problems in that freezing water." She strode to the *Lurlial* and soon came out again dressed in a warm varokian robe and slacks. Conn had not yet surfaced.

"He can't take that cold much longer," Tandra said. Before Orram could stop her, she stepped out of her own warm suit and dove into the icy lake.

Deep in the crystal water Conn was doubled up with his head clasped between his knees, convinced that he must be experiencing every kind of pain known to the elllonian mind. In vain he tried to shut it out. Tllan's rejection—a rejection he had never experienced before —compounded his self-recrimination, and that, together with the maddening, unresolvable emotions he felt toward Tandra, triggered a death-wish. His mind was beginning to close upon itself when he felt Tandra's firm grasp around his neck and shoulders. He did not resist as she towed him to shore, supported him with Orram's help in a bowed limp to the *Lurlial,* and bedded him into an *uuyvanoon.*

Warmth crawled over Conn's body, and he felt the pressure of something else enter his water. At first he knew only love—then Tandra. Here in his water. He pulled a large volume of the soothing liquor into his lungs, and at last, as she massaged his dangerously cooled body, he was able to savor the awareness of life again.

"You're treating me like an elll," he whispered in a water-logged lilt.

For a long while she massaged him, until he finally nestled underwater against one of her breasts and cupped the other in his palm, muttering something about elllonian women not coming equipped with pillows. Soon he was asleep.

When Llorkin found them a few minutes later, he gasped and stared and then rushed off to write in his piles of plastic. Orram looked in, smiled broadly, and went on. Almost an hour later Tllan passed the room. Tandra called quietly to her, "Ease Conn's head off of me, will you, Tllan? I'm wrinkling up like a prune in this warm water."

Tllan slipped her hand beneath Conn's head and lifted it gently as Tandra slipped out of the basin. Together they walked into the hall.

"How could you go to his water, Tandra?" Tllan said. "He has been disgusting—and especially unkind to you. Of course, Llorkin has failed to reach him, and the ellls at base have done all that they could. He has refused to join in the adjustment since Ellalon. The pool isn't enough for him anymore; he's been indulging his loner tendencies too much."

"Is it fair to call it indulging? Conn extends himself very far as an individual: he went beyond normal elllonian limits with me and Orram and with Bob Carliano; then he was able to reach Junah's mind when no one else could. Are all loners like that, Tllan?"

"I suspect so. No one knows yet."

"Unusual, antisocial individuals like Conn would not be easily accepted if such mutations appeared in human society," Tandra said. "And of course ellls would not be accepted. Bob Carliano was right. You would be put in a zoo—your wit, your intelligence, your elllonian emotions cause only for amusement or scorn."

"Orram thought you were no longer so bitter," Tllan said uneasily. "Lately you have been more in tune with life. You are so accepting, so full of awe. Now you seem to speak with hate."

"It comes in waves. I hate what I am. I hate myself for the way I let man's concern for money and convenience make me live. I no longer *want* to be man." Tandra's voice grew suddenly tighter. "Why should I take Shawne back into their fouled nest? That's what they made of Paradise. They took Eden and didn't rest until they had made Hell of it. Well, you can have your Hell, mankind! And may you rot in terror with it!"

Suddenly a fin grabbed Tandra's shoulders, whirling her around as another flew hard across her cheek, knocking her against the *Lurlial's* moss-hung wall. Conn stood over her, his face distorted with rage and stained with tears. He shook violently as he fought to control himself. "Will you ever stop thinking of yourself!? You *are* man! You and Bardeane—you're just the same!"

The words tore at Tandra, but she said nothing.

Conn turned away, his prehensile fin held limp.

Orram had watched the entire encounter. He immediately followed after Conn. "You have hurt her more with your words than with your fin. What you have said is not true."

"What do words matter? She didn't even flinch."

"You want her to be like a varok? She is somewhere between us, Conn. Sometimes hidden and repressed like a varok, sometimes open and volatile like ellls. Remember, we are all imperfect, and more or less reprehensible, in unique ways: in the ellls' insistence on sensual expression, in the varok's susceptibility to emotion, in the human beings' need for individual uniqueness and cultural inviolability. Are you going to make the same mistake she made? Can you love her as human?"

Conn's eyes widened with understanding as the concept walked through his mind. "I don't know. God! Orram, I really don't know."

During the long, free days by the pine-scented mountain lake the elll, the varok, and the human being searched for the keys to the loner's mind—with little success; Conn remained incoherent under a load of unfamiliar emotions that most ellls would ask the school to share rather than carry alone.

In the evenings Conn, Tllan, and Llorkin would climb into one *uuyvanoon* and school as best they could until Shawne and Junah would ask them to join in playing varokian children's games. Tandra and Orram reserved that time for themselves. They walked together at sun-

set enjoying the changing light, discovering small creatures and plants along the shore of the lake, and exploring the frontier where their minds seemed to meet.

One evening as Orram gently probed the resistance of
Tandra's mind she tried to open it to him—and finally
succeeded. He gasped with the sensation of falling into
the abyss of her consciousness. He pulled back hard to
regain his equilibrium and finally settled himself on its
periphery as an observer. From that moment they found
words unnecessary.

In the open moments beneath the pine trees, Orram
bathed deeper and deeper in the tides of Tandra's consciousness, finding not only love there, but much to love
—and more: Tentatively at first, then with growing
sureness, her fund of reason while he lowered himself
into the dark caverns of his own emotional potential.
First, his annoyance with Conn; then deeper frustration
with the elll; then intense desire to see him reconciled
with Tandra. Yes. He could bring himself back out of
it. No loss of reason. As with Ellalon's death, he could
experience emotion and maintain control. "Tandra," he
exclaimed ecstatically, silently, "what an incredible experience!" There was no answer, only a slight surge of
positive mood, which Orram incorrectly interpreted as
awareness on Tandra's part that she had given him her
mind.

Tandra, for her part, never realized that she succeeded in opening her mind so well. She felt nothing.
And it did not occur to her to probe the varok's willing
mind in turn. How would one do such a thing? It was
unthinkable.

Conn watched his relationship with deep concern for
Orram. He sensed the varok's strong desire to joint
Tandra's mind, and he knew that that desire, which for
varoks normally implied sensual sharing as well, was
pitted against Orram's resolution to deny himself such
sharing with Tandra. Orram's fear of imposing himself
on her was as strong as that desire. Few ellls knew, as
Conn did, that such emotional denial in a varok could
manifest itself physically—that involuntary muscles
could act in direct opposition to those controlled by

emotions, resulting in excruciating pain such as that suffered by a panicked woman in the labor of childbirth.

So it was with Orram. In ever more frequent waves the force of his determination to leave Tandra untouched drove against his desire to lose himself in her yielding mind, until suddenly, on their sixth walk in the mountain's crisp beauty, he could contain his desire no longer; and his conviction paid the price of pain.

He had taken her hand as they left the *Lurlial,* and their forearms met accidentally as they both reached to examine a perfectly shaped pine cone lying in a snowbank. Laughing, they struggled for possession of the cone, until Tandra won it and raced for their favorite tree to bury it in the soft bed of pine needles. Orram ran after her, grabbed her around the waist as she knelt down, pulled her over and back on the soft ground, then lay quietly beside her, reluctant to let her go, knowing he must. Suddenly, he was contorted with a spasm of pain. He doubled up and writhed away from her, his face contorted with agony. He uttered no sound.

Tandra sat up and grasped his shoulders. "Orram, what's wrong? Orram?"

For many seconds he could not make his voice work as the pain tore through his groin. Finally, he forced breath from his throat: "A moment. I will be all right."

"No, no you won't. You're in terrible pain. I can see it."

"*Aeyah,* Tandra." His mind leaned into hers and his emotion found expression as he groaned with pain and humiliation. "We're fragile, we varoks. I have no strength for you."

"Orram, it's senseless to suffer so." As she spoke, she placed her forearm against his and her words began to melt the denial that tore at his body. "No accusations can hurt me."

"So you know," Orram groaned.

"I look for nothing beyond us here. Let me love you."

"*Alyakah,* my Tandra," he said, and the joy of conscious passion swept him out of the stranglehold of pain into full, welcome release as their bodies sought and found each other in easy acceptance.

For a long while they lay in their conjugal embrace—the varok's mind open and expectant, but unprobed; the human's contented with giving a moment's help, expecting nothing more—until they felt the cold air attack them. Then, shivering happily, they dressed each other and huddled beneath the pine tree watching the stars grow brighter in the deepening night.

Like most ellls, Llorkin functioned best when he was involved with a group. So it was natural that he should make his belabored pronouncement while the *Lurlial's* passengers were all together in the galley, relaxing with a meal of bitter-sweet varokian fruit and chewy, dried *kaehl*. "After some deliberation," he announced, "I have formulated my recommendation to Director Artellian that Dr. Grey terminate her service with us now."

Tandra started.

"There are several reasons," Llorkin continued. "It is certainly most logical and efficient. It would save us another trip to Earth when Dr. Grey's period of service was to have ended. There is no reason for her to return to base. Her microbiological work is largely done, and Shawne is here. Since further contact with Earth is pointless, further discussions with Dr. Grey on how best to aid in such a contact are also pointless."

Shawne, Tandra thought. At least they could keep Shawne.

Junah interrupted: "The fertility tests have not been completed. They are very important."

"I have received communication from Generalist Killah," Llorkin said dryly. "Another human egg has been fertilized, and eight divisions have been observed."

"Orram! Tandra!" Tllan jumped up with excitement. "There may be a chance!"

"Whoopee," Conn grunted.

"I, too, regard it as tragic," Llorkin said. "It can only confuse and encourage an already complex relationship between Master Ramahlak and Dr. Grey. Another reason for my proposing an immediate termination of Dr. Grey's services is that her personality has involved two of our directors in disturbing, indeed, disrupting, affairs. Her continued presence is detrimental to the mental serenity of Conn and the physical and mental health of M. Ramahlak."

"Horseshit," Conn muttered.

"I have good reason to believe that M. Ramahlak is in an irreconcilable position. You, yourself, have expressed concern for his health, G. Conn. In the interest of the base I recommend that Dr. Grey be returned to her home immediately."

"And I propose that she be offered a staff position at the base with full rights under the EV Dictate," Junah said without emotion. "She has been invaluable to us as a microbiologist and social critic, and her broad insight into the human situation is essential to our most effective handling of Earth's continued education."

"Terrific," Conn said. "You went nuts for Orram less than four weeks ago, and now you want to keep Tandra around forever."

"Conn, don't be foolish," Tandra said.

"Don't call me a fool!" he screamed, the words tearing through Tandra like a cold chisel.

Suddenly Junah stood before Conn and extended her hands to him.

He was startled by her intimate invitation. Timidly he grasped her fine brown hands and waited while her patches read the tone of his mind and tasted the flavor of his emotions. He tried to hide it from her, but it was useless.

"Don't misplace your concern, Conn," Junah said. "I no longer grieve for what I know could never be, but you are grieving—a strange, longing grief, mixed with anger. Why, Conn? Why are you grieving? Orram is no longer in danger. He and Tandra are mated."

Conn jumped to his feet and faced Orram, his eyes narrowed and wild. "When?" he demanded. "How do you know, Junah?"

The galley fell silent while his furious question reverberated harshly. Then his brow deepened with regret. He touched Orram's shoulder, "I'm sorry. Forgive me," he said, and left the room.

"Conn!" Tandra called and followed him.

"So this is how you get your free ride off Earth."

"Conn, will you listen to me?"

"No. You listen to me! What do you care of me?! Do I go on watching you with Orram, loving you both, yet cut off because I can't sniff brain waves? Our minds mated once, too, Tandra—mated in music and foolish star-games. But that's not enough. I live by touch. Where do we fit in? Are we isolated, we ellls, alone in this solar system with two identical mammalian species, wagging our tails and hoping for a few scraps from your table? Do we have to watch a universal mating from the sidelines, yearning for a communion we can never share? Go home, Tandra! For God's sake, go home to Earth and quit tormenting me."

He turned away into his room, his tortured desire etching his face with skewed ridges as his emotion battled his enraged intellect for supremacy.

Then, a moment later, the boiling emotions were gone. He turned back to the hall, expecting to find Tandra still there, waiting for him to invite her back into his life—but she was gone.

When Tandra rejoined the others in the control room, Llorkin was repeating his views into the communicator. "I have therefore concluded that Dr. Grey should be returned to her home immediately."

Tandra heard Artellian's voice emerge loudly from the central unit. "Is Tandra there? I would like to talk with her about this."

"First let me make this counter-proposal," Junah said. "I believe that Llorkin's premises are exaggerated, and that Tandra is needed as advisor in human affairs and as bacteriologist. I propose that she be offered a staff position with EV Science. I will have the case ready for presentation as soon as we arrive back at base."

The others made room for Tandra by the communications center. "Yes, Artell?"

"What do you think? Do you want to go home now, Tandra?"

"I have no home. But I don't understand what is happening to Conn, and I have done nothing to simplify life for Orram. Perhaps Llorkin is right."

"The choice is yours, Tandra. I can't guarantee that you will be given an EV position, but I'm sure that Junah will make a formidable case."

"The original purpose of my visit to base has been accomplished," Tandra said, as if detached. "Contact has been made."

"Agree!" boomed Tallyn's voice from the speaker. "If care for Earth, you will return. Knowledge of us needed there. Go now. Otherwise you look to us too much, work on more emotions and never go."

"Exactly exactly exactly," shouted Llorkin. "She will precipitate Orram's emotional demise—aggravate Conn's neurotic trauma."

"I assume that you can substantiate those charges," Artellian said. "Tandra?"

"Orram?" Tandra looked to the varok for help.

Her eyes were very dark and brilliant, but too full and difficult. "I want you to stay," Orram thought, sure that he was telling her since his mind was yielding, completely open to her expected probing. Then in soft sandpaper words he said, "Why try to change what you cannot change? Why project yourself on the world—when you hate to—when you feel you will be trying to make impossible what you know is already inevitable?"

Tandra understood his words as a challenge to her integrity—kinder than Conn's but just as direct. She failed to recognize the open blueness of his eyes, to see into his mind. There was no choice. "I'll have to return," she said, her throat tight and unwilling.

Orram nodded. He was sure that Tandra had read his desire and had rejected it. Apparently, he had assumed too much. Though she had opened her mind to him, she was not varokian, merely accepting; loving, surely, but driven essentially by intellectual needs and desire for growth. He had imposed on her far too much. He would say no more.

The crystal blue depths of Orram's eyes finally let Tandra go, and she felt the impact of that release as surely as she felt the estrangement from Conn. Abruptly, she turned to speak into the communicator. "I would like never to leave you, Artellian. I would like too well to forget everything but you; so I better go back now—immediately."

14
Earth

She sank back to Earth only half-conscious of herself and everything around her, knowing what she must do, knowing it would stop nothing. But being swallowed up again by the man-dominated planet was much worse than she had expected. The tiresome gray-black sky above, the concrete beneath, the dull, matched buildings closed in on her, shuttering her in so that escape to silence and beauty seeemed hopeless. Even the pines were gray. Where was the crystal blue of her childhood? "Remember the Milky Way, Shawne? From the observation deck it spilled across the sky like fairy dust." How could she keep these memories alive in the child? There at base you knew what you were made of—what you were a part of.

But what was she a part of here? The faces around Tandra were pale and strange. The eyes were blank and difficult to read. The ears were large and pink, apparently used only for pulling and scratching and hanging things on.

She searched her mirror for some clue to her identity. She was undeniably one of the creatures called man, but the vision in the glass was more alien than the shadowy ghosts of Conn and Orram staring at her with unseeing eyes from the television screen.

She soon stopped watching their presentations. The loneliness they accented was far too painful.

She sought out Jesse Mendleton and found some relief with him. At least he understood her concern for Shawne. Already the child was becoming indifferent to the life around her; she was beginning to assume that she should have all the manufactured accoutrements that the others assumed they should have. Tandra feared that Shawne's awareness would be dulled, that she would lose the sensitivity to nautral phenomena that the ellls had taught her, that simple things like the gentle touch of the ellls' moss skin or the dancing reflections on the pool would no longer be enough. Tandra resolved to save the remnants of elllonian influence in the child if she could, if she had enough time, so she quickly set aside her fear and her yearning grief, as an elll might, and hurried through the motions of her assumed task.

She told everything that she could bring herself to tell about the aliens. She wrote tirelessly and granted all interviews, hoping to saturate the curiosity of the reporters and their readers; she accepted all speaking invitations; and she conferred with a never-ending, invariable assortment of government officials from throughout the world.

Most affable was the President of the World Federation. A glimmer of real hope surfaced in Tandra. Here was a man of influence who understood. Of course, no treaty with the aliens would be proper unless it was written and signed by a body representing all of Earth's peoples equitably, which, he was sorry to admit, was not true for the Federation yet. He smiled warmly and spoke of the need for perspective, for the growth of the human mind toward accepting the give and take of balance, which he defined easily as total recycling and equitable distribution of the fixed pool of Earth's resources and a stable or declining population count. Economic de-escalation to such a steady-state? A foregone conclusion. Disruptive? Yes, during the adjustment, but far less disruptive than the present course to human degradation and death. We should get on with it as soon as possible. "Won't you help, Dr. Grey?"

She believed him. She took him literally, as she would a varok. She devoted all her time to helping the environmental lobbyists. Her message was sure and inspiring. The President was behind them. He not only understood the problem but was committed to attaining the steady-state as quickly as possible. They could drop their defenses, forget the hypocritical reality of political maneuvering, and state baldly what was required. The environmentalists swelled with hope; many awoke from the deadening apathy that had followed their growing disillusionment; some dared to admit their sympathies with the stabilists. They reformulated their proposals in less compromising language and believed that they would now be realized. Tandra Grey—confidante of the aliens—had reassured the Federation President that his deepest beliefs were logically and practically correct for the planet Earth. Nothing could stop them now.

Meanwhile, the telecasts continued from the moon. Conn and Orram shared the duty of programming. Historical and cultural presentations were easy; world model confirmations and projection analysis were not difficult; but practical suggestions for implementing stability that men would seriously consider were impossible.

As the months grew bleaker, Conn watched every detail of Tandra's work. At first he couldn't understand it. He had expected her to do nothing. But with Orram to guide him, he eventually forced his thought patterns through their necessary logical channels and learned to understand the complexity of her mind.

To verbalize his own rampaging emotions was more difficult. He wore a wet-sweater all of the time now, for he rarely entered the pool. Orram was almost enough. But not quite. For, though they tried every technique known to varokian psychology, they could not merge the identity of their minds. Orram easily read Conn's mood, but he could not follow the elll's mind through its great complex of deductive channels. Cautiously he conditioned himself to accept and empathize with Conn's raw emotion, but the risk was ominous—and more so because it involved the resolution of Conn's ill-defined jealousy. Gradually, however, they grew as close as those species could, with Tandra a compelling, silent link between them. And still, words were as difficult for Conn as touch was difficult for Orram. Conn learned to drop his sensual caution with the varok and to rely on Orram's warnings, but occasionally he would rage uncontrollably with frustration at himself or at his unsatisfied sexual arousal and schooling instinct. Then the bemused Orram would drive him to the pool. "I am not a hermaphrodite, my dear friend, and I flatly refuse to fill *all* your needs. *Uleoon!*"

"Besides, the pool makes my chest feel heavy and uncomfortable," he said to himself.

Jesse Mendleton sat between Tandra and Maurice Glene, Chairman of the World Life Coalition, wondering what to say next. It wasn't going well. They seemed to agree in outlook, but they couldn't reach an understanding on matters of policy.

They agreed that the governments of Earth had waited too long before starting the adjustment to steady-state economies. As a result, a vital resource—which might be food or water as well as an industrial mineral —had often disappeared from an affected area or industry very suddenly, with disastrous results to the population dependent on that resource. Tandra and Glene also agreed that the legislation that the environmentalists had won—effective pollution controls and conservation measures—had been largely ineffective, for they were too easily suspended in crisis situations. There was no end to such situations. Their conclusion was that only radical enforcement of limited production and consumption would slow the progress toward total economic collapse and world-wide anarchy. The "natural disasters"—massive death from starvation, noxious substances and drought—which the World Federation seemed to welcome as providing some relief, could not be prevented. The people of Earth had chosen to let the death rate climb, not to lower the birth rate.

Philosophically, Tandra agreed, she was a stabilist. The effects of an immediate, though traumatic, adjustment to a stable condition were far less destructive than continuation of the open-ended world market. But to close the world market by force—by the violent destruction of the principal means of production—was insane. She would never agree to aid the stabilists if that were their policy.

"When will you see the President again?" Glene asked.

"Why do you think he will see me again? What more can I say? He knows what must be done."

"Does he? You have great faith in platitudes."

"Platitudes? The things he said became clichés long ago, but he meant them."

"Did he? Men such as he rarely mean what they say. He appeared to agree with you in order to draw you out."

"I find it hard to believe that I was being used."

"You did exactly as he hoped: you believed him, spread the good word to the stabilists; and they showed their hand. Now he knows what he's up against."

"He is no varok, Tandra," Mendleton interjected. "He is quite capable of believing himself when he agrees with you."

Tandra turned to Mendleton with an appreciative nod. "He does resemble Orram," she said. "Perhaps I was too ready to trust him. The solutions would have been relatively simple with his help."

"You are impatient, too, in your own way," Glene said. "Now perhaps you can understand our pragmatism, with tension so rapidly building toward violence. His latest act of diverting large areas of North America from agriculture to strip mining may tip the balance."

"Under what authority has he condemned this land to strip mining?" Tandra asked. "Every arable acre is needed for food production. It must be a bureaucratic mistake of some kind."

"We live in a state of emergency, Dr. Grey. Bureaucratic mistakes are a governmental necessity now."

"But what he is doing contradicts all his convictions."

"To the contrary," Glene said. "This grab for emergency fuel is the proof that his real interests lie with industrial growth. He has no intention of initiating the conversion to a steady-state. He will apply Band-Aids

forever in order to keep his friends in business. Advocating the reallocation of demand to a reasonable level
is too much of a political risk for any man, convictions
or no convictions."

"Then you have given up all hope of an orderly slow-
down? I am certain that the President understands varokian stability economics. He knows that the world's
total stores of vital resources can be accounted for and
recycled equitably."

"Of course he understands that. But he understands
immediate economic pressures far better." He paused.
"All right. We'll give you a little more time. Go to the
President again. Convince him that anger is running
high, that we may lose control soon. He can't seem to
understand how many people are caught up in this
momentum toward violence."

"Neither can I," Tandra said. "It is no solution."

"You can't just tell men to love life and live with less
—to live like varoks—Tandra," Mendleton said sym-
pathetically. "It would be a nice solution, but it won't
work."

"No one has seriously tried it. I have seen no reasonable proposals for implementing a stable economic
state. How can you know it won't work?"

"You can't force a man to live a smaller existence
than he can buy," Glene said thoughtfully. "People
won't live for some indeterminate, stable future. They
have seen no sudden horror in demographic projections.
Crises come and go, things change, but one learns to
change with them. And though the statistics of death
show high numbers, death from malnutrition or lung
poisoning comes slowly and quietly to individuals."

Tandra felt herself withdrawing. "Perhaps you are
right."

She rose from her chair and wandered toward the
door. "Shawne has been too long among those who
care too little, Jesse. Man has become alien to everything I believe, an enemy to everything I care about.
Mr. Glene, I will see the President once more—once
more only—then I must take Shawne away—quickly,
before she forgets the ellls."

* * *

"Time has gone very slowly for me these last few months," Orram said as he arose from Killah's examination table.

"I miss her, too," the elll said, assuming that the varok was thinking of Tandra. He did not look up, but reviewed once more Orram's records.

"Of course," Orram continued. "At first I thought that Tandra's absence was the reason for my lethargy. Then this cough began. It has deepened, I believe. I feel very very tired, Killah, all the time."

"You have lost some lung capacity, Orram. The growth has spread into the fourth section. It is like no malignancy I have seen in varoks; I don't want to operate. And yet it has come on you too gradually to be common disease. I'm not sure what to prescribe yet, except bed rest. Let's give your body a chance to throw this off. Meanwhile I will check Tandra's books. Perhaps you have picked up a human organism, something like TB."

Orram agreed to put aside his work, and he rested well; but the feeling of weariness was not relieved. Soon he was forced to try to sleep as much as the coughing would allow.

Though Killah was continually frustrated by his failure to culture any organisms from Orram's sputum, he decided that Orram indeed might have tuberculosis, so he spent many hours synthesizing the human drugs PAS and streptomycin and started administering them to the varok.

When there was nothing obvious left to do, Killah and the ellls grieved for Orram's loss of life-joy as they waited anxiously for some improvement, but their Master-varok continued to grow gray and thin. They felt helpless and wished Tandra would return to them.

"You must make your followers realize, Dr. Grey, that we are all concerned for the environment, but the economic health of the world is of first priority. Furthermore, our energy needs continue to grow."

Tandra winced at the clichés, especially the word *needs*. Maurice Glene had been right. The President was a master politician and little else. He knew how to mouth the proper philosophy at the proper time. He had used her to gain time, to learn who among the environmentalists were active stabilists. "You are going to let them strip all this acreage in spite of the loss of arable land, in spite of the knowledge that the stabilists are prepared to stop it at any cost."

"You are a friend of the aliens. The stabilists rely on your advice."

"That is no longer true. You have betrayed them through me. Your promises of beginning the industrial readjustment have been ignored and now ruthlessly broken by stripping this land for its coal. You favor the insatiable appetite of the powerful at the expense of the starving. The stabilists will no longer listen to anything but decisive reversals in policy. The bombings have already begun again. Most of the people are with the stabilists now."

"I can't believe that. This insurrection will easily be put down."

"You are going to let violence and nature do the leveling job, aren't you?" she murmured, only half aware of him now. "You can't conceive of denying invention or leaving power unused, as the varoks do. You will do nothing towards stability, towards giving Shawne peace and beauty and reliable roots and freedom from mindless change."

"Dr. Grey, it is economically dangerous—"

She walked away from him unhearing, oblivious to the insult she dealt him as President.

"I hold you responsible for any more violence, Dr. Grey," he called angrily after her.

"What makes me keep ranting?" Tandra wondered bitterly as she looked out at the sea of hard faces before her. "There is no way I can make them understand." But she continued in a final effort to dissuade the stabilists from violence. "You can't force a steadystate solution. It must be more gradual than that; the adjustment must be planned. Men must learn to temper their needs. More violence will teach nothing. You've got to care for men's lives in the process of reeducation or they will learn nothing but hate."

"It's too late to care about a few men's lives!" someone shouted.

Tandra continued. "You must look beyond yourselves. You are generating hate that will continue for your children." She was very, very tired. There was nothing more to do after this. It was time to quit and take Shawne away to some place quiet and clean and safe.

"She's been bought!" Uncompromising stares met her bewildered eyes.

"Try to understand me," she begged. "You must become devoted to living simply. Deny the spoilers their market. Then your children will learn and others will see and understand."

A groan of irritation rose in the crowd, and several people stood up to wave her off the podium.

"What?"

A comforting hand took Tandra's arm and invited her to step down. Eagerly she took it, looked into the despairing eyes of Jesse Mendleton, and welcomed the final knowledge he gave her: that her effectiveness had run out, that she was finished at last. Only a few jeering comments followed them out of the hall; and in very little time she was forgotten—by all but too few—but she would never know that.

Now for a place to raise Shawne, raise her strong but sensitive, with a real knowledge of what life might mean if one learned to love all of existence, including oneself.

Almost a year had passed since Tandra's return to Earth when suddenly Conn missed the steady input of information concerning her political activities. He asked the Midpacific Space Center for help in contacting her, but they claimed that they could not find her. Conn panicked. Why would she suddenly drop out of sight? He went to Orram. The varok had lain quietly determined, clinging tenaciously to his life, but gradually weakening through the long days. He could not talk without great effort. His only advice was the name of Jesse Mendleton. But uttering that name brought on a torrent of wrenching coughs that sounded as if they would split his lungs. At this Conn became incoherent with grief, blaming himself for driving Tandra away—and for Orram's unfathomable illness—and linking them somehow in the morass of his panic.

Hours later Killah found Conn still grieving. He tried schooling with the loner, but there was no help for Conn in the pool, so they climbed out onto the deck and talked.

"He can't take much more damage to his lungs, can he, Killah? Varoks have a greater oxygen requirement than we do."

Killah's eyes grew wide with empathy. "I'm trying everything I can to keep him conscious, Conn. Once they lose touch with reality varoks can suffer brain damage and die of oxygen starvation quite suddenly. That's why he's under high oxygen pressure continually now. I've given him the injection mask."

"Great God, you mean if he loses consciousness we'll never get him back?"

Killah nodded soberly. "I wish Tandra were here. I need her help. Junah has already initiated proceedings to clear Tandra for a staff position with EV Science. What would her presence do to you, Conn?"

Conn's grief was momentarily flooded by hope. Killah felt his answer in the high ultrasonic.

"If Llorkin blocks Tandra's candidacy I will issue a legal restraint on the grounds that he is obstructing base objectives—and if Orram dies, I will charge him with murder," Conn stated.

"His objections are no longer valid," Killah said. "It's

now quite obvious that she can cope with mentalities and cultures alien to herself—even those on her own planet."

"Killah, this request to clear Tandra shouldn't be routine. Let's label it urgent. Artellian!" he shouted to the Master ellil, surfacing from within the pool. But Artellian did not hear. Impatiently Conn stuck his head between his legs into the water and bellowed ultrasonically.

Immediately, Artellian surfaced and sliced toward them. "What was that for?" he asked. "The pool is still quivering."

"This request for Tandra's staff position should be urgent. And we need a *full* clearance for her so she can try to reach Orram if he should lose consciousness."

"Reach him?" Artellian asked.

"I have good reason to believe that if Orram loses consciousness Tandra can make at least diffuse contact with him. There is known human potential for low frequency reception and transmission, and Tandra has tracked with Orram."

Junah approached to listen, as did Llorkin and the other ellils in the pool.

"Tracking is very limited, Conn," Artellian argued. "You're asking that we clear Tandra for complete defined contact. That's equivalent to consummation."

"Artell, you know that last year Orram reached Tandra with diffuse mood-reading," Junah said. "But you may not know that it became a common form of communication between them, culminating in their mating."

"You see? You see?" Llorkin shouted. "She broke him. That's why he's dying. She broke him. He had resolved not to mate with her unless they could consummate a marriage. She broke his resolve. Varoks can't stand that, you know."

"Your rantings contain some truth," Conn said, forcing his eyes into a disconcerting calm roundness. "Now sit down and listen!" he screamed. "Orram had gone so deep into her mind that he went into catatonia on one of their sunset walks. He wanted to beat it down with anesthetics, but Tandra realized what had happened and offered a hell of a lot more than physical relief. Her message was loud and clear: complete acceptance, insistent love in the present, no strings attached. He damn near lost himself in her mind it was so wide open."

"Did Orram feel that more detailed mental contact was possible with Tandra?" Artellian asked.

"He had hopes that they could consummate."

"I suggest that we delay no longer," Artellian said. "Llorkin, do you have any substantial objections to offering Tandra a full clearance and a staff position with EV Science?"

"She is *human*," Llorkin snapped. "I insist on conducting a complete psychological analysis."

Conn catapulted to his feet and slammed his hand against the moss-lined deck. "Llorkin, will you get your goddam head out of your ass-hole?! Tandra isn't human any more! We may lose Orram!" The wild anger of the lonely elll had nowhere to go but back into ellonian grief: Throughout the night he sobbed and thrashed and paced in and around the pool, then back and forth to Orram's room, hour after hour, until Killah feared for his sanity. And still he refused to school, even when they suddenly realized that Orram had lost consciousness.

"I have talked directly with Jesse Mendleton," Artellian told Junah a day later as they sat quietly by Orram's bed. "None of his news is good. Some time ago Tandra left Shawne with Mendleton and drove away. He said that Tandra didn't know where she was going— only that she had to find a place for Shawne—and that she would return for the child as soon as she could. The Federation police are also looking for her, but so far they haven't connected her with Mendleton. He was smart to keep our contact with him secret through all the turmoil."

"Why do the police want her?"

"For sabotage, and apparently treason, also. A stockpile of weapons and explosives was found in her house.

Mendleton believes they were planted. They need a scapegoat for the recent bombings. She is accused of fomenting civil war."

"I remember Mendleton telling us about her last appearance with the stabilists. . . ." Junah was so intent with thoughts of Tandra that her patches missed Conn's approach.

Artellian continued, "Mendleton feels that Tandra will be safe while she travels; she won't be in heavily populated areas. Right now he's more concerned for Shawne. There have been charges of neglect. Tandra didn't want Shawne exposed to the schools, so she kept her home. He has heard that the child will be taken from Tandra very soon, while she's away."

With those words there suddenly crashed into Junah's perception an intense wave of fury. Conn! Where was he? Junah whirled to face him. His eyes glared with determined rage; then he turned and ran toward the hangar.

Junah and Artellian stood stunned for a moment before they guessed the loner's intentions.

"I had better go with you!" Junah called, running after Conn. But she was too late. The *Lurlial* had already crept out of the hangar.

Conn shut off the braking engines at forty thousand feet, activated the glide wings, and waited while the silver bat soared silently into the murky lower atmosphere of Earth. He scraped to a stop on a wide grassy slope and set off on foot in the direction of an insistent beep in his helmet. He shuddered at the hideous excuse for air and fitted his isolation helmet for oxygen, to prevent any of the human waste from clogging his lungs. The terrain was not rough, but he stumbled with fatigue and the unaccustomed pull of Earth's gravity. Finally, he saw a figure standing near a waiting car on the road below. The figure signaled for him to stop. It was Jesse Mendleton. Impatiently, Conn waited while the man climbed to met him.

"Conn?"

The elll grasped the man's arm gratefully. "Where's Shawne? It's my fault she's lost a whole year of her life down here."

"There. In my car."

"And Tandra? Where's Tan?"

"I'm not sure. She called yesterday, and I told her to be at her old homestead. I don't know if she will be. There's so little time. You'd better just take Shawne now."

"We'll *make* time," Conn said. "I've got to get her out of here. The steady-state philosophy hasn't had its martyr yet. She's become the symbol of human failure, and now it's time to hang it up on its cross. That's the way of human history, isn't it?"

Mendleton nodded grimly. "The human race is busy committing suicide, and they don't want to be reminded of the fact."

They came to Mendleton's vehicle, and he stood baffled when Conn suddenly began happily circling around it, bobbing up and down and making mock threats. Shawne was jumping up and down on the seat inside, happily joined in the game. Then Conn disappeared, the baby jumped out to pounce on him, and he captured her with a long-armed hug.

"A whole year's growth I've missed, Shawnoon. You're huge! Let's go find your mother, okay?"

Mendleton noticed that the elll's grief for Tandra's lost year did not reemerge during the ride; it had been expressed. Conn was completely, joyfully engrossed with Shawne now.

Miles later they drove onto a dirt road that wove haphazardly through an old orchard past houses built of scrap plastic and automobile shells. At last Mendleton recognized a pattern of juniper trees on the hill above an old frame house, and there he coasted to a stop.

Conn stepped out of the car, glad for the dimness of the night, which allowed him better vision. He whispered to Shawne and Mendleton to stay quiet, then tried the door to the house. It was locked. He circled the house trying the windows and back door. He stopped to listen. Something had moved inside. He tapped on the door. No answer. Quiet.

"Tan?" Conn whispered through the door. "It's Jesse Mendleton. I've come to take you home."

The door swung open, and Tandra stood there, frightened but expectant. Conn tore away the screen door and clasped her in his arms. He pulled his helmet off and nuzzled under her chin, forgetting the taste of the air for an intense moment. Then he tilted his head back, inviting the same treatment.

"I had almost forgotten how soft and open you were," Tandra said. Open and vulnerable—so unlike the hard, stubbled faces of men, which stare coldly as they speak half-truths and believed them.

Tandra kissed the elll beneath the chin very gently. "Hedonic glands there, Conn," she whispered.

He smiled down at her and took her face in his webbed fingers. "How I've missed you! When I think how you crawled into my water . . . You went more than halfway to know me again. Then I woke up in some goddam mental blind alley and found you really gone. I would have sold my soul to have you in the *uuyvanoon* again with me. The pool was no longer enough, so I walked the Earth with you this miserable year, followed your every move, began to understand your every thought, learned to tolerate your damnably human emotions. And I longed for you. My pool is dry and empty without you."

Tandra moved closer into his arms and spoke with gentle pressures and undulations along the length of his lean, tiled body—spoke more clearly and easily than she thought possible the language he had begged for many long months ago.

"I think I've finally sorted out pride and jealousy and bitterness and love, Tan," Conn said, "all these individual emotions that you stirred up in me. But now what do we do? I am still an elll. An elll's deepest relationships always involved sexual contact within the school."

Tandra's pelvis thrust slightly forward with his suggestion.

Conn exploded with joy. "At last I have my answer! You not only love me, you accept me! Totally! With no hint of repulsion! That's enough, Tandra. That's all I need."

"And you no longer hate what *I* am." She swam deep and easy in his emerald gaze. "I love you only for yourself now, Conn, as a part of my very being; and no cultural assumptions or intellectual inventions will ever confuse the expression of that love again."

"What a goddam mouthful that was!" A broad smile rumpled his face. "Have you had enough down here, Tan? Will you come home now and stay where you belong?"

"Stay?" Tandra asked hesitantly. "Shawne must go with you, but perhaps I should stay here. We don't even have an international materials inventory yet—"

Conn put a soft, dry finger over her lips. "Those are hollow words, Tandra. Don't try to rejoin the human race for my sake. You can't assume the role of caretaker now. It's too late; you're wanted for sabotage and treason. They won't allow you to do anything more now, and I won't allow you the role of martyr."

Tandra's eyes widened. "It is more painful to give up on Earth than I thought, Conn. She was once so beautiful. Now, with these bombings we add more horror to the rape—and we don't even care. We were given a precious gift, and they continually abuse it. They use it and destroy it; they take it utterly for granted!"

"Listen to yourself, Tan," Conn said, smoothing the quick tears from her eyes. " 'We' has become 'they.' Come home with me now. Our little gal Shawnoon is in the car waiting for us."

They drove as quickly as they dared, a strange car filled with mixed emotions: tension and relief and curiosity and joy and apprehension. (Why was Conn so hesitant to talk about base, about Orram? Tandra wondered.) And over everything was a fear that the *Lurlial* might have been discovered.

Finally they reached the long, flat hill which hid the *Lurlial* from the road. Everything seemed undisturbed.

Mendleton followed uncertainly as they circled cautiously toward the ship. He stood apart as Conn and the others climbed in. Minutes passed. There was too little noise. Suddenly the elll reappeared in the hatchway.

"Better come along with us," Conn urged.

"To the base?"

"Why not?"

Mendleton could find no answer, and no desire to reject the invitation. With great relief, he climbed in, and within minutes the stocky silver ship rose with a tremendous quiet power toward the moon.

Quivering with impatience, Conn eased the ship into orbit and finally sent it plunging toward base, while Mendleton sat beside him at the controls admiring the broad fingers darting competently at the command of the swiveling helmet, seemingly independent of the lanky, mottled-brown figure they belonged to.

"There," Conn mumbled peevishly, stripping off his isolation suit. "Call me if anything moves on this data readout." He pointed briefly to a calibrated set of concentric circles, and without another word heaved himself out of the control room and down the passageway in search of Tandra.

He found her braced against the weightlessness in an *uuyvanoon,* enfolding Shawne in her arms and staring out of the porthole. Conn grasped the edge of the sleeping basin and knelt beside them, but only Shawne turned to greeet him.

"Tan?" Tentatively, afraid to intrude, he placed a hand on her shoulder.

She took his fingers eagerly and clung hard while she watched the Earth sink beneath her.

"Tan, it's all right," Conn said. "Life finds a way to go on. Eventually Earth will reclaim her own."

"I wish I could be so sure," Tandra said. "I wanted you to see it, Conn, the way it was . . ."

While Conn stared at the back of Tandra's bowed helmet, emerald drops of empathic grief and longing gathered on his brow plumes. Suddenly he cried, "Tandra, I am too alone!"

She tore her gaze away from the swirling blue and white orb below. Her mind locked deep and sure into the once-fearful crystal green of his eyes, and his gentle touch of moss brought her home to him again.

For many hours, then while the *Lurlial* glided toward Earth's moon, the elll clung to the human being watching Earth grow ever smaller, shimmering silent and alone in space.

15
Home

"I have another passenger, Artell. Jesse, where are you? Watch the gravity," Conn laughed, steadying the man as he emerged from the *Lurlial*.

"You're very welcome here, Jesse Mendleton," Artellian said. "You've been an invaluable friend. Seems a bit rude to shut you up in quarantine right away, but we had better play safe."

"I don't mind," Mendleton said.

"Tandra, welcome home," Artellian said, embracing her warmly with his large golden-green arms. "I was afraid we'd lost you. *Aeo-o* Shawnoon!? You are getting very large." He picked her up with a surge of joy and set her tenderly on his hip.

"Conn," he continued gently, "your privileges and duties under EV Science are suspended until your criminal actions are reviewed. You are confined to base; automatic penalty for violation will be permanent expulsion."

Tandra turned to Conn.

"You might say I—borrowed the *Lurlial*," Conn said with a wry smile. "When Jesse reported that they were going to take Shawne from you, I blew my cool." He straightened out of his slouch and put his arms heavily on Tandra's shoulders. "Llorkin was threatening to block your return. I had to get you out of that horror down there, Tan. But I had to bring you home for a second reason." His eyes were wide and glistening. "I haven't been able to tell you, Tan. It's Orram. He's dying."

The shock lasted one long terrible moment. Then Tandra grabbed Conn's hand and ran into the soft silver-red halls of the base. As she released the sealed doors and stepped into the isolation room adjoining Killah's lab, she saw the unconscious shell of the Master varok lying on its back, its face gray-sallow and thin and its breathing noisy. She grew deadly pale.

Killah pulled her away from the restless form as it continued its struggle for breath. "Come, Tandra," he said, grieving for her pain. "Review what I have done with the sputum samples. I need your help. I don't know what to try next."

They retreated to the lab and with great difficulty Tandra set her mind to work. "Tell me about Orram," she said as Killah prepared a sample of Orram's sputum for microscopic examination. "When did he get sick?"

"It's almost impossible to pin down, Tandra. He began feeling tired about a month or two after he returned from leaving you on Earth. Then he began losing weight. The cough didn't become severe until a few weeks ago. I wasn't able to culture anything from sputum until recently. But now I may have a few colonies on these tubes."

Tandra peered at the minute drops of yellow on the surface of the semi-solid nutrient. "Could be TB. Are they acid-fast rods?"

"And gram positive," Killah nodded.

"What drugs do you have him on?"

"He's on PAS and streptomycin, but he should have responded by now, shouldn't he? I put him on the drugs when I first suspected TB several months ago."

"Let me look at these slides." Tandra's fingers deftly pulled the microscopic vision into focus. Then they slid to the manipulator, and her mind wandered visually through the bulbous, cloudy blue microscopic world until her eyes and her fingers were arrested by a magenta flash. She swung the slide back and stared at a cluster of broken red rods scattered in a bluish tangle. "Kill, have you ever had a uniform acid-fast take?"

"No, I don't think so. But my technique isn't accurate with your stains. I can't distinguish their differences visually, you remember."

"And those colonies were grown at twenty-five degrees centigrade, weren't they? Let's put them under the scope."

With a delicate scalpel they lifted one of the tiny drops of ferocious life into a scope sampler and set it under the lenses of the low-powered scanning microscope. The colony was like an aged dew-drop, wrinkled and yellow.

"Not much doubt now," Tandra said. "But I want to look at that smear again."

She returned to the high-power microscope and continued her survey of Orram's sputum. Another magenta tangle. She closed in on it. "There, Kill. We're in luck."

He switched on the infrared source light and peered down through the maze of lenses. "Branching forms. Then it could be fungal."

"Yes. It's not TB. It's nocardiosis, but I don't see how he could have picked it up. It's usually found in soil and not directly transmitted between persons."

"Could he have picked it up on your trip to the mountains?"

"Improbable," she said, remembering their happy scramble for the pine cone beneath their tree, "but most likely. We should have stayed in isolation garments up there."

"Can't help that now."

"Let's get him onto sulfadiazine right away, Killah."

"It may be too late, but help me find the chemical formula for sulfadiazine. I'll see how close we can come."

Through the artificial night and into the next day they nursed Orram and worked at synthesizing the new drug. The hours were not long enough, the minutes far too short, as they labored over their banks of intricate tools and rows of culture tubes and watched with mounting terror Orram's ever more difficult breathing. Finally, the drug was ready.

Cautiously, throughout the next week, they eased the varok onto the foreign chemical. Heart rate up slightly. Then down again. Some nausea. Tandra slept on a moss pad by his side, refusing to leave even when Killah or

Conn was on watch. Often Orram's coughing allowed none of them any sleep.

They pushed the dosage up, but his cough became steadily worse. The rare fungus was notorious for its resistance to treatment. Many days passed with no reason for hope.

Most work lay undone at the base while the ellls and the varoks teamed to provide relief and support for Killah and Tandra. Conn's hearing before the Directorate was held informally over dinner one night, and the order to pick up Tandra and Shawne was made retroactive. Llorkin abstained, as little able as any other elll to swim against an emotional tide that concerned the safety of children.

The Directorate then wanted to clear Tandra for patch understanding but she could not be persuaded to leave Orram until she was convinced that she had done all she could. Then reluctantly she told Artellian that she was ready. She was willing to try and reach the varok mentally, if they thought it was possible. Exhausted and discouraged, Tandra sat in the middle of the floor in Artellian's office surrounded by Conn, Artellian, Llorkin, Tallyn, and Killah—who were sprawled at odd angles around her—and Ahl and Junah, who sat straight and tense, concentrating on every aspect of Tandra's consciousness, probing as deeply as they could.

"Exhaust all doubts relating to our mutual trust with Tandra," Artellian announced succinctly, and the Directorate began its work:

Killah was brief; he said that his mind had been made up long ago. She should be on the staff.

Tallyn stated that his prejudices toward Tandra were largely dissolved. He had come to respect her for her attempts to reach Conn before she had returned to Earth and for her persistent efforts there during the last year. Nevertheless, to erase all doubt, he would wait until Conn was finished.

Junah, through a series of questions, examined Tandra's personal reaction to her psychological collapse and return to reason. No prejudice or confusion there—

rather, a clear understanding of varokian personality and profound appreciation for their cultural problems. "Just one more question," Junah asked softly, then waited. "Do you read me?"

Tandra looked hard at the varok and almost blurted out that she felt acceptance pouring from the alien's patch organs. But she remembered Orram's caution concerning patch information and remained silent. "I'm ready for your question, Junah," she said.

"You have already answered it, Tandra. You have been aware of our security regulations and quite cautious even here. Now you should know that all members of this Directorate have been cleared to know about patch capabilities; and they are aware of your ability to read diffuse patterns and to transmit them."

Llorkin and Ahl in turn then drilled tirelessly at Tandra's mind with questions that had no answers—or too many answers—questions that invaded every corner of her life and consciousness. She soon became very, very tired, began to seek refuge from the continual barrage, and found it difficult to control her annoyance as first Llorkin's questions grew thinner and then, before they stopped, meaningless. The varok, Ahl, continued relentlessly, as was customary, pursuing her breaking point. But before long a clear message reached his patch organ: please, it begged, let me go to Orram; my integrity will break only with physical exhaustion. Abruptly, Ahl ended his questions and nodded to Conn.

Folding his long legs across each other and curling his brow into a thoughtful knot, Conn began to shape his thoughts into words, but he failed. "Orram is losing too much time with this damn nonsense. Come here, Dr. Grey," he said, pulling her down onto the floor beside him. "Talk to me in a way I can understand. There have always been too many words between us." He wrapped his long arms and legs around hers and pressed his lean, tiled body against her softness, half expecting her to protest their public intimacy. But instead, she shifted slightly so as to increase contact with him.

Artellian glanced around the room. "Tallyn?"

"No questions," he said, nodding his massive, wildly plumed head with satisfaction.

Ahl stretched back in his chair and pulled thoughtfully at his silvered hair. "We are neither gods nor worthless specks," he said. "Let us take joy in our mutual consciousness."

"Tandra," Artellian said suddenly, "do you consider yourself a good security risk?"

For a long moment she said nothing.

"Should we share our technology with the Federation if it should become a stable and representative world government? Varoks have developed photovoltaic technology to a high degree of miniaturization and efficiency. But I don't think you realize that our backup systems are powered by controlled nuclear fusion. Shall we give Earth the extra time that our technology can provide?"

Tandra's face paled as she realized the magnitude of Artellian's challenge. "You have never seemed so powerful. You could have imposed yourselves on Earth long ago." She gazed around the warm green and silver-brown circle of once-alien faces. "No. I am quite sure, Artell. Man is not mature enough to utilize such power responsibly. If you provide Earth with unlimited power now, the problems of overpopulation and overuse would continue unchecked, so that suffering would only be magnified in the end."

Artellian stopped pacing and extended a golden webbed hand to Tandra. "This hearing is closed. Your trust in us is no longer in any doubt whatsoever."

"My trust in you?"

Artellian's great eyes yawned wide with affection. "Go to Orram now quickly," he said.

Tandra and Junah exchanged a glance, then arose together and crossed the hall to Orram's isolation room. In spite of the oxygen-injection mask, his breathing remained irregular and labored.

"You have communicated diffusely quite often, Tandra," Junah said. "Transmit to him now in much the same way. I can't tell you how, since you have no patch organ. Yours is apparently a learned response. Whatever you have done before, do it now more intensely, with concentration—only beware of letting your consciousness dominate. This may be an elusive thing for you, like a speck of dust in the eye. It might help to touch him as you begin to make contact. You have guessed most of the patch organ's functions." Junah paused and then continued carefully. "You remember that Conn checked your EEG pattern before he first contacted you. That low voltage detector and analyzer was modeled on our patch organs. What most ellls don't know is that we can read not only diffuse moods, as you have done, but we can also execute specific mind readings on a conscious level if both parties will it, and on a subconscious level if conditions are favorable— that is, if there are no strong mental blocks in the way. This is how our marriages are consummated. Submission to and identity with another person allows a complete sharing of minds."

"Can't you reach him more easily than I?" Tandra asked.

"No, I'm sure not. He was attuned to you, searching for you. Open your mind and go to him, Tandra."

Tandra leaned over the bed where Orram's feverish body struggled for its oxygen. She held his limp hands in hers and tried to flood his patches with a call to herself. The call envisioned everything that he had meant to her, everything that had passed between them. She struggled against her wandering mind, trying to focus her thoughts and emotions, but the focus eluded her, and she found her mind yearning diffusely or grieving already.

Gradually, as the hours passed, her consciousness left the room, its sound and its feel, its warmth, even its light. The focus narrowed and magnified her self-awareness, striving, yearning, loving Orram. Tentatively, she moved away from the focus and tried to lead it, extend it toward him. Then, as the focus steadied and grew sharper, she stole brief instants to listen for a reply, for any projection from the unconscious varok. There was nothing. She returned to reinforce and concentrate awareness of her total being, before she attempted to hold it again while she built on her extension to him. Finally, Orram, the concept of being that was Orram, grew in her mind and held and grew steadier and stretched toward her own self-extension. She strove to focus the concepts of both of them, to make them meet. But then she became anxious and lost the entire vision. She sank to the floor. She had seemed so close.

"You must sleep, Tandra," Junah said. "If you do reach him, you must be able to hold him until he has come through this crisis."

Tandra slept for several hours. She dreamed that Orram was slowly sinking into quicksand while she reached out for him, their hands just failing to touch.

She awoke with a start, quickly cleared her mind, pressed his fingers to her temples, and sought to recreate the concentrated self-awareness. It came back quickly. She was alone again in limbo reaching to Orram, but now she searched continually for a response from him. She strained toward the impression of him, and she imagined his response. She tried to bring her image of him toward herself. They leaned together a little more —almost touching—just a little more . . . Suddenly the vision evaporated and she felt herself in the presence of Orram's awareness; he had been waiting for her. She had been too narrowly focused. Joyfully, she basked in his knowledge, his dread, his love, and she provided a link with reality, a directive to his body, a strength he no longer possessed as they remained together through the night and into the next day.

And for several more days, afraid to break the subconscious communicative trance between the woman and the varok, Killah administered emergency sustenance to them both. Late on the fifth day, they emerged slowly into consciousness. The room materialized around them, regained its walls, then Killah's medical instruments, the bed pad they shared; and finally they rediscovered their bodies, suffused with joy as they touched and saw and heard each other again.

*   *   *

Through the next few weeks, as Orram began to regain his health, Tandra and Conn rarely left him, and
gradually they reestablished more and more easily their
intimate awareness of each other—until it became
habitual and constant.

Long forgotten incidents came back into Tandra's
memory. As they talked, her childhood, seen in perspective, became a vivid scenario, pleasantly relived with
Orram and Conn. Indeed, she shared more of it with
Orram than she realized as he explored her thoughts
with her, sometimes finding them before she got to
them herself.

One day, when the oxygen injector was finally put
aside, Orram began to tell her about Varok: about the
moist warm evenings when several moons could be
seen between the swirling gas clouds; about the ever-
changing light, now deep orange or red, then yellow or
green, now dense, then thin and fragile.

He described his family: his aging mother, still the
master of the gardens, tending each fruit tree and moth
with extreme care; his adopted father, a writer of some
distinction and his mother's mate for some ten seasons
already; his brother by his mother's first mating, approaching the middle age of sixty with unusually little
direction in his life—and his son, Raeral.

The knowledge of Orram's adolescent son on Varok
was nothing more than a pleasant surprise to Tandra,
for she was already comfortable with the varokian family structure, whose composition was determined solely
by individual choice, and could have included Orram's
former mate, his son's mother, as easily as not. Orram
smiled to himself. Tandra was gradually entering his
mind, but she did not realize it yet.

"I remember my early childhood as being the most
pleasant of my life," Orram said. He had loved to watch
the sky change from masses of dimly lit color to black
luminescence. Then he would lie on his back on the
warm ground and feel small, bushy plants beneath him
as he watched the black sky for an occasional glimpse
of the moons. Later, at new light, he would spend hours
looking for crystals buried in rocky cliffs near his home.

Overwhelmed by the secrets they might hold, he would hide among the huge rocks and pick at them with a stick, searching for a glimpse of color or a planar surface. As Tandra listened, Orram's voice gradually faded to an echo, and she became that boy: stooping over a crumbling hillock of rock, looking for a better tool than the stick, remembering the laser pencil he carried around his neck, using it to pick at the fragile minerals until at last he found another crystal. "It's an emerald!" Tandra shouted. The little girl then led the young varok back to her mother's dresser, where she stole a peek at the beautiful emerald ring her mother kept there. Together they carefully slipped it over their small finger. Gently, so as not to destroy the union, Orram guided Tandra's mind back to the present. There, in the medical isolation room at EV base, she saw herself through his eyes—and with her own. She was totally with him—joined with him in mental consummation.

Conn found them some hours later still wrapped around each other breathing in unison, a shared dream drawing a smile across their lips. He guessed correctly what had happened and tried to retreat from the room, but before he reached the door Orram spoke. "Conn, don't go."

Tandra stirred at the sound of Orram's voice, sought his consciousness, found his mind extending toward Conn, and sat up to welcome him.

"No, Tan," he stammered. "Privacy is sacred to varoks. I—"

"Don't you think that we know that?" she smiled.

Orram sat up with difficulty and extended his hand with Tandra's. "Please, Conn, we want you to be a part of us. Join us if you will, or leave us if you must, but don't reject us for superficial reasons."

Orram's soft words erased Conn's doubts. His brightly framed emerald eyes widened with gratitude as he took their hands and let them pull him onto the bed and into their arms.

Such a tender scene, wrought with profound significance for three excellent beings and their respective species, should have found a fitting ending behind a velvet curtain. But the varokian hospital bed support, made lightweight for space travel and never intended for three adults, collapsed with a crash. The ensuing exclamations and hoots of laughter brought Killah bursting into the room.

"What are you doing?" he shouted, delighted at the chaotic tangle of bed and beings.

"By *l'Ran,* we don't know!" Orram exploded, "But whatever it is, it's good"

"We're schooling, Kill, old fish. Can't you tell?" Conn laughed. "I've found myself a dry school!"

His period of quarantine finally over, Jesse Mendleton had rapidly become a happy addition to the base. His bemused appreciation for everything alien had given a light touch to the previously leaden days. And now that Orram was out of danger they could all relax with pleasant memories of their first contacts, joyfully recounting the difficult, subtle exchange of information they had accomplished before Tandra had beeen chosen for direct contact.

In spite of all this experience, Jesse went into a state of high excitement when they received a video signal from Ellason.

"It's Raeral!" Conn hooted, as he pushed Orram's medical chair toward plate center. "They must have sent this transmission all over creation and back."

Orram reached for Tandra's hand. "Kneel in front of me," he said, "and I'll give you the translation." He sat tense and unmoving while his son reported on his progress toward the Concentrate and on the general state of varokian life. Then with exposed palms the boy saluted his father across almost twenty billion kilometers of space, and Orram's hand pressed hard against Tandra's as she felt within him the tug of desire for home, for his son.

Suddenly the hazy picture centered on a group of ellls

submerged in dark red fluid. They hung suspended by the gentle waving of their feet and back fins. One heavy-set figure with a magnificent crest approached the transmitting plate and began to speak. His words leaped and tumbled fluidly, but he wasted none on formalities.

"Thought we'd send you a piece of direct news to make you homesick, Art. You probably need a leave, and Conn must be dried up like a varokian *kaehl* by now. EV Science wants you to convert base to a minimal automatic monitoring operation and prepare to come home. The expense of full operations is no longer justified. We have learned much from the initial decline in Earth's life-quality, but you needn't pay the price of watching the major die-offs.

"Your telecasts sound good, but too divisive, as we predicted. We're convinced Earth knows what it's doing. The choice to allow massive natural catastrophes is obviously deliberate. We've seen no cut-backs in production to force population stabilization.

"Don't waste any time getting home, Aen. Artellian, pack up everything of security interest. As for the rest— the human beings will find base eventually. They might as well have something to play with.

"Congratulations to staff Senior Microbiologist Tandra Grey. Security registered. I assume she will accompany you to Varok. *Uleoon.*"

The plate went blank.

Tandra sighed deeply as the last glimmer of her persistent hope faded. "So much for Earth," she murmured. "I don't know what I was hoping for."

Artellian drew her face into his broad hands. "No tears, *alyakah*. Life is lived by many other stars. You have gone beyond Earth, eh? Men will leave a fascinating fossil record for those to come."

Late on June 24, while the crew lounged intently around the pool, Artellian witnessed the formation of the Oran-Grey-ElConn Family, with mutual rights un-

der EV Law essentially similar to those of power of
attorney on Earth.

When the formality was completed, Conn took Tandra's hand, found her third finger, and slipped onto it a
graceful swirl of moon glass that beautifully enthroned
a small sapphire, a large diamond, and an enormous
emerald. "For sentimentalistic female scientists, a token
of love—so that none will misunderstand." He grinned
enormously. "Some useless human customs have a certain unmentionable quality. I apologize to Orram that
the stones are not quite in true proportion to our planets'
sizes. Orram, I have made one for you, too."

The varok accepted his ring with visible emotion.

"Shawnoon, here is yours," Conn said, slipping a tiny
duplicate onto her pudgy finger. "And," he sighed, "I
have made one for myself." He produced the fourth
ring from his palm and handed it to Tandra.

"I don't think you'll stand it," she laughed.

The crowd of ellls pressed closer to watch her push
it onto his large reluctant finger. "M-m, no," he murmured as it touched his delicate interdigital web, "I
want it to stay there. It feels like a—um—like a kind
of pool."

With that the ellls mobbed them with noisy shouts of
congratulations. After a long, clamorous, haphazard
meal, Tandra and Orram stretched out on the mossy
deck next to Conn, who lay with his head in Tllan's
lap translating into English the words to *La l lea,* the
tender mating duet of the ellls:

You are to my life its living.
Come now, confirm it to me.
Renew my life with touch, with roll, with wave.

You are to my breath its breathing.
Come, share your touch with me.
Restore now my being with yours, with mine, with all.

You are to my self its growing.
Come now, lock your body in mine.
I know not of life but through you, with you, in you.

You are to my soul its homing.
Come take now my love in yours.
I am what I am for I'm with you, I know you, I love
you.

Throughout the day and into evening they lived life's
most precious gift of moments, and the celebration never
really ended, though the varoks sensed the approach
of embarkation, and the ellls grieved their kind of grief
for the splitting of the crew.

It was decided that Tallyn would command the *Ranat*
and Conn the *Lurlial* for the voyage to Varok. Tallyn,
Tllan, and Llorkin would go on to Ellason with Aen,
who wished to spend his last share of life on his home
planet. Orram, Conn, Junah, Artellian, Killah, and Da-
oon would travel to Varok, guide Jesse Mendleton and
Shawne and Tandra around that planet for several
Varokian years and finally, late in life, return with them
to Earth—that is, if Earth were still habitable—for still,
as always, far too many of Earth's human creatures
wanted far too much—of everything.

Glossary

adjustment Intense schooling of ellls, in which intense pressure signals and ultrasonic messages are rapidly exchanged underwater over extended periods of time so that accommodation may be made for the absence of a member of the school or for the addition of a new member.

aeo-o Elllonian expression of intense pleasure.

aeyull Elllonian expression of intense pain.

ahlrialka tree Huge spreading, plant-like growth on the hot acid plains of Varok; it produces dense, tasty reproductive lumps.

alahranon The colorful, swirling mists that surround Ellason, whose surface is almost totally covered by warm oceans.

aloon Elllonian noun, usually used with affection to mean something like wet slob or water bum.

alyakah Varokian word for a mature, well-integrated female who would be desirable to any creature as a mother or wife.

arl A large, brilliantly winged, moth-like creature of Varok, eaten by ellls and varoks and considered a delicacy.

Arlaht Varokian land craft adapted for lunar exposure. See *Nalkah*.

brilln The tiny, brilliantly-plumed waterbird of Ellason.

challall weeds Delicious, rigid, leafless plants which grow on the low hills of Ellason.

consummation Total mind link, achieved by varoks of the opposite sex who have no mental reservations between them, so that complete subconscious mind-scanning can occur.

dankah   A potent, intoxicating tea, made from the Varokian plant of the same name.

ꟼ ⱶ ⌣, (Deācuh)   Elllonian noun for isolation, quarantine, or loneliness and torture, all of which are synonymous in the minds of ells.

Directorate   Full title: Elll-Varok Luna Base Directorate. The council of ells and varoks at EV Base which makes policy decisions on behalf of EV Science.

Dove Two   World Federation-built three-man interplanetary space shuttle.

el eggs   The large, blue eggs laid by elllonian females every six Earth-weeks.

Ellason   A heretofore undetected self-heated planet of Sol with gravity equivalent to about two Earth-g's. Its orbit is three times as far from Sol as Pluto, hence laser communication necessitates a delay of seventeen and one-half hours, Ellason being some eighteen thousand, eight hundred and seventy-seven million kilometres from Earth. Continental masses on the warm, black giant are small, and the deep, black seas are enormous, glowing with ruby-red warmth near the heart of the planet.

elll   An adaptable, aquatic, life-loving species of Ellason, equipped with a formidable array of sensory organs.

Elllonian   The system of throat sounds laboriously devised by the varoks and ells to be spoken by ells in the varokian audible range to facilitate communication between those two species.

Elll-Varok (EV) Science   An organization of ells and varoks that directs the scientific experimentation and observation conducted by those species and acts as depositor, summarizer, and interpreter of accumulated knowledge and verifiable fact.

EV Base   Earth-Moon observation station of Elll-Varok Science, set into the edge of a crater eleven kilometres in diameter, located northwest of crater Schlüter at 1.5° north and 89.5° west in the d'Alembert Mountains of Earth's only moon.

EV Dictate The working agreement between the species of Ellason and Varok, which defines obligations, responsibilities, options, and assumptions inherent in their dealings.

Generalist Abbreviated as G. An earned varokian designation signifying the acquisition of thorough, detailed knowledge in a broad area of related studies, as, for example, physics, chemistry, astronomy, geology, from the area of physical sciences. Between Specialist and Master.

Gurahn Mythological beast designed by the *ll-leyoolianl* to represent the total experience of the planet Varok.

hedonic glands Sensory organs whose stimulation gives pleasure, and often sexual stimulation, to ells.

hoats A tangy, black edible root of Varok which sports feathery chartreuse leaves.

integrate An ellonian concept to describe the state of being when an individual of another species becomes a part of the elllonian school in a way that implies total acceptance of the ells; in general, to accept oneself as no different from those around one.

kaehl A delicate, easily tamed Varokian animal with silky, pink, branched hair that drapes in long strands about its tiny body and over its large, red nose, causing it to trip habitually as it attempts to run. It incubates its eggs in an abdominal pouch and protects itself with an acrid spray from its sour gland. The dried meat is tasteless but nutritious.

kaehl-din Elllonian invective. *Din* means fecal matter, *kaehl* spray. In general, any repulsive substance.

kaehloid Literally, furry beast. The elll's nickname for species with hair.

la l lea Elllonian; title of the tender mating duet of the ells; literally—have a mating with me.

leel, la oon Elllonian; literally—female, you do water (swim, woman).

llaoon grass A soft marsh grass of Ellason.

ll-leyoolianl A species of creative great-fish of Ellason who perceive the significance of experience and express it in a manner most easily understood by their communicants, often by modeling clay representations of their ideas as progressively complex symbols.

Iohn bird A plump, football-shaped animal with large webbed feet, stubby wings, a ridiculously small, billless head, and a coat of deep red and pink parasitic moss that drips with a heavily perfumed liquid. One of two species on Ellason capable of flight.

l'Ran The Elllonian word for the blue star-planet, Earth.

Lurlial Varokian-built exploratory space cruiser, fourteen metres long, bat-shaped at full glide extension, with capacity to carry eight two-metre beings comfortably, eleven if necessary. The craft has an indefinite range, minimal noise, needs little landing space, and has an extremely low radar cross-section.

Master Abbreviated as M. Highest honorary recognition by varoks of expertise in a broad area of study, with some understanding of all knowledge, demonstrated by wisdom and restraint in integrating and in applying to real problems the acquired concepts. Artellian is one of twenty living ells to have received the honor; Orram, one of two thousand varoks.

Midpacific Space Center An international Earth launching site and control center for space exploration, funded by the World Federation.

Mutilation The period of time in Varokian natural history in which the varokian species mutated from magnificent and normally sensual winged intellectuals to unduly sensitive bipeds incapable of experiencing emotion rationally.

Nalkah Varokian-built land craft which rolls, climbs, or hovers as needed for rough terrain. This model was modified with lunar exposure seals, pressurized with an oxygenated atmosphere, and provided with heat shields. A crew of one to six can be transported in considerable comfort in its elllonian-designed couches.

oeln fish Edible fish of Ellason, large and gray, with cool arrow-shaped patterns visible to ells as dark lines in the infrared environment of Ellason.

oon Elllonian suffix implying water or wetness.

pallonions Ellasonian credits. A promise of postponed payment in goods or services whenever requested. Agreements are honored and enforced between all members of species capable of keeping promises.

pallons Elllonian unit of measure, about twenty-three metres, the length of an elll's arcing leap through the water from a fast swimming start. The similarity of this word to the word *pallonions* is probably a result of the ancient ellls' sense of irony and humor.

patch organ Round, featureless plate of tissue behind the ears of varoks which detects, amplifies, and interprets low frequency electromagnetic signals, particularly voltages produced by mental and nervous activity of nearby organisms.

Ranat Thirty-metre varokian space cruiser designed to carry forty passengers over long distances.

reading Sensing another individual's mood, emotion, or trend in thought. One function of the varoks' patch organs.

release The ability to experience emotion and to function rationally simultaneously. Normally an ideal state achieved rarely by varoks and only with the aid of a consummate partner.

school Any number of ellls who inhabit a particular environs or locale and who relate by schooling. The ellls' normal social structure.

schooling Functioning collectively and sharing awareness as if a group were one individual.

sonarplate apraxia A debilitating disease affecting the hexagonal plates of ellls, caused by an RNA viral-like agent. The untreated disease results in loss of sonar meshwork function, hence loss of ultrasonic reception and communication.

"Songs to Life" Ancient varokian poems written anonymously during the Mutilation. The first verse of the poem quoted by Ahl at the end of Chapter X is as follows:

Though long denied Life's gracious gift of flowing free,
In currents wild and lifting down, thrown tumbling,
Lifted up, thrown down, and swept without control,

Our minds unlocked, in gray mists swirling bright with
　　crystal hue;
Through elegance denied and flight subdued,
We find Life's beauty in her gifts
And take her favors where they fall.
Though all our visions racked our minds with pain;
Though sound grew dense and ruined quiet senses;
Though mind-filling silence became unknown and un-
　　knowable;
And new life came to us, unfresh, imperfect yet yearning
　　for consciousness,
Heavily distorted, torn by savaged genes
And thrown upon misery to writhe in horror for years
　　denied;
Though Life came not with joy or promise,
But used us for her mindless purpose—
Or too mindful—none can know—
We still survive, thankful for new strength,
Molecules still conscious in forms perhaps wiser.

Specialist　Abbreviated as S. Varokian designation for
　　those acquiring specific knowledge in one field of
　　study, such as physics.

stabilist　A person belonging, usually covertly, to a
　　revolutionary group on Earth advocating the destruc-
　　tion of the means of production if necessary and the
　　violent overthrow of the World Federation in order
　　to achieve a stable (steady-state or no-growth) econ-
　　omy.

tad　An English word used by ellls to mean any young
　　being or new life.

tracking　Sensing and imitating the precise muscular
　　movements of another individual, one function of the
　　varok's patches (in conjunction with spinal nerves).

udan　Varokian style bidet-toilet.

uleoon　Ellonian affectionate farewell, from *u* (go),
　　lea (mating) or *leoo* (live) or *leoon* (love), and *oon*
　　(in water, deliciously wet).

uuyvanoon (*-l*, plural)　Sleeping basins on varokian
　　space-ships designed by and primarily for ellls. They
　　are made of a tough, flexible synthetic imbedded with

a thick growth of moss, shaped like a bathtub, and provided with a warm water inlet and a sealed cover for space flight. From Elllonian: *u* (go), *uyan* (beyond), *van* (knowledge), and *oon* (in water).

uyen l'e advant . . . Elllonian; Furthermore, I am convinced . . .

Varok   A dense, barely habitable, hidden satellite of Jupiter, thought to be associated, at least visually, with the Great Red Spot. It is six hundred and twenty-nine million kilometres from Earth; communications delay is fifty-eight hundredths hours.

varok   A degenerate species of the planet Varok, having lost its ability to fly and to tolerate emotion rationally.

Varokian Concentrate   An institution of Varok open to qualifying individuals of any species who are admitted as students to acquire, by high-speed microvolt implantation into the memory, established fact, noninterpretable information, and thought techniques. The integration and application of this knowledge is acquired at other institutions through continuing studies, leading to the designations Apprentice, Specialist, and Generalist.

Vrankah   A dance invented by ellls and performed by varoks only in close sympathy, usually in consummation; often used as a public announcement and celebration of legal commitment between varoks. The dance requires spinal anticipatory patch organ reading—tracking—by one partner as the other matches the rhythmic clapping of the ellls with his feet and tells a symbolic story with his hands.

wet-sweater   A shirt made of the most moisture-retaining, softest, and most delicious of Ellasonian mosses, kept alive by periodic moistening and feeding.

World Environmental Charter   A document signed by many nations to insure the safety and cleanliness of the world's oceans, waterways, air, and soil, whose provisions were subsequently ignored or suspended for reasons of emergency shortages, international security, or economic disaster.

World Federation   A world government with limited

sovereignty but growing enforcement capability, formed primarily out of economic necessity.

World Life Coalition   A religious organization working for the enforcement of the World Environmental Charter, actually a front organization for the stabilists.

The riveting novel of suspense in the tradition of
The Day of the Jackal and ***Three Days of the Condor****!*

THE NINTH MAN

JOHN LEE

In 1942 nine Nazi saboteurs landed in America.
Eight were captured; one was not. He was *The
Ninth Man*. His assignment: to carry out a plot
to assassinate the President of the United States,
Franklin D. Roosevelt. Alone, the German escapes
the net of U.S. Intelligence. Alone, he begins a series of
crimes that will bring his death plan to the Oval Office
of the White House. Only Captain Blaszek of the White
House security staff suspects the existence of *The Ninth
Man* and the subtle workings of the plot to destroy that
came directly from Adolf Hitler!

**Soon to be a major motion picture from the producers
of JAWS!**

A DELL BOOK $1.95 (6425-12)

BESTSELLERS
FROM DELL

fiction